TWEEN

SAMMI LEIGH MELVILLE

For content warnings, go to
https://sammileighm.com/content-warning-for-tween/

Contents

CHAPTER ONE

Don had already decided that when he died, he died. That's all there was to it.

He had grown up believing otherwise—in fact, his entire family still believed otherwise, still devoutly Muslim—but somewhere down the line, he'd fallen away. There was no point, he thought, in continuing to worship Allah when you had the sinking feeling that once your body decomposed, that would be the end of you. Not that he had ever found any fault in Allah... he just wasn't really sure if he believed or even cared about Allah's existence. In fact, it seemed to him that those who did care (or cared about any god) did so because they wanted somewhere to go when they died. They wanted to avoid decomposition. They couldn't handle the end being the end.

Don thought he could. He had learned very early on in life that there was a time and a place for everything, including death. And Don had never really been the type of guy to go scale a mountain, or cure cancer, or really any big act that would put his life on the map in any way. He just didn't need that fulfillment. Hell, what was "fulfillment" anyway?

He didn't hate his life, of course. It didn't consist of much—between doing deliveries for Sal's Pizza, playing video games, and occasionally walking his landlord's dog, there wasn't really one particular thing worth mentioning—but it was still a satisfactory life, in Don's eyes, at least. He was comfortable just getting by. And if his life were to suddenly end, then it must have run its course. Oh well. It was hard to care about the impact of apathy when he was the one who was apathetic. When the day came to die, he would embrace it just like he had embraced every other day in his life: with a bag of Cheetos and an open mind.

So, he thought he could handle the end being the end.

Unfortunately, it turned out that the end was not the end.

This not-end began with a tree. A large oak tree, to be precise—when such an item crashed onto the highway, the two-ton pickup truck cruising along was going to very quickly try to veer out of the way to avoid damage, and it would consequently slam into the '96 Chevy Impala in the other lane. That was just the nature of things. One could not deny that it was a spectacle of timing, a seemingly orchestrated act of fate, or coincidence, if one subscribed to that worldview instead.

If there was one feeling Don could pinpoint from the moment he died, it was confusion. The crash was extremely disorienting. One moment he was jiggling the knob on the heater, and the next thing he knew, his legs were being ripped to the side, the world was spinning, and his head was hitting the side window as the car tipped and landed in the ditch beside the road, headlights flashing through the trees. There wasn't really enough time to feel pain; it was just—it's cold, what the hell, and gone.

But that confusion was nothing compared to the confusion Don felt directly after death, when he crawled out of his sideways Chevy, turned around, and saw himself still slumped in the driver's seat, blood flowing from his temple, his legs gone... along with the front of his car.

Don took a step backward, stumbled a bit, and fell to a sitting position, noting that what felt like his legs were not actually visible in front of him. If he reached out, he was sure he would touch them, but he couldn't see them—nor could he see his hands. Was he invisible? Was this some extreme version of phantom limb syndrome?

He stared dumbly at the scene before him. There was a shout, and he looked up to see the driver of the truck sprinting towards him—no, not him, *him*—and checking to see if he was all right. He got his answer pretty quickly.

The trucker and the dead man continued their little play in front of Don, but Don was not a very good audience. Don could not concentrate. His mind buzzed, not exactly with emotions or thoughts but just... buzz. Though his head swiveled to and fro, trying to take in its surroundings, his eyes refused to cooperate, sliding out of focus as if disconnected from his brain, unable to admit something was wrong. *I'll see what I want to see, and at the moment, that is absolutely nothing. Thank you.*

Don had never had a panic attack before, but he wondered if he might be having one now. His sister had described it to him once, an "out-of-body experience" that seemed to line up nicely with the current situation. Or maybe he was dreaming. Because he sure as hell couldn't be *dead*. But with all this buzzing in his brain, he couldn't tell apples from oranges, and the trees and shrubbery surrounding the highway seemed to tower over him in blurry streaks, coalescing into thick, unbearable walls that threatened to close in.

He wasn't sure how long things stayed out of focus, but as the shock dulled, Don became aware that there were eyes staring at him through the bushes on the side of the road. No... not eyes. They looked like eyes, but they were more translucent. Disembodied. They couldn't be eyes. But they did blink.

"Oh, come on," a voice muttered softly. "I told you this was a waste of time."

"Well, how was I supposed to know?" another voice said. "I'm new at this. You're supposed to be the expert."

There was a laugh. "If I was an expert, would I still be here?"

Don clumsily rose to his feet. "Hey!" he called. The voices hushed; the eyes pulled further into the bushes.

"Hey!" Don cried again. It was silly, but he didn't know what else to say. He had just died.

"Aw, fuck," one of the voices said. "We can't just leave him by himself out there."

The voices muttered incoherently to each other, and after a moment, a pair of eyes came forward, floating out into the ditch. This pair of eyes approached Don, stopping just a few feet away, as if wary that Don would somehow lash out with his nonexistent body and attack.

Don attempted words. "What... ah... what's happening?"

As they came closer, Don saw that they were hazel eyes. They rolled slightly, seemingly exasperated by his incompetence—at a time like this, Don thought he was doing his best—then flicked back to gaze steadily at Don. "You're dead," the voice said.

Don swallowed. Okay. "I was kind of... guessing that." He tried to gesture with a sweeping motion at the mutilated car, then realized that gestures were moot at this point. "With the car in front of me and all. But what... what happened to me?"

There was a sigh, and the eyes flicked in the direction of the bushes. "Look, I actually don't want to explain this. Can someone else take over? I want to go look for the next one."

"Fuck you, Oswald," a voice called out from the bushes. "You're the oldest, so you get to explain."

The eyes belonging to Oswald squinted. "Okay. Fine. So, you're dead."

Don nodded enthusiastically. "Yeah. I got that."

"And... and look, I really don't need to explain this. The world is fucking full of ghost stories. You can figure it out from there."

"Okay, but... ghosts aren't real." As soon as the words came out of his mouth, he knew that the disembodied eyes floating in front of him were not going to like him.

"Well, believe what you want, man. You're stuck here now." Don could almost perceive a twinkle in the eyes before him. "You're a tween now."

Don stared at Oswald's eyes. "I'm… a what?"

The eyes hesitated, squinted a bit. As if their owner was a bit sour that he had to answer the question in the first place. "Did you have any sort of religion before you died?"

"Um… I grew up Muslim."

"Huh. Yeah, I have no idea what Muslims believe."

"Surprise, surprise," Don replied, his own candor catching him off guard. Apparently, dying had made him caustic.

Another sigh. "Look, fucker, nobody's happy about this, so stop making fucking jokes. It's your own damn fault, anyway."

Don sputtered. "No, it's not!" he cried. "I had the right of way!"

"No, it's… I mean, that you're here. That you didn't move on."

"Why?"

"Because…" The eyes glinted. He gave a little snicker. "This is awkward, huh? Because you weren't important enough."

"Uh…" Don laughed, for lack of a better response. "Fuck you."

"Nah, man, I'm fuckin' around," Oswald said, unable to keep the amusement out of his voice. "I mean, I don't know for sure why you didn't move on. Fuck, maybe it *was* because you weren't important. I don't know." His voice carried off towards the bushes. "Yo, someone come over here and help me explain!"

"Fuck you, Oswald!"

As the woods echoed with peals of laughter, Oswald leveled his gaze resignedly back to Don. "Look. It's an energy thing, all right? You didn't have enough, so you didn't trip the system, and now you're stuck here."

Don shook his head. "Okay, you're speaking gibberish now. I'm going to talk to your friends."

He marched over to the bushes, but the eyes blinked and vanished, their laughter trailing through the woods in front of him. That had been a mistake. He had let go of one frog to catch another—he should have known they would all submerge and leave him in the lurch. He sighed and turned around, searching for Oswald. "Oswald?"

There was no answer.

"Oswald? I'll listen, I promise. Please, just—"

But Oswald was gone.

Don slumped to the ground again. The police were arriving, and an ambulance—well, they were useless now, Don thought.

"Hello!" he cried out, approaching the disheveled trucker and the cops who were talking to him. "Hello, terrible driver. Hello, murderer. Can you hear me?"

No one even glanced in his direction. Don sighed, and walked around the scene of the crime, taking it all in. The truck was parked off to the side of the road, a small bit of smoke rising from its slightly dented hood. It taunted him with how intact it had stayed. Don tried to get another look at his own broken body. Soak up that image, now, he thought. It may be the last time you see yourself.

Don tried to shake that thought from his head, and approached the fallen tree. It lay, splintered and gray, at a haphazard angle on the road, despondent and guilty. Don followed the tree to its trunk, a distorted, rotted mess that looked like it had been in decay for years. Naturally, it had chosen that exact moment to fall and ruin Don's life. Must have been a hell of a wind, Don thought, a blip of anger breaking through the shock.

It didn't feel real. Don wandered in circles around his own death for hours, as the EMTs slowly extracted the bits of his body and hauled them off in the ambulance, and the scene slowly disassembled from "travesty" to "old, dusty road on a Wednesday night".

So what the movies said was true. He was a ghost, stuck haunting the world he had been ripped from. No one could see him or hear him—except for other ghosts, it seemed. He wondered where Oswald and his cronies had run off to. He wondered what he should *do* now. Didn't ghosts always have unfinished business? Wasn't that why they were ghosts in the first place?

But Don had no unfinished business, unless you count the game of Dark Souls he had saved at home. He very sadly noted that he would never be able to beat that game. Should've played it when it actually came out.

* * *

Cherry opened her eyes and blinked at the beams of sunlight peeking through the blinds. They seemed insistent on aiming directly at her. She rolled over, sighing. A glance at the clock told her it was 4:43am. She picked her head up off the pillow, felt the woozy spin of sleep deprivation, and groaned. Not only had she been unable to fall asleep until three in the morning, but now she was waking up before her alarm.

Might as well get up before it went off. She pivoted her legs to the side of the bed, grabbed her glasses from the bedside table, and sat silently, willing herself to wake up the rest of the way.

The alarm blared, and Cherry reached over, plucking her cell phone up and swiping the sound away. Today, she thought, would be a productive day—she would not lounge around in bed until the last minute like she had every day that week, making herself nearly late for work. And she had to run to CVS before work, so she was already going to have to rush. Finally getting a nine-to-five was great on the wallet, but not great for Cherry's time management skills.

She had a voicemail. She groaned. If there was one thing she hated most in the world, it was checking her voicemail. Actually, that wasn't true. But her mother had told her that speaking with qualifying words took all the fun out of life, so she embraced the lies her mind spoke out.

So instead of checking the voicemail, she focused on her Fajr salat, the repetition of bowing and kneeling, pressing her face and palms to the floor. Any recollection of the call fell out of the back of her mind until right before she rushed off to work, when she realized she hadn't put her makeup on. And when she finally did listen, putting the phone on speaker while she quickly applied eyeliner, she was unsure of what she had just heard. There was a man talking about an accident, and her brother's name, and suddenly Cherry had to sit down on the toilet seat because she started to understand what the voicemail was about.

The only image that popped into Cherry's mind as she sat there in her bathroom was a memory of her and Don when they were little, driving to Auntie Sadira's house. Cherry always sat in the front passenger's seat, because she was older, and little Donny would sit directly behind her, kicking his feet against the seat and driving her crazy.

But there was one particular instance in which he wasn't kicking. He was seven, she was ten. She reached her hand up and behind her, hanging over the top of the head rest to wiggle her fingers at him. Felt his hand reach up and grab her fingers, bending them back a little in jest.

She protested, and he laughed, stopping; but he continued to hold onto her hand, just for a moment. And Cherry didn't want to tell him that she hadn't just been saying hello—she was, in fact, consumed by the anxiety that had crept up on her in her childhood, which caused her mind to pick out the smallest, most inconsequential details of a moment and amplify them into horror shows. Cherry had, in fact, been checking to see if Donny was still alive. Maybe he had just been distracted, and that had stopped his kicking; or maybe something worse had happened. Maybe he had started to have a seizure, or maybe he had somehow swallowed something that blocked his airway and made him black out. She couldn't be sure until she reached back to check.

There was something instantly relieving about feeling her brother's fingers grasp onto her own—that sense of closeness, that feeling that only human touch could evoke. Here he was, grabbing onto her hand, and she hoped he would never let go, when just moments before, she had been yelling at him to stop singing the Lamb Chop theme song at the top of his lungs.

Cherry felt the cool tile of the bathroom floor under her toes, and the realization washed over her that she would never get to grasp onto her brother's fingers again. At least not like that. She could, perhaps, touch his hand after he had been wrapped in funeral shrouds, but at that point it would feel cold and rubbery, and not really him anymore. All she had left was a wisp of a memory.

Cherry had not really been close to Donny after middle school; the two had completely different interests, and to be quite honest, Donny could be a real pain. Even when they were old enough to understand what teenage angst was, and more importantly, how to deal with it, their relationship continued at an arm's length. Now, Cherry was thirty years old, and lived in the same town as Don, and yet they only saw each other during the holidays. It was a time management issue, really. They both had their separate lives and could not really be blamed for being too busy for each other.

And yet, Cherry would now only blame herself. She should've put in the time. She could've really gotten to know Donny, couldn't she have? She could have convinced him to go out for coffee, or she could have popped in on him when she passed through his neighborhood—all of that was very possible, so why couldn't they have done it at least every once in a while? That was her fault. No one could excuse Cherry from the guilt she was feeling now. This was on her.

The thoughts rushed through her in rhythm with the beating of her heart and the panic that suddenly rose in her chest, and suddenly Cherry was running back to the bedroom, flopping back down on the bed, her back pressing into the mattress and her hair covering her face, having not been tossed gracefully as she landed on the bed. She didn't care. She hoped she choked on the chunks of hair slipping into her mouth. Then she'd get to see Donny again.

Actually, she didn't even know that for sure. She had no idea what place Donny had been spiritually, or what level of Jannah he might end up in—that judgment was for God and God alone to make. She bit her lip. There had been moments when she had wondered about his spiritual choices, but she was always too afraid to press him about his faith, and he didn't exactly offer up the information. He never showed up to Friday Khutbah; that much she knew. She was sure if she had asked about that, he probably would have just said he had work. He had, at least, been a good person, she thought hopefully... maybe that was all that was, just a hopeful thought. She really had no idea.

But no... even if she was to be hopeful about his soul, she needed to not believe that dying right now was her best option. This is mourning, she thought, this is what mourning feels like and it's not going to get you to work so you need to snap out of it. This was not a convenient time, Donny. You did not die at a convenient time.

And more guilt. And the realization that, again, this was what mourning felt like, it never made sense, she needed to just cry and let her emotions flow, and maybe call Mom, and would she have to be the one to arrange the funeral? After all, she was the closest physically, and ya Allah, she would probably have to deal with the body, and make all the arrangements, and she wondered if he'd had a specific way he wanted to be buried, or if he would have been fine with a Muslim funeral, she should probably just call off work, and—Cherry couldn't breathe. Cherry couldn't breathe and the air in front of her face was boiling and she was pretty sure the walls hadn't been that close before.

And then, Cherry felt stuck. Her thoughts stopped, her mind paused, her inner voice was caught in her throat, and she closed her eyes, and she faded into the bedsheets around her, and Cherry slept.

Cherry slept until noon.

CHAPTER TWO

Don took the slow walk back to his apartment, nearly oblivious to the morning bustle of the town around him. He wasn't sure why he was going back to his apartment anyway, apart from the fact that it was the only thing he could think of doing. When in doubt, go to a familiar location. Maybe when he got there he could at least slow down the waves of panic he was experiencing.

A thick mist had settled over the ground in the few hours since his death. Odd, he couldn't feel it on his skin as he walked.

He was a few miles away from home—he had made this walk once before, when his car had broken down on the way home from work, but then, he had been so tired he barely even remembered the journey.

He remembered every moment of it now.

Maybe the shock of the situation was starting to kick in, because everything around him seemed to be buzzing, even more than before, vibrant and bristling with energy. He wanted to shut it all out, lie down in his own bed, turn off the world, and forget about what had just happened.

It's funny, he thought, you don't expect to mourn yourself when you die.

Okay, Don, he thought. Let's take stock. You're dead now, right? So why the hell are you here? Why are you a fucking ghost?

There was a lot to think about. Had he done something wrong? He had grown up learning about Jannah and Jahannam, but he didn't really believe in that anymore, and besides, didn't this prove that the concept of a heaven and hell was bogus? Unless there was something he just hadn't learned, ghost-wise.

Ghosts, he thought. Ghosts were not a Muslim viewpoint, that was for sure. He found himself hoping, strangely enough, that if atheism had in fact turned out to be wrong, maybe the religion of his childhood had found some piece of the truth. But the stories of the Quran seemed to directly contradict that hope, at least where ghosts were concerned.

What were they? Christian? Don's only frame of reference for anything Christian was the movies, where ghosts were sometimes tied to a priest or a creepy old church. But then, so were vampires, and Don was pretty sure that Christians didn't believe in vampires. He also vaguely recalled some conservative Christian kid in his ninth-grade history class muttering under his breath about how bogus ghost stories were, so he was pretty sure he could rule out Christian ghosts, or at least American Christian ghosts.

He vaguely remembered something he'd learned in a religion class in college about Jewish people believing in ghosts—but he was pretty sure the ghosts that they believed in centered more around possession than disembodied spirits, and as far as Don was aware, he hadn't body-hopped. And the ghosts of Jewish lore were either malicious spirits or guardians, neither of which he could particularly relate to.

So he wasn't a Jewish ghost. Don racked his brain, but of the countless religions he had heard about or even studied in religions classes, he really didn't know all the different perspectives of the spiritual realm. It was going to be pretty difficult to figure out his situation if it required having paid more attention in school.

Maybe he was some kind of secular ghost, not connected to religion at all. He had heard plenty of ghost stories in which the ghosts had unfinished business, and he was beginning to wonder how that could be accurate, since Don had never even really *started* anything. Maybe he was a ghost because he hadn't talked to his family in a while, out of sheer laziness? That seemed like a bit of a stretch. Or maybe he had somehow been preventing someone from reaching their full potential, and was being called out by whoever ran the afterlife. Don still didn't want to believe in a god, so there had to be someone else in charge.

Or maybe he had just been forgotten. Maybe he was supposed to move on to the afterlife, and the angel of death or whatever had failed to make his appointment. Maybe he'd missed his ticket to Jannah.

Maybe he'd missed his ticket to Jahannam.

Stop that, thought Don. You've spent the last decade or so believing that none of that was real—there's no need to start just because of a little accidental death.

Although, he mused, the fact that he was still around at all must have meant there was *some* kind of afterlife. He hadn't ceased to exist when he died, so he must have been wrong about something.

So, okay. Let's humor religion, he thought reluctantly.

He wasn't ready to guess which one topped all the others in this scenario, but he could at least focus on the fact that he didn't get proper procedure. If there was anything like that. That made more sense, since the others who had been at the crash site had been disappointed. They thought that he was going to move on, clearly. But expectations meant that they either knew what was going on—which was not the case, judging by his conversation with Oswald—or that they knew something about him that made him special enough to be disappointed over when the time came. Unless he had unwittingly been the hero of some young adult fantasy novel come to life—which, dear god, he really hoped wasn't the case—the idea of a bunch of people finding his life interesting enough to follow him around seemed very difficult to imagine. Their expectations could not possibly be attached to him as an individual. So maybe they didn't *expect* him to move on, they were just *hoping* he would. Then the disappointment he had seen would be... what? What would they possibly be disappointed about? Had they wanted something from his death?

Oswald had mentioned something about energy. The only thing he could think of that would even come close to relating was the equipment that those celebrities used on that ghost hunting show. They would record audio, and use those machines that would pick up heat energy. So maybe that's what they meant—maybe the ghosts at the crash site had been waiting to see that kind of energy.

But that didn't make sense either, Don thought. Because they were disappointed that there wasn't that energy. So… did that mean he didn't have the energy they had been looking for? If he had been recorded by one of those machines, would he not even show up? A ghost, but not even able to haunt those still living.

Well, this royally sucks, Don thought.

Okay, so, supposing Don had no energy to speak of… whatever that meant… that meant he really was stuck here. He wouldn't be able to communicate with the living to figure out what he needed to do to move on. He was going to wander around aimlessly, not even able to have fun being a ghost, forever invisible to everyone else.

Except for other ghosts. Oswald and his friends had seen him. And he had seen them. Or at least their eyes. Don decided that when he got back to his apartment, he needed to take a good look in a mirror and see if he could see his own eyes. He wondered if what he saw would be different from what living people could see—he hadn't seen any reaction from the EMTs, screaming bloody murder about a bunch of floating eyes at the crime scene, so he had a hunch.

When he was only about a mile from his house, he approached an intersection in which a fender bender was in process. The drivers of the cars had hopped out and started shouting at each other, smoke billowing from one of the drivers' hoods.

Don felt a bit like they were showing off their ability to not get into a complete wreck.

"False alarm," a small voice said next to him.

If Don had been in possession of a physical body, he was sure he would've jumped a foot in the air. He turned and saw a glimmer of something: a pair of eyes, beady and nearly masked by long eyelashes. Just like the eyes at the crash site, these were nearly translucent, but they had a kind shine to them that Don was able to see.

"Are you—what do you mean?" Don asked, careful not to scare the set of eyes away. For all that is good and sane, he lectured himself, this is your time to get some answers, so be a pleasant human being.

"No one died," the voice came again. It was a woman's voice, and almost certainly belonged to a shy woman, given the volume of the words and the way that she sounded like she wanted them to echo back inside of her. Of course, it was hard for words to do such a thing when there wasn't a body to echo inside of. "It was just a fender bender… I was hoping it would be something more, but, um. They're just being dramatic."

"You were hoping it would be something more?" Don asked suspiciously.

The voice was silent for a moment, the eyes blinked and disappeared. A moment later, they reappeared, this time turned toward him. "Are you new?"

Ah, he was a rookie. Great. "Yeah."

"I'm about a year in."

"What—?"

"I mean, um, as a ghost. Sorry, are you *really* new?"

"Yeah."

The eyes turned back to watch the accident. "Oh. Sorry. How did you die?"

Don blinked. The whole conversation was just a little too cavalier. "In a fender bender," he said wryly. The eyes swiveled back to him, measuring him. Perhaps it was harder to read a joke when you didn't have the facial expressions to match. "It was a little worse than a fender bender," he whispered.

"Me too," came the reply. The eyes shone with a hint of understanding. "Worse, I mean. I'm Lydia."

"Don."

"Don." She sounded as if she was saying the name to memorize it. "Um, well. It took me a while to get my bearings back when I died. A couple of weeks."

"All right, can you please just tell me what's going on?"

"Um, limbo, I guess? I don't know, there wasn't exactly a manual."

"Limbo." Don felt the word fall dumbly out of his mouth, and silently chastised himself for repeating words like a parrot. "That's a Christian concept, right?" he said, almost to himself. "Like Barzakh, but Christian."

The eyes squinted. "I don't know what that means."

"It's... I grew up Muslim. I don't know, I don't really know what limbo means to Christians. If it's like stage one of wherever you're going to end up after Judgment Day, then it's like Barzakh."

"Um, okay. So, limbo isn't really stage one, it's just kind of, um. An in-between." She hesitated, squinting. "Wait. Stage one of um, heaven or hell?"

"I... I don't know. Honestly, this doesn't fit the bill for either Jannah or Jahannam. Which means it probably isn't either, huh? Does this fit the bill for limbo?"

"Um. I'm Protestant, not Catholic, so I only remember a little about limbo, but, um... well, we're living in a time after Jesus, so not really."

"Oh." None of that made any sense to Don, but he let it drop. Lydia seemed to be trying to navigate subsects of her own religion that she hadn't ever dealt with before. If she didn't fully understand it, then he wasn't going to get anywhere with it. But he did feel compelled to figure it out. It seemed more and more unlikely that any of his previous knowledge would be of any help there. Apparently the same went for Lydia. Maybe religion had nothing to do with it, in the end. "Well, this is exhausting. I mean, I know I'm dead, but I didn't think it would be this draining, you know?" He sighed. "What have you been doing for the last year? Have you just been walking around, haunting people?"

"I, um, I wasn't sure what I was supposed to do when I first got here," Lydia said. "I thought maybe I was still here because I had, um, unfinished business."

"That's what popped into my head, too, but I can't come up with anything! But that's how it always is in movies, anyway, right?"

"It's not that," Lydia said. "I, um, I've talked with a few people—people like us—who convinced me that wasn't the case."

"How do you figure?"

"This one woman I met was positive that she had unfinished business. She'd died right before her son graduated college. He was, um, the only one in the family to get close—to being a college graduate, I mean—and she was so proud of him, and she thought, I won't be able to move on until I see him reach his goal. So she went to his graduation, and she watched him walk across the stage, and, um... nothing. She was still here."

"Well, maybe that wasn't really her unfinished business. I mean, maybe that's what she thought she needed, but it was something else."

"Maybe. But... theoretically, unfinished business would mean that we would continue on, in limbo or whatever, forever, or until we finished, um, whatever business it was that we needed to finish. But that doesn't seem to be how it works. I've talked to several people who say we... we fade away after a while. You know?"

"There wasn't exactly a manual," he mimicked.

She blinked. "It's a lot to take in, I guess."

"What do you mean, fade away?" Don didn't like the sound of that.

"I don't know for sure. No one does, really. But people… fade."

"Like, die? Again? Like, move on? Couldn't that be the same thing?"

"You can see my eyes right now, right?"

"Yeah."

"So imagine if you didn't even see that."

"Okay."

"People fade. Until they're not there anymore. Or, um, I don't know, maybe they still are there, but just… even less able to communicate."

True loneliness. Don shuddered.

"Or maybe they do move on. I don't know."

"Did the people you talked to fade?"

"I don't know." She sighed. "I mean, um, I didn't see them fade, or move on, I just… didn't see them anymore after a while. But most of them seemed to be collecting, so I would like to think they probably moved on."

"Collecting?"

"You really are new, aren't you?"

"I just said, didn't I?" Don snapped. "Look, you talk about not knowing much, yourself, but at least you've been here a year, at least you've had the opportunity to learn, so stop making fun of me for not knowing what the hell is going on."

The eyes blinked out again momentarily, then reappeared. "I'm sorry," Lydia mumbled. "It's just, I haven't talked to someone this new in a while. Anyway, there's a running theory… and by that, I mean, basically a good guess, that the key to moving on is to start collecting."

"Collecting… what, exactly?"

There was a hesitation. "Um… Life." She hesitated. "Well—energy."

Don was getting frustrated. Whatever happened, he thought, to a good old-fashioned explanation, instead of hemming and hawing around the subject? He sighed. Oswald had mentioned energy, though, so maybe he had been onto something. "What did the last… collector? What did they say?"

"She said that, um, she knew someone who just faded away."

"Who wasn't collecting?"

"Mmmhmm."

"And we're collecting energy?"

"Yeah."

"I have a feeling this isn't going to make any sense until I see it in action."

"Well, I can't show you now."

"Why not?"

The eyes swiveled back to look at Don. "Because nobody died here. There's nothing to collect."

Don was liking the sound of this less and less.

"I'm sorry, I'm not doing a very good job of explaining this. If it makes you feel better, what I'm trying to tell you doesn't even fully make sense to me most of the time."

Don sighed. In a way, it did make him feel better, but it also made him feel worse. If Lydia had already been floating around for a year now and didn't have the answers, then how was he going to fare?

"There's a place over by Englewood Beach that I go and sit," Lydia said after a moment. Her voice was tentative, like she was reaching for straws to make him feel better. "There's a jetty, and a little dock. It's um, it's nice. If you'd like to come." And Don could not see any reason why he shouldn't go to the beach. He was a goddamn ghost, after all, and he couldn't feel the cold weather, so he might as well go sit in the sand and while the hours away with someone to talk to.

It was still hazy when they got there. There was a little girl bundled up in a purple coat, standing with her mom, skipping rocks on the water's calm. That was always the nice thing about Cape Cod, Don thought, even though a lot of people thought of it as a con… the water was calm. The bay protected them from the harsh reality of the ocean beyond. Don had visited the ocean in California with his family once, and the strength of the waves crashing into him was not very pleasant. The west coasters loved it. It had made Cherry cry. She had kept whispering, we'll die, we'll die. Don hadn't thought that, but he did remember not liking the feel of such strength, unfettered. He was used to the shelter of the bay—still able to savor that salty sea taste, but no pummeling to offset the joy. The soft break of lazy waves on wet sand was enough to soothe and lull you into a calm, meditative rhythm, in which he could still hear himself think.

Now, as he and Lydia sat on the jetty, dangling what would have been their feet over the rocks, Don realized the waterfront was too quiet. The sounds of the little girl and her mom, laughing and squealing on the shore behind them, the plunks of rocks and the tickle of water rippling, were not enough to distract Don from his feelings of despair, and it became suddenly apparent to him that that's what he wanted: a distraction. He still wanted to know what was going on, and what to do, but he did *not* want to think of the consequences of his death. That could wait for another day. Right now, he wanted to do what any sane person would do when facing a catastrophe: he wanted to sleep. And he realized he couldn't exactly do that anymore.

"You're making strange noises," Lydia said next to him. In all his inner turmoil, Don realized he had started to hyperventilate.

"I'm just breathing," he spat defensively. The idea made him pause. "How can I do that, anyway? I'm dead, how can I breathe?"

"You're not," Lydia said simply. "Breathing, I mean. But your soul is, um, it's used to the *idea* of breathing, and so it continues the motions, even if it doesn't have a body to physically do the act. You're breathing just as much as you are talking out loud right now."

"What, so I'm not talking out loud?"

"Can those people hear you?" Lydia blinked.

"No. But you can."

Lydia's eyes swiveled to meet his. "I'm dead."

Don sighed. More and more questions flooded his brain, and he wasn't even sure if Lydia knew what she was talking about. But here he was, listening. "So, we can't be seen or heard by the living. We can barely even see ourselves. And—hey, on the way over here, I couldn't feel the mist. Is that another perk of being dead?"

Lydia glanced at him. "Would we, um, call that a perk?"

"Oh, I was one hundred percent kidding. But I guess not being able to feel wet in the rain might be considered a perk. So yeah, I stand by that."

Lydia was silent for a long moment. "I haven't felt anything on my skin for a year now. Not the mist, not the sun... nothing."

"Oh. So... not a perk, then."

"There was one point where I might have felt a gust of wind. That was a strange revelation."

"You *might* have felt it?"

"I mean, um, you just hyperventilated. I'm allowed to be unsure about a gust of wind."

"It's like those GIFs, where you hear the splash when the body hits the water, but there's no actual sound attached to it."

"Yeah. Or, hey, maybe I did feel the wind. There's always that hope."

"But how?"

"I had just collected."

Don sighed. "So we're back to that."

"I'm sorry, I'm overwhelming you. I promise I'll wait to talk more about collecting until your corpse is at least embalmed."

"*Jesus.*"

"I, um, may have also become numb to morbidity." Don saw her eyes glitter, and felt his own invisible lips twitch into a smile.

"I bet you did feel the wind."

"I really do think it's possible," Lydia mused, staring out at the water. "But then... you know. That was a few months ago, and here I am, back to my faded self. Makes you wonder... if we'll ever, um, feel again. You know?"

"At least we don't have to feel pain."

Lydia was silent for a moment. Then suddenly, she let out a little tinkling laugh. "Imagine if we finally make it to heaven, and everyone's excited to see us, and we get hugged by all of our loved ones, and Grandma Rosemary comes right up and swoops you in for a big hug, and, um, since you haven't felt anything for months and months, that tight squeeze just feels like a million bricks laying on top of you."

Don snorted. "Wow, what a great perception of what heaven's gonna be like."

"Yeah, well."

"I don't even believe in heaven, but getting squeezed by some auntie doesn't sound like it's going to sway me to think otherwise."

"Oh." She stared at him. "So you... you must be *very* confused, then."

"A point that we've already established, thanks. But I am gonna point out that I haven't been proven wrong yet."

"We'll see about that," she teased.

Don gave her a sidelong glance. He didn't know why he even bothered looking over at her. It wasn't as if he could actually properly see her.

He frowned. "Hey... when I died, there was this guy..."

"A guy, you mean, like us? Or, um. Alive?"

"He was like us. And... he called me a tween."

Lydia blinked at him.

"What does that mean?" Don prodded.

"I don't know," Lydia said.

"Okay, but you paused, so I don't know if I believe you."

Lydia laughed. "I was pausing out of confusion and, um, curiosity? I mean, I haven't heard that name before. I mean, other than as a—"

"A not-quite-teenager, yeah."

"Um. Like I said. There wasn't someone waiting with instructions when I died. I didn't, um, get a tourist guidebook with the set of terms we're supposed to use. It's possible that this guy just made it up." She paused again. "It makes sense, though. Being between life and death. Tween."

"He was a real asshole," Don muttered. "And also, none of this *really* makes sense. All of us are just making things up as we go along, aren't we? I was living, and I was fine, and then... and then I died, and this world doesn't make sense anymore," Don muttered.

"I'm sorry," Lydia said soothingly. "Don't try too hard to understand it. At least not now. You've, um, you've got the time to figure it out. Right now, just give yourself some time to get used to being here. And try to be content with that."

"How can I be content with that?"

"I, um. I don't know how to tell you this, but I'm not super good at consoling people, and I don't know what you want to hear from me."

Don let this sink in for a moment, and then began to laugh. It was a full-throated laugh—or maybe it was not a laugh at all, given the news he had just received—but nonetheless it echoed across the water, creating its own ripples, not physically, but emotionally, for all the dead who sat by shorelines in the near vicinity. They heard Don's laugh, and the small, tinkling laugh from Lydia that followed it, and for a flash of a second, there it was. There was hope.

Don didn't know why he was even laughing. Perhaps it was still the shock. But in that moment, the laugh felt good, and the laugh felt right. And Don was really glad that he had met Lydia.

It was good to have a friend when you were dead.

CHAPTER THREE

Cherry's fingers slid back and forth along the lining of her hijab. Up, down. Up, down. She felt the texture of the fabric on the tips of her thumb and forefinger, the small bumps of the hem, which, even sewed as deftly as they were, could not escape the electric alertness that Cherry felt. She could feel *everything*. Up, down. Up, down. She knew it was probably the blunt she had smoked on the way to her mother's house that made her feel this—her mother had given her a very suspicious look when she arrived, and Cherry prayed that the conversation would never be brought up—but she also supposed this vibrant alertness could stem from the fact that she was alive… a feat that not everyone had managed in the past week.

She recognized this as a nervous tick—up, down—but she didn't think that stopping would actually help her in any way, and in fact, the action was somewhat soothing, so she allowed herself to continue. She was in mourning… she was allowed to soothe herself in her own little ways. It was funny to her how she could use that excuse for anything—*I'm in mourning, I'm allowed to…*

The funeral had happened the day prior, before her mother had even made it back to the Cape. Ironically, it was her insistence on proceeding according to Muslim tradition that had prevented her from being at her own son's funeral. Tradition was to have the ceremony as soon as possible after the death, since embalming was extremely frowned upon, and the earliest flight from Florida had a long layover that detained her until the next day.

Imam Aasim—a man who had known her family since before Cherry had been born and yet still insisted on calling her brother Donald—had led the funeral prayers. It was a quick and painless ceremony: thank you for coming, Allah Akbar, the calls to silent prayer, and yes, there will be food at the Rind household starting tomorrow. Inna lillahi wa inna ilayhi raji'un; surely we belong to Allah and to Him shall we return.

Imam Aasim had checked in with Cherry after the burial, asking how she was feeling. "It's all very emotional," her reply had been. Even though she felt like a cold, steel bell, hollow and dull. A shell. Her face felt painted on, only there to prove that she had loved her brother, that her mourning was as expected.

And just like that, the service had ended. Cherry had breathed a sigh of relief, which to others sounded like a gasp for breath, like she had been crying. She felt a stab of guilt again.

Why was she not sadder? She had these moments where she was overcome with grief, but they felt more like when you watched a really sad movie and the emotions were plied out of you by the soundtrack and the color scheme and the words that aimed to wrench your heart from your chest. And those moments would quickly fade, leaving Cherry to feel like that empty shell again. She felt cold and heartless—so, so irritable—and she didn't understand it. She thought she was more of a person than that.

But now her mother was here, and the mourning period was upon them. Cherry had taken Monday off from work, allowing her three days to sit in her mother's parlor, welcoming the guests who came to pay their respects. What a fun long weekend.

She didn't recognize many people who were coming through. That was weird. After all, she and Donny had grown up in Yarmouth, and back when their mother had still lived here, the three of them had been very active in the community, both in their own town and in Osterville, where the mosque was. Granted, the main force behind their interaction in the community was usually their mother, and as soon as she began making her snowbird escapes to Florida every year, that socialization quickly stopped. Cherry had her own friends from community college, and Donny was, frankly, disinterested in everything that wasn't video games. So maybe the absence of their mother made the community forget about Donny.

The thought brought a pang to her heart. It wasn't that Donny wasn't—hadn't been—likable, it was just that he did tend to stick to himself. She had always faintly worried about him that way—clearly not enough to do anything about it, to hang out with him herself, but she always wondered if Donny had any close friends. Perhaps not, she thought with resignation, staring at the scattered few who fumbled their way through the door. Maybe these were the only people who deemed her little brother important enough to see him out. Or at least felt comfortable coming to a Muslim household to mourn.

There were still people there, though. There was the little old woman who lived across the street from Donny, who Cherry could only guess had made a perfume from the scent of her cats. She and Cynthia, the woman who had rented Donny the apartment attached to her house, were sitting in the corner, chatting with each other. There was Donny's boss, Mitch, who seemed very uncomfortable in a collared shirt. A few of his other coworkers, and also—and this brought Cherry a wave of ironic joy—Donny's UPS man, who had introduced himself to her almost immediately after he walked in. Cherry supposed he felt awkward for coming, and yeah, it was a little weird for your UPS man to show up at your funeral. But Donny bought a lot of video games. Cherry knew this was still a thing after all these years, because Carl—that was the name of the UPS man—told her how many conversations they had had about the games he was buying, and it touched her heart to think that Donny had somehow made friends in the most unexpected of ways.

The fact that there were a few people that Cherry didn't recognize at all relieved her most of all. These people allowed Cherry to imagine Donny as a social little bee behind her back; that despite her worst fears projected on her brother, he had actually been the life of the party. For this very reason, Cherry hoped to not have to speak at length with any of these people;

where most people would want to connect with those who had stories of their loved one, Cherry preferred thinking that there were these hidden connections, that she had just been the inattentive sister.

During the first day of mourning, it became clear that would not be the case. She would have to talk to these people. People tromped right in, eager to speak with her and her mother, bringing flowers and frozen meals, asking inappropriate questions like, "How bad was the accident?" and, "When was the last time you spoke with him?"

Really, any question felt inappropriate to Cherry, who mostly wanted to just crawl into a cupboard and shut the door. She numbly accepted their brief condolences, letting her mother take the brunt of the conversation, watching them shuffle on by with tissues clasped in white-knuckled fingers. It made Cherry wonder if the tissues were there to elicit an emotion. Maybe these other people were feeling the same way she was: that this was unimportant, that Donny had already died, so why did strangers have to put up with each other and try to talk to each other? They would never see each other again, so there was no point in speaking now. The act was empty. So they held their tissues as a way of saying, "See? I cried tears. I care."

Cherry's mother, on the other hand, didn't seem to have any problem showing her true emotions, staunch and proper though they were. Mina Rind, who had moved from Iran to California to Cape Cod in the span of three successful years back in the 80s, who now casually maintained a winter home in

Florida like it was no big deal, had absolutely no problem being a normal human being. She cried at just the right times, smiled at just the right times, even made small talk at just the right times. She stood with her chin held high, peering at Donny's death guests like they were beacons of hope in a river of sadness. She gave the people what they wanted. They wanted to feel helpful, and she let them know they had succeeded.

That was her mother. It was no surprise she had become so successful over all those years: she knew how to work a crowd. But Cherry still sensed something in her mother's eyes. That challenge. She had known her too long to be entirely convinced by the show. With every "thank you for coming," with every "glad you could make it," her mother was challenging her guests to live up to her expectations. Did you love my son as much as I loved him? her eyes asked. Cherry was sure others didn't pick it up in her mother's demeanor, but the challenge was there. And with their responses—I'm just here for the snacks, I'm just here because I couldn't come up with a better thing to do on a Saturday afternoon; all unspoken but interpreted by Mina Rind—her eyes gleamed with a satisfaction: I loved my son more than anything. I loved him more than you.

Cherry understood the origin of that glint in her mother's eye, even if she couldn't stomach the feeling. She needed to feel as if her closeness with her son was special; and it was. Cherry honestly didn't know how close Don and Mom had been over the last few years, though it didn't really matter. The mother-son bond never really went away. But she was sure that the same thoughts were going through her mother's head that had gone through hers: why didn't I try more? Why didn't I connect with Donny more before he went? So she could see why she might need that extra boost of pride, of stability, on a day like this.

Cherry bit her tongue and kept smiling her sad smile at each guest. She hoped that the remaining people waiting in line would get bored and decide to skip the condolences, and maybe she would be able to leave early. Go home, go to sleep. Sleep felt so alluring right then.

The front door opened, and Cherry's friends, Dee and Thiago, entered. Dee had managed to comb back her Brazilian curls and wear a plain black shirt and slacks, though Cherry noted with a smile that her combat boots still peeked out of her ensemble. And Thiago... Cherry rolled her eyes and smothered a laugh. Thiago had put on a bowtie. That had been a huge argument in college, whether a bowtie was too playful for a funeral. Cherry knew Thiago's insistence on wearing it today was meant to make her laugh, and break her out of her "sads", and she had to admit, a smile did tug at her lips a bit. She walked over to hug the two as they approached.

"Sorry we're late," Dee offered uselessly, as there was no such thing as being late to an event that didn't actually require its guests to show up on time.

Cherry squeezed Dee's thin frame mercilessly. "I'm just glad you're here at all."

"What, did you think we weren't going to show up?" Thiago asked. "Nah, Dee was wicked hungry, so I kept bribing her with the promise of treats."

Dee shoved Thiago, who laughed in as quiet and respectful a way as he could. Cherry gave him a hug before pointing them in the direction of the snacks on the table. "Come find me after, though," she made them promise, then shuffled back over to her mother.

Mina Rind had an eyebrow raised. "You went to college with them at 4Cs, right?" she asked, and Cherry nodded. "I believe I've met Dee, but not the boy."

Cherry heard the curiosity in her mother's voice, and groaned inwardly. "That's Thiago," she said. "You met him at graduation. I'm surprised he made it today, he's been out in Fall River for the past couple of months."

"Fall River?" Mina frowned, and Cherry waited for the statement about what he possibly could have found appealing in Fall River, but it didn't come, thankfully. "That's not that far away," her mother whispered, "and maybe he was looking for a chance to visit."

Cherry chose not to respond to that.

"Did either of them know Donny?"

"They both met him once. Is it okay if I invited my friends to support me if they weren't personal close friends of his?"

Mina clucked. "You don't need to have such a defensive attitude. Of course your friends can visit. I hope to see more of them in the next few days."

Cherry's fingers found the edge of her hijab again.

A young man about Don's age entered the parlor, glanced around, and made a quick beeline for Cherry and her mother.

He had timed his entry perfectly, as there were no other people pestering them about their loss at that moment.

"I'm so sorry for your loss," he said, clasping Mina's hand respectfully. "Don and I were neighbors at UMass. He was a really good guy."

Cherry thought about this for a moment. She didn't remember Donny ever talking about his neighbor in college, but then, she hadn't really kept in touch with him then. It was disconcerting to think that maybe this guy knew more about her brother's life than she would ever know. "What's your name?" she asked.

"Mark. And you must be Cherry," he said, reaching over and shaking her hand eagerly.

"Cheryl," she corrected.

He nodded, his cheeks flushing. "Sorry, that's just what he would call you."

Cherry felt her heart rip in two at that moment, spitting blood out of its valves and quivering at the words that Mark spoke. She pulled her hand away, and folded it under her elbow, and without even looking at the man, she knew he was trying to come up with something to say to soothe the energy of the conversation.

"He really had some great things to say about you," he said softly. As if that was going to make her feel better.

Her mother made small talk with Mark, while Cherry thought about how warm the room had gotten. She tried to remember the breathing exercises her therapist had taught her in high school: breathe in, hold, one two three four, breathe out, hold, one two three four. The endorphins released during this process were supposed to calm you down. Breathe in, hold, one two three four, breathe out, hold, one two three four.

"…okay?"

Cherry blinked. She had left the room for a moment. "What?"

"I said, are you okay?" Mark asked.

Beside her, Mina reached out and touched her wrist, a look of concern flitting across her face. Cherry realized she had started to tip over, and the jarring question helped to steady her.

"I'm fine," she said. She smiled. "I'm so glad you came."

Cherry's tone of voice gave indication that this was Mark's cue to move on, and he did, to her relief. She needed a moment to recollect herself.

That moment didn't happen. "We brought you food," came Thiago's voice behind her, and Cherry and her mother turned to see him and Dee with paper plates stacked full of cheese cubes and grapes in each hand.

"I'm gonna guess you two haven't eaten all day," Dee ventured, thrusting one of the plates towards Cherry. Thiago silently offered one of his plates to Mina, who took it gratefully and nibbled on a piece of cheese. Cherry wearily rearranged some of the crackers on her plate.

"So are the two of you still in the area?" Mina asked, as if Cherry had not just answered that question moments before. The woman was up to something, for sure.

"I am," Dee replied, "but Thiago's fled the Cape." She elbowed him playfully.

"What drew you away?" Mina asked, eyes wide from feigned shock that anyone would leave such a perfect habitat. As if she didn't do that every year.

"I got a job out in Fall River," Thiago replied. "First time living on my own, it's very weird."

"And in such an unsteady neighborhood." There it was, Cherry thought, making a mental check mark next to the Mina Rind Comments on Other People's Living Situations bingo card. "Are your parents still on the Cape?"

"Yeah."

"They must miss you. Do you visit here often?"

"Yeah."

Cherry smirked. She could read the two of them like a book right now. Her mother was trying to wheedle information out of Thiago, and he had very quickly caught on. She wouldn't be surprised if he only gave one-word answers from this point on.

"Hey, I bet the hors d'oeuvres table needs replenishing," Cherry said, nudging him pointedly.

"I'll help," Thiago chirped, and nudged Dee.

Dee looked up, oblivious to what had been happening. Her eyes widened slightly, and she shoved a grape in her mouth. "I guess me too," she said.

Mina called her thanks after the three of them as they made their way out of the stuffiness of the parlor and into the kitchen.

"I can't believe this is just a winter house," Dee muttered, grazing her fingers over the polished marble countertops. "Imagine if my mom spent this much on a kitchen she only used a few months out of the year."

Cherry laughed self-consciously, opening the fridge and pulling out the Ziploc bags of cheese cubes. "Well, it used to be a full-time house. And trust me, the rest of the house isn't as lavish."

"Um, you have a parlor," Thiago reminded her, opening the box of Wheat Thins on the counter and pouring it into a big bowl. "That's fancy talk for 'living room'. Oh my god, do you have a living room *and* a parlor?"

Dee snorted at his comment.

Cherry groaned. "Guys, come on."

"Okay, but seriously, why don't you live here again?" Dee asked, giving Cherry a look. "You're literally paying how much to rent that shitty apartment of yours when you could just stay here while your mother is in Florida?"

"Because then when she came back, I would be living with my mother." Cherry gave a sardonic grin. "She was actually about to just stay here instead of going back and spending the rest of the winter in Florida, but I convinced her that she didn't have to sacrifice her time. Narrowly escaped that... I thought I was gonna have to put up with a couple extra months of her constantly checking in on me."

"You'd have survived. I still live with my mom," Dee reminded her. "I put up with it. That's the only way I'm gonna get through grad school loan payments."

"Okay, okay. I like my freedom, let's just leave it at that." Cherry chewed on her lip.

She knew that Dee and Thiago meant well, but she was never going to feel comfortable with her friends pointing out how well off her mother was. Of the three of them, Cherry was the one practically leaking out privilege. Growing up on Cape Cod was a constant reminder that the world hadn't really finished having the argument of whether immigrants were allowed to settle down in a place without paying their dues of kitchen staff jobs and lawn care businesses, while white-skinned office workers complained that the Cape was losing all their jobs to outsiders. Her mother had been one of the outliers, having not lost any sort of status in coming to this country—she had managed to make the transition without having to jump through the hoops of America's system, armed with a job that allowed her respect and dignity, instead of having to prove the education and status that she had already acquired back home like so many other immigrants did. Cherry couldn't help but feel sometimes that her circumstances left a bad taste in her friend's mouths... her friends who, as second-generation immigrants, had experienced their families going through ten times the hardships with their chins raised high. And that was great, that they had made it to where they were, but they had gone through a harrowing cycle that she had managed to avoid, and why did she feel so incredibly guilty about it?

She knew this was her anxiety peeking out, or maybe even funeral malaise, but she felt it nonetheless. Not that it had prevented her from experiencing prejudice—there was plenty of that to go around. But still, the whole topic made her uncomfortable. She very much wanted to do things on her own, and she knew that even that thought was drenched in privilege.

"By the way," she said, turning to Thiago and deftly changing the subject, "I'm pretty sure my mother expects us to start dating."

Thiago's eyebrows shot up. "Forgive me in your time of mourning, but ew."

Cherry smiled. "Right back at you. But, you know... just in case she starts asking who your third cousins are, where they summer, and whether or not you want kids."

Thiago's face turned beat red, and Dee cackled. "So, I guess you still haven't had that conversation with your mom yet, then?"

"She has too many assumptions about who *her daughter* is, and I... I don't know, I've never cared enough to tell her she's wrong. And I'm not about to start now, not while my brother's body is still practically warm."

"Wow. Dark, but okay," Thiago said.

Cherry cringed inwardly. The comment had been so offhand, she hadn't even thought about how disrespectful it was. Real nice, Cherry, she thought. Way to show him you loved him.

Dee gave Cherry a sidelong look, and squeezed her shoulder. They finished organizing the hors d'oeuvres and carried them back out into the parlor.

* * *

Don watched his mother and sister mingling with the people around them. His family. They were the last reminder to the world that Don had once existed.

It had frustrated Don that he hadn't been able to actually go to his own funeral. He knew it was a once-in-a-lifetime opportunity—ah, the phrasing of that—but by the time he had convinced himself to go, he knew it would be too late. Not being able to drive as a ghost was very irritating. The Cape was a small place, but it was still nearly a half-hour drive from Yarmouth to the mosque in Osterville. Take away fossil fuels, and the amount of walking Don would have needed to do was astounding.

He had also been terrified to see the lump of his broken body under that white sheet. He was really glad he had missed that part.

But even if he didn't get to attend the funeral, he knew he would be remiss if he at least didn't swing by for the days of mourning. As glad as he was to have missed seeing his corpse, he would have to deal with seeing the faces of his family. It was traditional to reserve your grief to some extent, but his mother looked willing to push the limits.

It was always a bit more difficult to gauge Cherry's emotions. He knew, though, in the way that she held onto the hem of her hijab, like she always did when she was nervous. He wondered if she knew that she did that. And in the way that she would mutter things to herself, no louder than a subvocalization, but Don knew what she was saying. She always told their mother she was saying prayers, but she was really repeating her breathing techniques to herself, like she learned when she was in high school. It had driven Don nuts when she had started doing it, but it was better than watching her have a meltdown.

Don glanced around the parlor, taking in the small crowd. It hadn't struck him until now that there weren't really any other people he would have liked to see at his funeral. Sure, maybe it would've been nice for that cute girl who worked at the convenience store to come, and he was very dutiful in noting who from the pizza place had made their appearance and who had not bothered to show up... but there was not really anyone in his life who he was aching to see.

He tried to take stock of his last few years of life. Hell, he thought, even just the past year. There had to have been something that he had done right, friends that he had bonded with, something to leave a meaningful impact.

He had always talked about going out for happy hour, meeting new people, going on a date or two. But he never did. It was humiliating to think now that his life really had been on autopilot for the past few years... get up, go to work, come home, sit on the couch, and play video games for a few hours until suddenly he had to remember to eat dinner before going to bed. If it hadn't been for his stomach grumbling, he wondered if he would have even remembered dinner most nights.

But he had enjoyed that life, hadn't he? He had a night job, which allowed him a slow, leisurely routine of waking up naturally with the sunlight—he was so proud to not have to use a godawful alarm clock—eating Cocoa Puffs on his couch, and playing video games before work, usually finishing whatever level or campaign he had been working on just in the nick of time. He loved that routine. It was his normal, his happy place. In the context of death, he could see how most people would see that as a low bar he had set for himself. But it was good to be happy, right? Even if he had purposefully made "happy" not all that difficult to achieve. Sometimes he would run errands; sometimes he would walk his elderly landlord's dog, if her arthritis was acting up—Cynthia had made an appearance at the funeral, bless her. Not only did Don count his errands for her as a good act under his belt, but he was very pleased to see that she had come out to mourn his death. He had always liked Cynthia.

But he was still there, which meant he must have done something wrong. Maybe there was only one version of happiness that allowed you to move on to the afterlife; maybe you *had* to have a more complicated form of "happy". Maybe you had to tick off the boxes to move on properly, and those boxes were very particular, like on The Good Place. Maybe the standards were so high that Don would never have made it, even if he had done all the good deeds in the world. But then, where were all the other dead people? Obviously, not that many people got stuck here like he and Lydia were. So that meant that, if there was some sort of standard, it was a really strange standard, widely specific in its exclusions.

Don let his mind wander, ignoring the guests that milled around him, sometimes even through him.

When he was alive, Don had, on occasion, ventured out. On his days off, sometimes he would go to the tavern down the street, Giardino's. He and his sister had gone to Giardino's all the time with their Uncle Bobby when they were kids. Uncle Bobby was from their dad's side, a born-and-raised Cape Codder who had an even thicker local accent than their dad, and a hell of a drinking problem; but he did love spending time with his niece and nephew. He always bought them Keno tickets, and told them stories about their dad, inadvertently, anyway. The place made Don happy, with its walls chock full of old photos and drawings—the big Figawi sign and the high school soccer team photos. They always got the nice server named Marie who had a Jamaican accent and always asked him how school was.

Don liked going to Giardino's as an adult. Uncle Bobby had passed on by then, and going without him had a different feel to it: he actually sat at the bar instead of one of the booths, drank beer instead of a Roy Rogers. He wasn't much for socializing when he was there, but he liked to people-watch at the bar. He had at least garnered some recognition from the bartender, who wasn't about to break their unspoken pact and start a conversation with him, but on occasion, would sidle up to the bar in front of Don, and listen in on the other patrons' conversations with him. It was a silent understanding: there would be no awkward small talk, just: "I'd like a Sam," and then two hours of mutually accepted observation.

Don wondered about that bartender. He honestly didn't even know the guy's name, and clearly, they hadn't built a rapport enough that he would even know that Don was dead, let alone come to his funeral. But Don wondered if the man would eventually notice his absence, after a few weeks.

What did it matter, really? There wasn't any way to communicate, or any way to go back and introduce himself. Don had forever lost his chance to make an impression on the people around him. If he'd wanted a crowd at his funeral, he should have planned ahead.

But being a shy, to-himself individual didn't mean he had wasted his life away. There were plenty of people whose deaths revealed they had been working on a Nobel Prize-worthy science experiment or had given all their money to the local charity.

Don grimaced. There was no way he could even attempt to compete with that. Let's face it, Donny Boy, he thought. You coasted through a semblance of life. You chose to enjoy other people's creations rather than creating your own—you chose to sit back and view, rather than lean forward and do.

Maybe that was what had gotten him left behind. Maybe everybody had figured it out, had done something active with their life, and there Don was, boasting his skills of people-watching and playing video games.

Don studied Cherry and his mother for another moment with a sinking feeling. It would most likely be the last time he would see either of them. After the mourning period, his mother would probably go back to Florida for another couple of months. And who knew if he would still be around by then? And Cherry... well, she would still be there. Maybe he would see her again, but he felt strange about the idea of just showing up at her door, hoping to catch another glimpse of her before he moved on. Or faded away. The thought nauseated him. He wanted to reach out to them, tell them that he was there, that… well, he didn't exactly know what to tell them. That he was all right? *Was* he all right? That was typically something that he had seen ghosts tell their loved ones in movies. It's all right, they would say, I'm in a better place. It's time to move on.

But Don wanted to scream, scream at the top of his lungs, It's not all right, I'm here, please wake me up from this nightmare and put me back in my body!

His body was broken in two and buried six feet deep. It was going to take a lot more than waking up from a nightmare to fix that. But he still found himself hoping that he would wake up anyway, and Cherry would call him on the phone, and he would say, "Whoa, sis, I just had this crazy dream," and she would laugh at him and tell him everything was all right.

That wasn't even a very Cherry thing to say. He knew better than to let his imaginings get away with him—they would only bring more melancholy to the situation. Snap out of it, he thought. You barely even talked to Cherry these past few years, why do you imagine yourself to be best buds with her now?

Don found it faintly annoying that dead people were not excused from the mourning process. No, he had to be a part of his own mourning party. He couldn't have just disappeared in a puff of smoke like a good atheist, oblivious to the hole his death had left in his loved ones' lives. Or hell, he would even take some form of afterlife at this point—ushered to a place of unmitigated joy and bliss, where again, he wouldn't have to think about all this. That would have been too easy a game for Fate to have played... instead, here he was, wondering how much they missed him, wondering if there was anything about his life that had really mattered. Wondering why he hadn't gotten a dog or something—anything to give his life meaning.

Well. At least Fate hadn't thrown him into someone's version of hell. Though this was looking more and more like his own version of it.

CHAPTER FOUR

D on had never realized how much life was equated with busyness.

It was as if humans refused to sit still; every moment had to be full of purpose, and if it wasn't, then what were you doing, sitting there? To "get a move on" was the peak of human existence. Don't you dare waste a single moment.

This was accentuated in the hospital hallway that Don and Lydia now stood in: nurses and orderlies speed-walking to their next patient, the shuffling of forms at the reception area as incoming patients were told to please take a seat and wait to be called, and the fidgeting of those in the seats, as if to wait was a physical impossibility—or no, an *insult*, which one could not accommodate without some sort of twitching and eye rolling as the moments ticked by.

Lydia had suggested they go to the hospital to give Don an idea of how to collect. It had taken a few seconds for that to sink in and register for Don: Lydia was suggesting they go to the hospital to *watch people die.*

What was worse, they weren't just watching, they had an objective. The whole thing just didn't feel right to Don.

But, as Lydia had timidly reminded him, it was either collect or slowly fade away, and Don knew exactly which terrible option he would choose.

"What does fading away mean?" Don had asked.

"I don't know," Lydia had replied. It felt like this was the millionth time they'd had this conversation, and it was beginning to show in Lydia's tone.

"But, I mean, we're already dead. The next step would be moving on to the afterlife. What if fading away is just the same thing? What if we just go on to the afterlife? What if collecting and fading are equal?"

"It's possible," Lydia had said. But the hint of doubt in her voice was unmistakable, and even if Lydia was not certain, it seemed that the only way *he* could be certain was to go the path well-trodden, or whatever nonsense that saying was.

He could take a guess, refuse to collect, and risk the possibility that he would just stop existing… or, he could do what every other dead person he'd met seemed to be doing, and ensure that he would stick around.

So Don and Lydia went to the hospital.

Don hadn't been in a hospital in a long time. The last time he had been there was when his father had died; at four years old, there was not much that stuck in his mind about the occasion, but the one thing that he did remember—more like couldn't suppress—was the smell. To little Donny, it smelled like powdered gloves and cough drops. He hadn't been able to comprehend the actual origin of the smells he took in as he'd walked down the white, sterile hallway, watching people in scrubs shuffle to and fro, watching squeaky phlebotomy carts pass by and clipboards bounce with the gait of those who held them. All he knew was that it didn't smell like home, and Daddy didn't smell like Daddy—he smelled strange, like someone had wiped him down with a sickly-sweet sanitizing wipe, the kind that Mommy used on the countertop when it was dirty, and maybe Daddy was dirty, maybe that's why he was here, in the hospital.

Don remembered how his mother had clutched his and Cherry's hands, one child on each side of her, like a fortress. They had walked through the hall and stood at the entrance to Daddy's new room—temporary room, Mommy said—and waited while Mommy broke down in tears, squeezing their hands even tighter. They could all remember the shouting just hours before, shouting in the living room while Donny and Cherry played in the dining room—but Donny and Cherry hadn't been in the room when Mommy shrieked and tripped over her pocketbook trying to reach the phone, shaking as she dialed and talked to the person on the other line. They had come into the room only when Daddy was leaning on Mommy, the two of them making their way to the door, and then there were flashing lights and men in blue collared shirts with a rolling bed, and—

Don blinked. The hospital wing that Lydia had guided him into was quiet. No, serene. There were no rushing nurses, no crying family members, just a bored looking secretary who held the button to keep the doors open for an orderly.

Don and Lydia swept into the hallway, numbly walking past rooms with quiet beds, sleeping patients whose TVs quietly flickered at them as if saying, "Try me out before you go."

This was the hallway of the resigned. They all knew death was coming, and no one was complaining. They all had made peace with their varying conditions.

Lydia had told Don that they wouldn't find much energy there. Or at least, she didn't think so… it was so hard to tell what exactly the rules were, it was simply that she was going off past experience. The two deaths she said she'd seen in that wing had not produced very much, but she insisted it was a good beginner's trial. Lydia was going to show Don the ropes.

They picked their way through the patients, peeking over nurses' shoulders at the charts, trying to guess who would be next. Don felt sick at the idea of what they were doing. Not that they would be *doing* anything—at least not to encourage someone along on their way—but they were still *hoping* for it. And that was a difficult idea to swallow.

Finally, they came to the bed of a woman, arms like twigs, her skin so papery thin that Don swore he could see the blood limping along through her veins. Her breath came in rasps. Her hair, which Don was sure at one point had been neatly cultivated to one side and pinned back, was now receding, mussed, like a tuft of grass that hadn't been properly tended to in a while. Which, he thought with a grimace, was probably uncomfortably true. Sure, the orderlies changed her clothes and kept her clean, but they didn't care how her hair looked.

Lydia's eyes swiveled towards Don. She was silent for a moment. Then, "This will be the one."

Don gulped. "You mean…"

"Well, um. I can't know. For sure, I mean. But she looks close."

Her eyes dropped suddenly from their place in the air, and Don realized that Lydia was sitting. She was setting up camp. He shuddered.

"What if it takes—?"

"We, um. We've got the time," Lydia whispered. She sighed. "There's nothing about this process that is quick and painless," she warned. "You're dead now. You don't get quick and painless. Maybe, um. Maybe we'll get that after we move on."

Don laughed nervously. "Maybe."

Lydia eyed him for a moment. "This one will be yours," she said slowly. "There's no use in splitting the energy, at least, um, not from what I can tell, for this one. But after this, we collect separately."

"Wait. Are you—?"

"It's not like we can't hang out," Lydia assured him. "It's just… I prefer collecting alone."

Don thought about it for a moment. He could understand why Lydia would not want to do this with an audience. He hadn't even seen the process yet, but it didn't sound like an ideal social activity. He supposed that meant that he really needed to pay attention this time around. If he couldn't figure out how to collect now, he would be on his own. "Okay. So what do we do?"

"Be patient," came Lydia's reply. "It's not really an action, more than it is just being nearby when it happens."

"Right. So, you have to be within a certain radius of... the death?"

Lydia was silent for a moment. She watched the frail woman before them, then stood, her eyes hovering over the chart by the end of the bed. "Her name is Patricia Lloyd," she whispered. "Age seventy-nine."

Don sat on the floor, appreciating the fact that she hadn't answered his question. This was a woman's life, and he had been treating it like a practice test in middle school. Just because he was dead didn't mean he had to be cold. "Hi Patricia," he said quietly, "I'm Don." That felt silly, but Lydia returned the gesture, introducing herself too.

There was something Don was still stuck on. He cleared his throat. "Ah, Lydia..." Lydia's eyes swiveled towards Don. She waited. "It's just... How do we know this isn't... I don't know, hurting her?"

"We don't," Lydia said simply. "No one honestly knows what exactly happens when you collect. Um. We just know that when a person dies, if their spirit, um, doesn't end up here, with us, then that means it's somewhere else."

Don toyed with that thought. He pictured the gates to heaven being slammed shut in Patricia's face, because someone had collected her energy before she made it there. "Are we... stealing it?"

"*I don't know,*" Lydia repeated, a little exasperated. "Look. You don't have to do this. You could decide not to collect."

"And then what? Disappear like your friend said? How do we know the people who disappear aren't just going to heaven after a while?"

Lydia blinked. "Maybe that's exactly where they go. Would you like to risk it?"

Don wished that Lydia could see the glare he was giving her.

Lydia turned back to Patricia, watching her ragged breath slowly lift her chest, then lower it back down again. "Can we please stop arguing?"

"I'm not arguing, I..." He stopped himself, sighed, and agreed.

The two of them sat, settling in, watching the woman in the bed, and the slow crawl of the hospital outside her door.

It took about twenty hours, the majority of which Don spent fidgeting his nonexistent body in impatient agony, but not daring to say a word, while Lydia sat serenely. He even heard her humming softly a couple of times. And finally—Don kicked himself for thinking the word—the old woman before them closed her eyes, and took her last breath.

Don stared at the dead woman, a shade of grief falling over him.

"It's happening," Lydia whispered. "Go."

Don glanced sharply at her. "What do you mean? What's happening?"

"*Look.*"

Don stared at the body carefully, unsure of what he was supposed to look at.

And then something strange happened: Patricia Lloyd began to glow.

Just a little; it was barely noticeable, and had Lydia not pointed it out, Don would've missed it—in fact, he wondered how many glows he had missed already simply by not knowing what to look for. It seemed to seep from the woman's pores, and for one brief moment, she looked like she was full of some sort of soft electricity, an organic energy.

Lydia took a step back, nudging Don forward. He felt a surge of panic—what should he do?

He saw the glow lift up off the woman and waft out and around him. Was this her soul? Was this energy what a soul looked like when it wasn't trapped here, stuck like he was? Would Patricia move on to heaven? How would she move on? Was there a door, would some sort of Reaper come to whisk her away? Don didn't think any of those questions would be answered. But he leaned forward, and did the only thing he could think of: he drank it in.

The glow was not a physical thing, but it felt like water going down his throat. It numbed his insides, cool yet warm at the same time, and he felt a tickle within himself. For a flash of a second, the world around him looked different—like he was seeing elation. It was a strange feeling.

And just as quickly as it began, it ended, and the world looked the same again. Patricia Lloyd lay, dead, before them, and Don felt strange. He didn't know if it was a good strange, or bad strange. No, he decided. It wasn't either sort of feeling. It was just… a feeling. That was it.

"Good job," Lydia whispered behind him.

He whipped his head around to stare at her. Now he felt the bad kind of strange creeping into him. He had just drunk someone's energy. *He had just drunk someone's energy.* What did that even mean? Was he stronger now? Was he an awful person for thinking that question? Would he ever know the effect he had had on Patricia's passing to whatever afterlife was out there?

As he and Lydia left the hospital, what he would later learn was often called the "after-collection gloom" hung over him.

CHAPTER FIVE

Don phased through the front door of his apartment and stood on the other side, frowning. He had hoped that would be fun, walking through, but instead, it left him feeling strange.

Or maybe it wasn't walking through a solid object that made it strange... maybe it was the room he had walked into. Don glanced around, taking in the stale, cluttered living room with new eyes. It looked exactly as he had left it on Wednesday afternoon. His coffee cup from Cumby's was still sitting on the coffee table from his last night alive. He had probably thought, I'll throw it away when I get home tonight. And now someone would see that coffee cup, they would come in to clean and get rid of his stuff and see it sitting there and think, the guy who lived here didn't really clean up after himself.

Not that the coffee cup was the only clue of that. A sweatshirt was bunched up in the seam of the couch, and a couple of cords hung out on the floor in front of the TV. He didn't typically have guests, so he didn't typically have a timeframe for when things needed to be put away.

Strange to think about the things he should have worried about when he was alive.

There was a rustling sound from the next room, and Don started, heart pounding. A reflex—whatever it was, he wasn't in danger from it. What could possibly happen, he'd get killed again?

He crept through the hall and peered through the doorway to his bedroom. Cherry was inside, sitting cross-legged on the floor with several cardboard boxes and trash bags laid out before her in a circle, sorting through a drawer.

She must have gotten stuck with cleaning out Don's things. It made sense… their mother had probably already flown back to Florida. If Don could venture a guess, Cherry had all but begged her to go.

Don felt a wave of guilt wash through him as he watched her pick through his things. No one should have to look through their dead brother's stuff. He glanced around, hoping he wouldn't find anything embarrassing, before realizing that the room was covered in balled up socks and stray boxers. An entire load of clean laundry sat in a pile, un-folded, next to the overflowing, dirty hamper. His mother had always hounded him about picking up his room when he was a kid, so naturally, he stopped doing it as an adult. Ah, well, she was his sister. She'd get over it. But Don had never felt as anxious as he did in that moment, watching his sister surrounded by the cluttered dump that was his home.

The rest of Don's room looked exactly as it had in his mother's house when he was a teenager. He even still had the same posters up on the wall, David Bowie and the Cranberries. Apparently decorating had been too much for him in his twenties; he'd just copied over his juvenile interests to maintain a semblance of style.

He glanced down at Cherry as she rummaged through his things. She was doing a terrible job of actually packing things away—she kept stopping and looking at each item she picked up, examining it and, Don could only imagine, thinking about what significance it had for her little brother.

Cherry had taken the little wooden car from its perch on the windowsill and was examining that now. It was from the Pinewood Derby that Don had entered when he was four years old, which was more a testament to his father's attention than anything Cherry might reminisce about Don. Daddy had helped him decide the shape of the car and talked to him about aerodynamics—as if a four-year-old was going to be able to retain any of that—sitting with him and guiding his hand while he scraped at the pine wood and shaved off little pieces until it finally started to look like a car. He remembered that his dad was excited about it, until... well, until he wasn't, anymore.

That moment was irreplaceable in Don's mind. He had been sitting at the kitchen table, painting his car, and Daddy was hunched next to him, squinting and muttering praises. "Looks good, kiddo," he said. "You're gonna knock the judges' socks off. Who is judging, anyway?"

Donny rattled off a couple of the teachers' names. "And Jesse's dad."

A shadow crossed his father's face.

"Jesse's dad?" he repeated.

"Mmmhmm."

"Why is he judging?"

"He's one of the volunteers, and they needed an odd number of judges."

His father's eyes got wild. He leaned back in his chair, let out a heave of a sigh, and dragged his hands across his face, hiding for a moment. When the hands came down, Don saw that his expression had changed to one of resignation, eyes closed, lips twitching into a frown. "What?" he asked.

"It's nothing," his father said. "You keep painting. At least you can have the best-looking car out there, even if you don't stand a chance of winning the race."

Donny narrowed his eyes. "You said I have a pretty good chance!"

His father sighed. "Well, that was before I found out the playing field." He was convinced that Jesse's father would cheat somehow. Rig it somehow, make it so the extra weight on his kid's car would be overlooked. He couldn't be persuaded otherwise. "Look, it's okay if you don't win, you know that, right? It doesn't mean that you're not a winner, you know?"

"Daddy." Don put down his paintbrush.

That was when his mother entered and yelled at her husband for being discouraging.

He kept muttering, "I just don't want him to get his hopes up," and then finally, he came back over and said, "Keep painting, Donny Boy. I'm sorry. I was wrong."

He wasn't. Jesse won first place at the Pinewood Derby. Maybe his dad had been right; Don would never know. Thing was, Don didn't even rank—the judges assigned second and third place to other kids.

Don had been heartbroken. He had gone home and cried, and his father had sighed and hugged him and said, "I know. Dreaming big always comes with its hitches, huh?" And that night, Donny and Cherry sat listening through the walls while a spectacular parental spat occurred in the next room over.

Don rolled his eyes. He never really had been into friendly competition after that. That was probably for the best.

It struck Don as funny now that he had kept the car. Maybe he did it because it was one of the last things he and his father had done together. His mother had probably had a hand in making sure he held onto it. And, well into his twenties, the car remained.

Cherry had a far off look on her face as she placed the derby car into one of the big cardboard boxes in front of her, already crammed with other items. Great, Don thought, something that will remind her of her two dead family members. He wondered if that box was a "keep" or "donate" box. Actually, scratch that, he didn't want to know. If it had been him, he would have just chucked it all. Nothing of his was *that* important, really.

He could picture it now: Mina would come back to her winter home in a month or so, go down into the basement to do laundry, see a big box labeled "Donny's Things", and then everything would all come flooding back—the memories, the sadness. And then Mina would get mad at Cherry for leaving it there, and Cherry would say, "I was just trying to save what was left of him, Mom," and then they'd get into a big fight, and god damn it, just throw the box away, Cherry. You don't want to go through that, now or ever.

This couldn't be easy for her. He wished he could make it easier for her. He wished he had picked up the night before his death, or somehow had a clairvoyant moment and just packed up or thrown out all his things. Cherry had never been overly sentimental, but she had a heart, and Don didn't think he would make it very far looking through *her* stuff before breaking down.

She kept plowing through, though, her face nice and blank as she divided up the contents of his life. At this point, Don wasn't sure if her stony silence was comforting or unnerving. She was sad, right? She had to be sad. Don really hoped she was sad.

He wasn't even sure why he had come here. There was nothing left for him here. He'd had this crazy idea that, if unfinished business really was the game, maybe he would see something that would give an indication of what his was. But all he saw was clutter.

Once one box was full, Cherry hoisted it up and carried it to her car. She was gone for just a moment, and when she came back into the apartment, she grabbed a water glass from the kitchen cupboard, filled it, and downed it. Blinking, she put the glass in the empty sink—Don was at least thankful he had done the dishes—and Don saw her jaw muscles clenching as she washed the water down with whatever intrusive thoughts were floating around in her head. So she *was* sad, she just... wasn't dealing with it. She packed away the memories quicker than she packed up the things that triggered them.

Back to work. Don sat quietly on the stripped bed while she sifted through, an organizational machine. One by one, items from his life disappeared from his shelves, and bit by bit, the bedroom became an empty shell. Nothing that Cherry transferred to the boxes reached out to him, begged him for completion in any way; nothing screamed "unfinished business". Cherry moved on to the kitchen, and then the living room, and finally tossed everything in the bathroom into a big trash bag. Fair enough.

And then she was gone; she climbed into her car and drove off, presumably with plans to come pick up furniture later. Or maybe she had told Cynthia to keep the furniture. Help furnish the place for the next tenant. Who knew?

Goodbye, Cherry, thought Don, watching her car recede into the distance. Maybe he should've gotten into the car with her, followed her to her next location. But why? So he could haunt her? Be a creepy dead man following the last of his kin forever around town until they died, too?

Don gave his apartment one last walk-through, ignoring that now-familiar feeling of despair, and sat for a moment on the couch, his mind buzzing with dead-end thoughts. This was it. Other than a few knick-knacks at his mother's house, the things that proved Don had lived on this planet were now gone.

He sighed. There was no unfinished business. Unless you counted living. He hadn't gotten to finish that—but then, who did, really?

In normal circumstances, when Don felt uncomfortable or out of place, he would get this gut feeling, a want to go home. But now, he wanted nothing more than to leave this place. He no longer had a home. He couldn't shut the world out, couldn't hide away where no one could get him.

All that was left was to fade.

CHAPTER SIX

Cherry heard the small scratching sound of a flier being pushed under her door. She heaved a sigh, and lay in bed for another moment, considering the idea of never getting up to check it. She guessed the messenger was one of two people: it could be Mason, the ex-frat boy who lived on the second floor and had ragers periodically, much to the dismay of the majority of the apartment complex—and yet he invited everyone, every time. Cherry liked to think Mason's sense of humor was such that he wanted to see everyone in the building at their most awkward, standing in the corner with a beer as his friends danced on tables. Or, it could be Edna, the frail, enthusiastic woman on the first floor, who—and Cherry beamed at this idea every time—would occasionally leave notes for people in the building to come to tea. Edna liked having guests over, and it seemed that the only way to have guests over was to invite them… Cherry appreciated this "go get 'em" attitude very much, but could never see trying it herself.

After a moment, Cherry rolled out of bed, shuffled her way to the entryway, and tugged at the small corner of paper. It was stuck between the door and the threshold, having not been pushed far enough inside. Cherry was very hopeful that it was a call to tea with Edna. She needed some decompressing time, now that her brother's funeral was in the past, and she felt that Edna would be extremely helpful with that.

Cherry opened the door at the same time as her across-the-way neighbor.

Her name was Jill. Or Jane. Or something with a "J", Cherry had never quite been sure. Upon first meeting her, Cherry had mumbled her way through introductions, her heart slamming into her chest, because *god*, Jess was beautiful. She was tall, with broad shoulders and a small, hawk-like nose, with her short blonde hair slicked back like a model. Her eyes had glittered when she smiled, and her voice had sounded like honey. "I'm Jenn/Jolene/Jade," she had said. Cherry had nodded. She had *nodded*. Like, yes, I approve of the fact that you are named that. That kind of nod. So, really, it was a bit ridiculous that Cherry couldn't remember her name.

Cherry had lived across the hall from Julie for three years now, and had only had two interactions with her: the first, aforementioned. The second, Cherry had been in the front hall, trying to force the wad of envelopes from her mailbox. This always happened. There would be days in which Cherry would get nothing in the mail, and then suddenly, she had a full box, and would have to jiggle the envelopes carefully to retrieve them without ripping them.

That day, she had not realized that Joan was passing behind her in the hall just as she made one final yank, rescuing the letters from the mailbox's grasp but consequently sending her elbow into the poor woman's shoulder.

Justine had seemed forgiving enough, and had even made a joke about it. "It's okay, really," she had said, "I was just thinking I only wanted the one shoulder, anyway."

But that had been the last time the two of them had interacted. Cherry had been sure it would never happen again. She didn't have the courage to cross the hall, knock on the door, and ask to borrow a cup of sugar, like she sometimes imagined doing, or ask if she wanted a running partner. Which was ridiculous because Cherry didn't run. She just knew that Jocelyn did, because sometimes she looked out her window and saw her following the winding path leading up to their building, in a tank top and leggings.

Now, Judy gave a little wave and a smile, and stooped to pick up the piece of paper outside *her* door. "Ugh," she said, reading the contents. "Not another one of these."

Cherry retrieved her own flier: it was, in fact, an invitation to a rager. She rolled her eyes. "I guess this means I need to buy more earplugs."

"You're telling me," Jackie said with a laugh, the honey still oozing from her voice. "I'm directly below!"

Cherry glanced up at the ceiling. "Oh, no, you're right!" she cried, and gave an empathetic frown. "I'm sorry."

"Not your fault." Jeanie tapped the edge of the flier on her doorframe. "Maybe I'll have to go out on the town that night."

She raised an eyebrow, flashed a smile, and went back into her apartment, closing the door and leaving Cherry to melt back into her own apartment.

She wished she'd said more. Maybe she could have invited Janet to go for drinks the night of the rager, to avoid the noise—or even better, she could have invited her to go for drinks right then and there.

Cherry leaned against her closed door, closing her eyes and trying to stop the dizziness that had taken over her. No, she thought, your brother just died. You shouldn't be trying to go on a date.

And besides, she thought, there was no reason that Jodie would actually want to grab a drink with her. She was the shy neighbor who wore—Cherry looked down at her apparel—sweatpants and an oversized sweatshirt, constantly. She never worked out. And she had anxiety attacks at the mere thought of emotional intimacy.

Cherry, facing the realistic conclusion she had drawn, nodded to herself, and threw the flier in the trash on the way back to bed.

* * *

Don sat on the edge of the jetty, staring out at the sun hanging low in the sky over the water. He had actually crawled out on the rocks this time, carefully—as if he needed to be careful without a body to bruise—picking his way down to the water. He liked this view. He wondered how far down into the water the rocks went before hitting sand—how far they continued to go, past the floor of the ocean.

The waves crested languidly on the rocks at his feet, and he gazed into them, studying the reflection of pastel swaths from the sky. It really was a gorgeous sight. He didn't think he had ever spent this much time at the beach in his entire life. Ironically, for someone who had lived five minutes from the ocean since he was born, he had so often taken it for granted and only rendezvoused with it as much as landlocked folks might do in their weekends on the Cape. He had never paid attention to how beautiful the sunset was, not really. Sure, his mother had pointed it out to him many times—"Donny, look! See how Allah smiles at us from the sky!"—but for some reason, the pinks and purples interacting with the horizon had never captivated him like they did now. Death had brought Don one thing, at least, and that was perspective.

Except, the sunset had also never made him sad. It was a reminder of the things that he would be leaving behind, should he ever manage to get himself out of this godforsaken tween state.

He kicked his legs uselessly at the water below. Not even a ripple came from the movement, but he still just barely felt the cool of the water flooding past his toes. Or maybe he was imagining it, he thought, smirking. Like Lydia's gust of wind. He mused that if he could at least imagine the water around his toes, maybe that meant he was barefoot. If he were to be corporeal, he thought idly, would he be wearing shoes? Would he be wearing *clothes*?

The thought made him chuckle, and he reached to "himself" to investigate. He grazed what should have been his fingers across what should have been his forearm, and grimaced. It was strange… maybe he could imagine he was feeling some sort of effect of the water on his feet, but he couldn't feel even a faint impact from his hand on his arm. There was more tangibility in the water than there was in his body.

Lydia was meeting him there. Now that he had learned how to collect, he had kept to his word, and tried to schedule himself for collecting time… apart from Lydia. It was like a job, he thought. He could work the nine to five and then still have his nights and weekends to socialize. Keep himself sane.

Maybe not exactly nine to five, though. Don remembered reading an article in The Atlantic years back which stated that statistically, 11:00 a.m. was the most likely time to die. He felt uncomfortable remembering that fact now, but it would come in handy for scheduling purposes: he would focus his collecting time in the morning—maybe he'd start at 10:00 a.m., or even earlier if he happened to feel particularly bored, just to give himself some lead time—and if he hadn't found anything by early afternoon, then he could make the decision whether to keep "working" or not.

So far, he hadn't been terribly successful at finding anything. He had gone back to the hospital, figuring that this would be a good place to start, but perhaps he and Lydia had just been lucky that day, and the other collectors had finished for the day… now, every time he turned a corner, he ran into another collector, wispy and desperately translucent, waiting for someone to croak.

The second death he witnessed at the hospital, three other collectors were within a ten-foot radius, and the death drew them like moths to a flame. He knew what to look for now, so the glow was immediately apparent to him, but splitting one death between four people made Don feel like a seagull fighting for scraps with the other gulls at the beach. He wasn't even sure if he could count this as a second collection, so little did he absorb, the other three slurping up the energy beside him—they might as well have had their mouths open wide, like Pacman eating energy pellets.

There was no way he was going to get any real energy if he had to fight with a crowd of onlookers.

So Don had begun to venture out, looking for new places for people to die. Where could he start? And honestly, how often was he going to get lucky if he wasn't hanging out in the hospital? He thought of the obituary page: it always had quite a few obituaries, but then, that was for the entire region. He imagined that being in the right place at the right time would take precision and intention.

So he made a mental list: there was that intersection where everyone always complained about the lack of stoplight. "They only put up a light once somebody's died," his mother had always said.

Then there was the ocean, which seemed a bit far-fetched— Don supposed that if it were the middle of the summer, he would have a better time of it. He'd just go to the beaches that didn't have active lifeguards on duty—but winter was still lingering, and swimming weather wouldn't be here for at least another month or so. And even then, once the weather warmed up, he didn't have much hope in the chance of a drowning, not when there would be that many people present to help someone who needed aid. It would be better if he came to the beach late at night—that was the time when sad people came to the beach, with thoughts of suicide on their minds.

This thought gave Don pause. Every day that he tried to collect, he felt more and more sickened by what he was doing. Don did not want to collect the energy of a suicide victim. He didn't want to collect *anyone's* energy—he preferred if they could keep themselves alive, if they could find help and not commit suicide, or slow down when approaching an intersection. Why did he have to be this person? Was moving on really worth seeing the horrors of this world?

Lydia was right. He could stop collecting and take the risk. Maybe fading away wasn't a bad thing—maybe it was just a different way of moving on. After all, before he had died, he had expected to just fade away. What was so different about that idea now? What about being a tween made him so hesitant now to fade away?

Don shuddered. Maybe it was the thought that fading away didn't necessarily include his conscious mind.

But still. He was not ready to stoop to the level of searching for suicide victims. Not yet, anyway.

He would not rule it out, but he would also not search for it.

Don could not wait to get out of this hellish purgatory.

Since the hospital, Don had not collected any more energy. But it was now evening, and he and Lydia had made a habit of meeting at the jetty at sundown. Sometimes Lydia didn't show up... there was always the chance that she had made other plans for herself that night. That was the problem with being dead... it made using a cell phone, or hell, even a planner, impossible. You kind of had to be old-fashioned about your social life, and just show up at your friends' favorite haunts, hope they'd be there.

Don cracked a smile at his unintentional pun. Goddamn it.

The last couple of nights, he and Lydia had just hung out and talked. One night they had even gone downtown and people-watched at Giardino's.

Now that Don was dead, the tone of the place had changed again. The Figawi sign was still there, and the same bartender still worked behind the counter; the Keno machine was still tucked away by the bathrooms. But now instead of people-watching as one of the crowd, he people-watched as a separate entity—apart from the crowd. As no one. It felt a little darker in the room, possibly because of that. But it was still familiar, and since Lydia didn't go out to drink much, he got to choose the location. So, Giardino's it was.

It was a nice break, getting to watch people without hoping they would pass. And it was nice to do it with a friend.

And some people were very entertaining to watch. There had been a couple sitting at the bar the other night, the woman softly swaying her hand in the air, like she was conducting the music blaring over the speakers. Or perhaps her hands were dancing. Her partner had looked annoyed, impatient, like he was waiting for her to stop connecting with the music and instead connect with him.

She had instead turned to the girl next to her at the bar, reading a book.

"What are you reading?" she'd asked.

The girl had shown her the cover. Don had not been able to see what the title was.

The woman had smiled. "I love to read," she'd said. "I had to have back surgery a while ago, and I couldn't move my arms enough to turn the pages, so my friends bought me a Kindle. It was so nice, but..."

Her partner had caught the girl's eye before quickly rolling his, making a jabbering motion with his hand out of the woman's view.

To her credit, the girl had ignored the man. "I have a hard time reading anything other than a physical book," she'd replied.

"Yes!" the woman had cried, thrilled that the girl had understood her.

They had turned back to their drinks at that point, and Don had tried to read Lydia's expression. Sometimes Don thought that if he really squinted, he could start to see the tip of Lydia's nose floating there in front of her eyes. This was probably just wishful thinking. But that night, Don had at least been able to tell that Lydia was touched by the interaction.

It was a sweet thing to be touched by. Don personally had wanted to pummel the man in the conversation. But Lydia had just let out a small sigh, staring at the two women with a kind of happy, nostalgic glint in her eyes. The joys of vicarious social interaction. Don had imagined that Lydia had had a close-knit circle of friends when she was alive, who maybe traded out beer for coffee, since Lydia didn't strike him as the type who went carousing... but he still bet she enjoyed her time with her friends. Even with the acknowledgement that she still had a friend even on this side, he had felt for her, not being able to have those interactions in the same way. He thought he was decent at conversation, and he was sure she didn't mind talking with him, but there was something about being unable to talk to whoever you wanted that could really put a damper on your mood.

Don glanced up and saw the sun starting to drift below the surface of the water. It was bedding itself.

Lydia was still nowhere to be found. Well, he couldn't expect her to hang out with him every night, Don thought. After all, he was sitting here worrying about her social life, but she probably did have friends apart from him; she had been collecting for a year before he had shown up. She had probably met every dead person in town. Or maybe she just didn't want to go to a bar tonight.

Still, Don felt a ping of self-pity. He didn't want to spend the night alone. He wanted to talk and enjoy somebody's company—more than just people-watching could provide. The only thing worse than only being able to talk to one person in a crowded bar was not being able to talk to anyone.

He sighed and stood, picking his way back up to the top of the jetty and traipsing back to the mainland. These were the moments in which he wished he could just fall back on his video games. Whenever he had felt insecure about socializing, he would just socialize with the latest game he had bought. That had always made him happy, and had been a lot easier than putting his neck out there, trying to make friends with people.

Don vividly remembered the social dynamic when he was a kid. He hadn't been a cool kid, or even an *un*cool kid—he had faded into the background socially, and this had been something he'd enjoyed: you wouldn't get picked on if people didn't know you were there.

Sure, he had tried to make friends, and had had reasonable success: his best friend in middle school had been Brian Whittaker, a tall, stocky kid who didn't say much in public, but when you got him talking about baseball, he wouldn't shut up. Brian had been the only kid in their class who had even known what baseball cards were—not many people seemed to collect cards anymore, especially kids, unless it was Pokemon or Magic the Gathering. But Don and Brian found life in baseball cards. They would park themselves behind the brick wall that announced the school's entrance, flipping through their cards and talking about the players of then and before, and commiserating in how difficult it was to find cards those days. They had even gone to a few Cape League games together, and made plenty of casual bets about who would get pushed to the Majors.

Brian Whittaker hadn't stuck around for too long. In ninth grade, he attempted suicide, and his family panicked and moved to Williamstown, where his aunt who worked in psychology lived. Don had always felt bitter about the move—not only did he think it was a stupid idea to have your own aunt be your psychologist, but he had always wondered, if Brian had been going through something, why didn't he bring it up to him? Wasn't that what best friends were for?

Maybe he hadn't known it was something he could talk about. Or maybe he flat out hadn't wanted to talk to Don about his mental health. Maybe he and Brian hadn't been as close as Don thought.

After that, Don had faded into the background. He had occasionally gotten together with people for board game nights, or to test out a new video game, and then, once the socializing was done, he would climb back into the walls and hide. He had made no effort to branch out, or try anything new.

Don wondered now about Brian. He wondered what would have happened if he had actually died all those years ago—if he would have moved on, or gotten stuck there. He was pretty sure Brian had been Catholic, and if he was remembering correctly, if Catholicism had any actual say in the matter, Brian would probably have been stuck. But Don was pretty sure he couldn't measure the afterlife by what living people thought of it, even if it was based on centuries of religious study—hi, had any of them ever died and found themselves in the not-so-afterlife?—so he really had no idea where Brian would have ended up. The thought made him uncomfortable.

In life, he would have found comfort in the unknown, but now he felt a creeping anxiety about it.

Maybe he'd just go to Giardino's by himself, like he'd used to. The people-watching would at least be a good distraction.

Don quietly meandered down the streets, occasionally passing the oblivious living in his walk. They hurried on by, glancing at the time on their phones, worried about being late to their next engagement. Don rolled his eyes. Being dead had taken all urgency out of his step. Well… okay, he hadn't had too much urgency before, he supposed. But if he were to look at a graph, he thought his urgency had probably gone down a little.

It was strange to him, he thought as he continued ambling towards Giardino's, that death had made him a reflective person. Every moment felt vital, felt alive—but not in a way that made him worried about getting things done. He could just take it all in. Maybe it wasn't death that taught him that—maybe it was the lack of cell phone, the lack of schedule, that made him feel so in the moment.

He sighed, wishing he might have tested this theory before he had died.

When he reached Giardino's, he found the bar dotted with regulars. It was a Tuesday night, and he hadn't expected it to be as bustling as it was.

He wandered through the bar, and finally settled on a couple sitting at a two-top in the corner. Or maybe they weren't a couple. Don could never tell these things, especially at a place like Giardino's, where people seemed to just exist, forgetting to put on airs like hand holding and arms around shoulders. You had to pick these things up from context.

The man was drinking a bottle of Busch. The woman had some sort of mixed drink and was sucking it with a straw. Both of them looked dazed, avoiding eye contact.

The bar noise gathered around the two like a wall, isolating them. Don thought maybe he should pick a new couple to watch... something uncomfortable was clearly happening. He was about to stand up when the man spoke.

"How's the drink?"

The woman's gaze slid toward him, her eyes suddenly fierce. "It's fine," she said thickly, and Don could see that her cutting eyes were a mask for the lump in her throat.

The man looked uncomfortable. "I didn't... I didn't mean anything by it..."

The woman crumpled a bit. "I know," she said meekly.

The man hesitantly reached his hand out, placing it over hers. "Hey," he said.

"James, please don't."

James squeezed her hand. "Look, I'm not gonna start a huge conversation about it tonight. But I—"

"*James.*"

"Honey. It's okay." He took a shaky breath. "We can try again." A tear trickled down her cheek. "I mean, not immediately, right? Because that's gonna... that's gonna hurt."

"I was just so ready."

"I know."

Don felt a pit of dread in his stomach. He looked beside the woman, saw the small, blinking eyes next to her. He felt a wave of nausea.

As the woman broke into tears, resting her head on the table, her partner enveloping her head and arms with his, those tiny little eyes fixated on them. They looked confused; they looked trusting.

Don stumbled out of his seat and backed away from the table, trying and failing to breathe properly.

The couple continued to mourn, their child patiently waiting by their side.

I don't want to be here anymore, Don thought, leaving the bar, wishing the cool air of the dimly lit street could wash over him and calm him down. He felt jumbled and frayed, and if he had been alive, he imagined he would be hot and uncomfortable, his body not really knowing how to react properly to what he'd seen. At least he was spared that discomfort in his death. He crumpled up against the side of the building, trying to steady his breathing.

This world is so fucked up, he thought, this world is so fucked up and I don't want to be here anymore.

And then, the realization, that nasty, nagging reminder: the only way to not be here anymore was to either collect or fade. And that made him hyperventilate some more.

He heard a snigger coming from the alleyway beside the bar and glanced over. A pair of hazel eyes watched him with amusement.

"What the fuck do you think is so funny?" Don spat out, anger flooding his system and temporarily dismantling his horror.

"You look like you've seen a ghost!" came the cackling reply. "Something in that bar got you spooked."

"I don't want to talk about it," Don snapped.

"Who said I want to talk about it?" the voice replied. It sounded familiar. "Don't you know better than to go traipsing around in a bar on a Tuesday night? That shit'll get you down. Now, a Friday night, that may be different. But Tuesdays... go to a fucking strip club, dude."

An image popped into Don's head of hundreds of sets of eyes, piling over each other as naked women danced at a club. It was certainly an image that jarred away his previous interaction.

"Thanks, I'm good," he replied.

The eyes ambled over, plopping down beside him on the sidewalk. "What's your deal? You new?"

Don rolled his eyes. "A couple weeks, yeah."

"Damn," the voice said. It was a young guy, maybe in his early twenties, or possibly about the same age as Don; at least it sounded that way. The voice still sounded very familiar. Don studied the eyes for a moment.

"Have we met?"

He laughed. "I don't fuckin' know, man, all I can see is your fuckin' eyes. What'd you used to look like?"

Don squinted at him. "What's your name?"

He squinted back. "Look, bud, I don't do niceties, so if you think you have some past beef with me, you can fucking knock it off right there. I—"

"Oswald?"

The eyes blinked. "Who are you?"

Don laughed. "Don't get too worked up," he said. "I don't have any beef with you. You were just there when I, um... when I died."

Oswald stared at him for a long moment. "You're gonna have to give me more than that, sweetheart, I've been collecting for years."

This guy was a peach. "Well, as I said, it was a couple weeks ago... it was a car accident."

Oswald's eyes widened. "Oh, shit! You're the dude who fucking split in half!"

Don gave him a look that could have killed, had it been bestowed on a living subject. "Yes. Yes, I am."

"Oh, fuck, man! How ya been?"

"I've been dead."

"Ah, that never gets old. Listen, you figure shit out? You good, man?"

"Yeah, no thanks to you," Don muttered. "A friend taught me how to collect."

Oswald laughed. "Look, I'm sorry, man, but I don't play mentor. That's not my shtick, never will be. I walk the face of this earth on my own terms, not for others' demands. It's nothing personal."

Don shrugged. He could understand that. "You were with two other people—"

"Oh, yeah, those losers. I dropped them about a week back. They were fine and everything, but, ah… I don't know, man, when you spend all your time with *anybody*, they start to get old real fast."

"Fair. I guess that's part of why Lydia and I collect separately."

"Who's Lydia? Is she your girl?"

"No, she's the one who taught me how to collect."

"Right, right." Oswald looked back out at the street. "Well, fuck, man, now I gotta know what happened in the bar."

"Why?"

"'Cause, I'm interested in you now. You're the newbie tween, and something's freaked you out. I miss those days, you know? Getting freaked out over the morbid-as-fuck way this place works."

"You miss getting—"

"Well, not the freaked-out part. But I miss seeing it through fresh eyes. Can't afford to let things get too stale, you know?"

"How long have you… been around?"

"Oh… years." Oswald laughed. "What'd you see, man, you see somebody you know? You spying on somebody?"

"I was just people-watching. That's not spying."

"Right, right. So, somebody you know?"

"No. It was… Look, I really don't want to talk about it."

"All right, man. Your call." Oswald stood, his eyes skipping out to the street a few yards. "Hey, what's your name, man?"

"Don."

"Well, Don, maybe we'll catch each other again. I'm gonna go check out the strip club. I need a show. You're more than welcome to join, but you look like you need a minute."

Don grimaced. "Yeah, I do."

"All right. Well, I make the rounds in this neighborhood a lot, so I'll probably see you again. Don't be a stranger. And dude… Don't let it get you down."

And Oswald drifted away, leaving Don with a pit in his stomach.

CHAPTER SEVEN

Cherry shuffled down the aisle, pushing the shopping cart slowly in front of her. So far she had circled the store twice, and the cart was still empty. Pick something, she thought, you need to eat something.

Once she had realized she hadn't eaten anything all day, she had forced herself to open the fridge—only to find a few spoiled items, and an egg carton with one egg in it. She had nearly gone back to bed, ready to deal with it in the morning. It could always be done in the morning. She'd said that for the past two weeks, and now her time was up. She would not let herself starve. She just had to find something she wanted to eat.

But every shelf full of produce looked unappetizing; the frozen food section was full of dull little cartons with drab photos of their content; and the bakery section smelled too strong. It was making her sick.

She idly reached out and touched one of the bags of sandwich bread. Who was she kidding? She hadn't made a sandwich in years. And buying bread for a sandwich would mean she would have to get deli meat, and the idea of deli meat made her feel sour inside.

Maybe she could buy a frozen lasagna. Lasagna was a food she could always eat, no matter what her mood—no matter what was happening in her life. She strolled back to the frozen section.

She stared at the frozen lasagnas.

Cherry's mind was completely blank. The thought of melted cheese would normally have excited her, but now it just sat in her mind, a gooey, sticky mess. It seeped into the crevices of her thoughts, shorting the circuits as it went.

She felt a buzz in her pocket, and pulled out her cell phone. It was Dee.

"Hey, what's up?"

"What are you doing?" came Dee's reply.

"I'm…" Cherry looked at her empty cart. "…grocery shopping."

"Good. How are you feeling?"

Cherry sighed. This was Dee's way of consoling her friend after her brother's death: she checked off the boxes, and played Mom. She and Thiago had probably had a meeting about it, and this was Dee's not-so-undercover task. "I'm fine."

"And you're going to eat something you buy?"

"*Yes,* Dee."

"What do you have picked out so far?"

Cherry stared at the freezer in front of her. "A lasagna." She opened the freezer door.

"Okay, cool, I'm coming over and I'm gonna watch you eat it."

"*Dee*—"

"Shut up, Cherry, I'm gonna do it. See you soon."

Dee hung up. Cherry sighed and picked out a box of veggie lasagna.

She was used to Dee pulling this. And it lifted her spirits, if only long enough to grab a bag of baby carrots on her way to the check-out. Add a little health to the mix, why don't you?

Dee was sitting on the steps leading to Cherry's apartment complex when she arrived, kicking the heels of her combat boots into the concrete. She smiled when she saw Cherry, and jumped off her perch and followed her into the building.

"Is that your lasagna?" she asked, poking the bag around Cherry's shoulder.

"Stop it," Cherry said, unlocking the door to her apartment.

Dee picked at the plastic bag curiously. "Can I have some too?"

"No," Cherry said flatly. She was kidding, of course; she knew she couldn't keep Dee from eating off her plate any more than she could force herself to eat at the moment.

The two of them shuffled into the apartment. The place looked like a tornado had hit it, but Cherry knew Dee would be cool with it. Usually, Cherry was a fairly neat person. Sure, the sweater draped over the back of the couch was normal, and there was usually a forgotten mug on the coffee table even when her brother *wasn't* dead, but she at least was normally able to keep her bookshelf in order, and the kitchen counter devoid of junk. At the moment, however, a Hershey bar wrapper was in the middle of the floor, the silverware drawer was left pulled wide open, and Cherry counted at least three T-shirts strewn around the room.

Cherry dropped the grocery bag on the kitchen counter next to a couple of used tissues, repeating "Dee doesn't care" in her head as her momentary mantra, and disappeared into the bathroom. She could hear Dee rummaging around. "I'm putting your lasagna in the oven!" Dee yelled, and some beeping ensued.

Cherry stared at her reflection in the mirror. Her hijab was wrinkled and lopsided, and her face looked puffy, her glasses smudged. But, like the state of her apartment, she didn't really care about her physical appearance either. Okay, sure, it made her cringe to see herself in the mirror, but she didn't care. Honestly. What did it matter right now? She unpinned and pulled off her hijab, and her dark, messy curls spilled out in front of her shoulders. She picked her hairbrush up from the counter, trying to remember if she had actually brushed her hair that morning. It sure didn't look like it. She'd better be careful, or this period of mourning would leave her with a giant knot that she would have to cut out. Even now, she couldn't bring herself to tame the locks. Her brush sat idly in the palm of her hand, her fingers finally slowly releasing it and letting it tip onto the counter below.

She would brush her hair later. Right now, she had a guest over, who, she repeated, *didn't care*, and she needed to get out of the bathroom and join her with that lasagna.

She stared at her reflection in the mirror some more.

After a moment or two, she folded her hijab with the little care she could muster and reached for the door. So be it that she was in a disheveled state, she thought. It would give a nice contrast to the days she was put together.

Dee was drawing on the magnetic whiteboard on Cherry's fridge. She winked at Cherry, then turned and drew in the final line of her Grateful Dead bear.

"You're getting better at that," Cherry remarked drily.

Dee stuck her tongue out at her as she crossed to the oven. "I actually am, so thank you."

"Hey, sorry my place is such a m—"

"I don't care," Dee sang, and Cherry nearly burst into tears. She turned away from Dee, closing her eyes and letting the wave of panic rush through her, and began to count her breaths.

"Hey, your lasagna is veggie, so I'm not gonna eat any."

Dee's voice brought her back into the room. Cherry smiled. "Yeah, you'll still eat some."

"That's not true! I don't want any of that fake-meat crap. There had to have been meat lasagna that didn't have sausage, you just didn't look."

"I like this kind. And you have never passed up the opportunity to eat food, vegetarian or not."

"I mean, I am a little hungry," Dee replied. "I guess if you have some left over after the crazy amount you eat."

Cherry rolled her eyes.

"So, uh, how are you feeling?"

Ah. Here was the pity, masked in the guise of friendship. Not a guise, she immediately corrected herself; boy, her therapist would be having a heyday with this inner dialogue.

"I'm fine, Dee, really," Cherry said. "You don't have to keep asking me that. Let's watch a movie."

"Sure, sure." Dee flopped onto the couch, hugging a throw pillow. "But if, like, you want to talk, then you know I'm here. And if you don't want to talk, then I'll still be here. Sitting on your couch. Probably eating your lasagna."

Cherry groaned and slumped onto the couch next to Dee. "Just put on whatever."

Dee obliged, screen-casting some old classic screwball comedy movie. Jimmy Stewart was claiming to have a giant rabbit for a friend, and that was the extent of Cherry's knowledge.

After a moment of letting her eyes glaze over while Jimmy cavorted around on the screen, Cherry sighed. "Feels weird that he's gone," she muttered.

She felt Dee's gaze on her. "Yeah. I bet." They were silent for a moment, and Cherry knew Dee was still staring at her, and she didn't know what she wanted to say, or if she even wanted to say anything.

"I'm sorry," Cherry said finally, "that I don't know how to talk about it."

"You don't have to."

"But that's what you want me to do."

"No," Dee said, abandoning all pretense of not staring at her friend and instead turning her whole body to look her dead in the eye. "I don't want you to do anything. You're the one who dictates how you mourn. You're *supposed* to be miserable, and in pain, and me being here isn't going to change that. You're still gonna feel awful, because he's still dead. And don't you dare say that my being here makes you feel better, because it doesn't. Because it's awkward. Because you don't know what you should be doing. But if I wasn't here, you wouldn't feel better either. You'd be saying, 'I shouldn't be alone right now,' or 'I think I would feel better if I talked it out.' But you wouldn't, because, ta-da—"

"That's exactly what I feel awkward about now, yeah, I get it, Dee," Cherry muttered, smirking. Dee was always spouting off some psychology talk—she was going for her graduate in psychology, and though she managed to abstain from most of the jargon, she still was quick to explain exactly what was going on in anyone's head at any given time. It was amazing, and yet minorly irritating at times.

Cherry watched the TV for a minute or two, contemplating. "I could just go to sleep. Pop some melatonin, pass out, forget the world. That would make me feel better. Or at least not feel."

"Yeah, but that's what you've been doing for the last couple of weeks, and there's a point where I wouldn't be a good friend if I didn't cut you off from that."

"Oh, so this is about you, then?" Cherry teased, laughing.

Dee rolled her eyes. "If you're sleeping, then you're not dealing with it. I'm not here to make you feel better. I'm here to make you deal with it. You don't have to talk about it, and you don't have to cry or whatever, but you do have to sit there in your waking state and feel miserable."

"Well. Then I'm glad you're here."

The two of them burst into giggles, and Cherry was still miserable, but she at least had company.

CHAPTER EIGHT

Every year on the first day of Eid al-Fitr, Mina Rind would wake her children up very early in the morning and give them each a small package wrapped in white paper. She would then usher them to put on their shoes and coats, and the three of them would climb into the car and drive to Veteran's Park Beach. They would open their little paper packages, which always contained halva, and they would pray their Eid salat and eat dessert for breakfast while watching the sun go up. Then they would get back into the car and drive home.

One year, Cherry sleepily made the comment on the ride back that she was glad they had moved the tradition to a warmer time of year, and their mother had to explain to Donny that this had stemmed from their father's Easter tradition. Since their father was gone, she wanted to keep the tradition, but she was absolutely not going to adhere to Christian cultural expectations in order to do it. So now it was their Eid tradition.

Now, on the opposite side of the bay, Don sat on the jetty at Englewood Beach, looking out across the water at his memories. He couldn't actually see where they would have stood as kids, but he pretended he could, squinting. There was where Cherry would chase after the seagulls as they began to fully wake up, and there was where Mina would tell Don not to get his shoes wet. From this distance, it was all just a blur. He was on the other side, now, watching the sun set instead of rise, and it was bringing about an awful sort of melancholy, especially after how his day had gone.

"You haven't been sitting here all day, have you?" Lydia's eyes appeared above him.

"How'd you fare?" Don asked as she squatted down and sat beside him on the edge of the jetty.

"Nothing today," she said, gazing out at the bay. Her voice had a rehearsed lightness to it, and Don suspected she was not willing to talk about something. She seemed disquieted. "You?"

Don shook his head. He was beginning to think he wasn't very good at collecting. But then, how many people actually died on the Cape every day? Maybe he should be easier on himself. He was still pretty shaken up about the incident at Giardino's, and had wandered around aimlessly for the better part of the day.

"Did you collect anything today?" Lydia prodded, and Don realized that he needed to get out of the habit of answering with gestures.

"Sorry. No. I shook my head—I didn't even think about it."

Lydia's tinkling laugh came to his ears. "It's okay, it took me a while too."

"I ran into the guy who was at my death," Don said.

"The, um, the one like us?"

"Yeah. Oswald. Real weird guy."

Lydia hesitated. "Oswald?"

"Yeah. Do you know him?" Don's mind flicked back to when he had first mentioned him, and Lydia had said she had never heard the phrase "tween". Oh well, maybe he hadn't said the term around her. Maybe he hadn't come up with it yet. Or maybe she was thinking of a different Oswald, and he needed to stop working himself up before she even responded.

"Kind of young sounding?" she asked. "Kind of um, cavalier?"

"Yeah. You know him?"

Another pause. "I met him once."

"Yeah? Sounds like you weren't a fan."

"I didn't say that." There was a pause. "But you're right, he was, um, was not my favorite."

"Why's that?"

"Just, um, his attitude, that's all." She sounded uncomfortable, and Don racked his brain to change the subject, though he was definitely curious.

"So, what'd you do with your night last night?" Don hesitated. "I mean, if it was personal, you don't have to—"

"I thought you said your *sister* had anxiety," Lydia interrupted, and he heard a smile in her voice.

"Yeah."

"Not you. Not at all."

"Shut up. What'd you do last night?"

Lydia laughed again. "If you must know, um. I visited a friend."

"Oh. Cool."

"A living one."

"Oh. Uh. How?"

"Well, I didn't try to talk to him or anything. I just went and checked in."

"Ohhh. Okay. Yeah, I kind of accidentally did that with my sister when she came to clean out my apartment."

"Oh yeah? How'd it go?"

Don grimaced. "It felt a little like I was spying on her."

"Don, we've gone people-watching three times this week."

"Yeah, but it felt different with someone I knew. Like, I was encroaching on her space. Felt more... I don't know, private."

"Well, um, it was your apartment. And it's not like you were watching her sleep or something. But I get what you mean. I try to visit people in public places."

"Where'd you go?"

"The park. He takes walks there. Sometimes he reads, when the weather is nice. He'll read anywhere, honestly."

"Who is this, an old beau?"

Lydia ignored the question quite deftly. "Sometimes I like to go and read over his shoulder. Not that I'm really interested in the book, per se, although he does pick interesting books, sometimes. Except when he rereads A Tale Of Two Cities, which he does a *lot*. But anyway... it makes me feel close to him. Like we're um, doing an activity together. Like we're hanging out."

Don thought about that for a moment. "But why don't you go follow him when he's talking to people? You could hear life updates, maybe. Maybe someone would ask how he's been doing, and he would answer, and you could hear what he's been up to. If you don't know through stalking him, that is."

Lydia took her time to answer. "Sometimes, it feels better not to know too many details about the living," she replied meekly.

Don let that sink in. He supposed there was no denying that. He knew a few things about the living that he wished he didn't know. "Hey, Lydia."

"Mmmm?"

He let out a deep breath. "I, uh… I saw a miscarriage last night."

"I'm sorry, what?" Lydia said sharply.

"I mean, not—I didn't watch it happening. But I saw the… results of it? There was someone, someone like us, with the couple. I guess I don't know for sure if it was a miscarriage. It could've been an abortion, or an early death, or… I don't know, it just seemed like they were talking about a baby."

"Did you ask them? The… the baby?"

Don frowned. "I… I kind of ran out the door."

Silence.

"You aren't obligated to talk to aborted babies, Don."

"I don't think it was an abortion—"

"That's not my point. You, um. You can't make everyone's problems your problems."

"But someone has to show them the ropes," Don whispered feebly. "Like you did for me. What if no one ever does for them? What if they don't even know how to talk, how to communicate, and they never understand what they need to do?"

"Don't beat yourself up about this, Don—"

"How can I not?" Don said, his voice echoing across the water all of a sudden. "It's so—it's so fucked up, Lydia. I walked away from a helpless *baby*. What the fuck."

"Don."

It was weird... he wasn't crying, because he couldn't physically emit tears. But his body still went through the motions of crying, screwing up his insides and leaving him with a breathless feeling. "I didn't think dying would be so damn hard. But it is, for all... for all the wrong reasons. I wanted it to be—I mean, I didn't want it to be hard, but I mean, if it had to be hard, I would rather it be hard like, oh no, I have to leave everybody behind, oh no, I'll never get to make that trip or get that winning lottery ticket or—fuck, Lydia. It's like I died, and then I just have to continue dealing with death. Forever."

"Not forever."

"Okay, but I'm upset, and it feels like forever, so let me just say forever."

"Geez, Don." He thought he could hear a slight tremor in her voice. "I don't... um... I don't know what to tell you."

"I know. I know, you never fucking do."

"That's not fair."

"I know. I'm sorry." Don took a deep breath. "That wasn't fair at all. I'm sorry."

"It's okay. You just saw a dead baby."

Don wasn't sure how Lydia's frail, mumbling voice could so quickly shift to deadpan, but once again, he was laughing. He felt shitty about laughing about a dead baby, but as soon as the laugh came out, he knew he had needed it. He had been rigid for the past several hours, holding everything deep within him, and now he felt it all rush out, like a popped balloon. He had to remember the importance of laughter, even if the joke wasn't all that funny.

"Hey, let's go to the cemetery," Lydia said suddenly.

"Why?"

"I want to see your grave."

"I repeat, why?"

"It'll be fun. We can poke fun at the inscriptions. We can see who your grave neighbors are."

"Is this a thing? Is this a thing that people do? Like, dead people?"

Lydia swung her eyes to level with Don's. "Don, I'm trying to desensitize you to this insane nightmare we're in. We're going to the cemetery."

It was windy when they got there. Cold gray stones stuck out of the ground, some at odd angles, across a large, winter-seared field. Little bows and flowers adorned some of the nearby tombstones. A plastic bag was winding its way around the branches of the tree not too far from where Don's grave resided.

"So that's where my body is," Don offered awkwardly.

Lydia eyed the inscription for a moment, then glanced at him. "Were you cremated?"

"I doubt it. That's a big N-O in Islam."

"I bet you were cremated."

"Why do you bet that?"

"I don't know, you just, um, seem like a body that would be cremated."

Don laughed. "I seem like someone who people would look at and be like, 'God, I hope they burn his body.'"

"Yup. That's exactly what I meant."

"Well, unless my mother somehow lost a fierce battle with the funeral director, I'm gonna go with no."

"I'm telling you, you were. You're a cremie."

"Ew, god, did you just make up an affectionate term for cremated people? That's almost as bad as 'tweens'."

Lydia's tinkling laugh echoed across the cemetery. "You know, I used to not be so morbid."

"Yeah. Death changed you." Don smiled.

The two of them stared at the grave in front of them, a twinkle in both sets of eyes.

After a moment, he cleared his throat. "Okay, so why are we here?"

"I told you. You're too, um, freaked out by the world. We're here so that you can get it through your head… you're dead, Don."

"I know that."

"But do you? You're acting like you can control things, and you can't, Don."

"I'm not trying to control things. I'm just…"

"Scared. I know. So don't be."

He laughed. "It's not that easy."

Lydia gazed down at his grave. "Your bones are dusted and broken beneath this stone. What remains of you is literally in a tiny box underneath the ground."

"Oh my god, Lydia…"

"You don't get to control the living. You don't even get to control the dead. You are gone, Don."

"I *know*, Lydia."

"Then stop being so scared every time something new and ugly happens. Expect it. This is what you should expect from now on."

"That's real dark, Lydia."

"We're in the dark." Lydia gulped. "All of us. All of us *tweens*, we're bumbling around, and we're, um, running into things, metaphorically speaking, not sure where we're going. We're just trying to get by. And it's not what we thought, and it's not how we like it, but we've got to carry on. Um. In order to move on."

Don sighed. "Okay, I get it. You want me to accept it."

He glanced around at the other graves. Rows and rows of tombstones littered the cemetery, many broken and knocked over. His section was one of the few that was all in one piece, not yet ravaged by time.

Forgotten graves, he thought. There are plenty of people who have come before me. They died years ago, they dealt with it, they moved on. I'm not the only one who has to go through these horrors.

And Lydia was right: being scared wasn't getting him any closer to moving on. He needed to grit his teeth and do his job. Rip off the bandage.

Don glanced over at Lydia. Her eyes held a far-off look.

"You okay?"

"What? Yeah." She breathed deeply. "I was just thinking about the couple who had the miscarriage. I wonder how they're doing."

Don studied her sheepishly. "I didn't actually think about them all that much."

Lydia's eyes slowly turned towards him. "You're right, you didn't." Her eyes trained on his face for a few lingering seconds. "Don, do you believe in abortion?"

"I—I did. I mean, I—I don't know what I think anymore."

"I do."

Don felt a prick of discomfort from her tone. "Why's that?"

Lydia stared at him for a long while. Her eyes pierced into him for what seemed like hours, before she said, "Did I tell you how I died, Don?"

Don started to respond, then faltered. He watched Lydia blink a few times.

"I was, um. Part of a very conservative Christian family. Abortion is… it's a big N-O."

Don shuddered. "Look, I'm—I didn't say I—"

"I'm not accusing you of anything, Don."

Don had a horrible thought. "Did you…" He gulped. "Did your baby make it?"

"I think that's enough cemetery for one day," Lydia said softly. She walked away.

Don feebly followed after her, unsure of what to do or say. She had just told him her death story… should he do the same? No, that was stupid. She had just opened up that she had died giving birth—the last thing he should do was tell her how his body had split in half in a car accident. That would sound like he was trying to compete with her or something.

Should he try to comfort her? Did she want to be comforted?

Death by childbirth. What was this, the dark ages?

Don had so many questions.

But he was pretty sure now was not the appropriate time to ask them. He just wasn't sure what *was* appropriate at the moment.

"I could use a drink," he muttered, more to himself than anything, but Lydia, overhearing him, gave a short laugh.

"I didn't drink before I died," she said, "But I could use a drink, too."

"Is there an equivalent of alcohol for tweens?" Don asked curiously.

"Not as far as I know," Lydia replied.

They heard a snicker to their right. "Sure, there is."

It was Oswald. Don recognized the voice before he even saw the hazel eyes. He had a feeling that now that he had actually made his acquaintance, Oswald was going to start showing up everywhere.

He must have been sitting on the top of a grave. The eyes hopped down and approached. "Don, right?"

"Yeah. Lydia, this is Oswald."

Lydia took her time in answering. "Hi, Oswald."

"Lydia, Lydia..." Don wasn't sure if he was actually trying to place a name, or if he was just being an asshole. "Why does that ring a bell? Oh! You had mentioned Lydia. Your girl."

Lydia blinked. Don rolled his eyes. "No, I believe *you* said that, Oswald. I used the word 'friend'."

"Po-tay-to, po-tah-to." Oswald snickered again. "You guys do know that there's a way to get high here, right? Not quite like being drunk, but... I'll pick whatever poison I can get."

"I can only imagine the lengths that you took to figure out a way to get high," Lydia said flatly. She walked away again, and Don followed after her, feeling extremely awkward.

Oswald tagged along like a puppy who had mistaken a passerby for his family. "Becoming corporeal," he said, not missing a beat. "That's how you do it. The more corporeal you get, the more corporeal... ism... you can use. And if you use it quickly, you get a high off it."

Don was very confused. "Being corporeal?"

"Yeah! Oh, duh. Newbie, I forgot. Yeah, the more energy you collect, the more corporeal you can become. Lydia didn't tell you that? Oh, maybe Lydia didn't *know* that, 'cause she hasn't gotten that far herself."

"Wait. So you can use the energy you collect for things other than moving on?"

"Oh, yeah!" Oswald cried. "Yeah, why do you think so many people talk about seeing ghosts? Those are just tweens like us who got enough energy to show themselves to people, or at least make themselves known. Not like, fully corporeal, but... like ghosts."

"Huh. So I could visit the living? I mean, and have them know it?"

Oswald rolled his eyes. "I mean, you can do a lot more than visit the living, but yeah."

"Like what?"

"Ever hear of poltergeists?" Lydia asked. She sounded like a schoolteacher, explaining a math problem to a student. Except that in this case, Don guessed, she was explaining why she seemed to hate Oswald so much.

"Yeah."

"Poltergeists, man." Oswald laughed. "They really know their shit. I wanna be called a poltergeist someday. That's a good goal."

"So, you can move stuff? That's what a poltergeist is, right?"

"You can scare the shit outta people, is what you can do," Oswald said. "A couple of months ago, I nearly gave a family of four simultaneous heart attacks when I made their chandelier crash down on their dinner table. All four of 'em practically jumped out of their skin."

"But why would you use your energy on something like that?" Lydia asked. She had a note of fury in her voice.

Oswald let out a laugh. Don had originally thought that Oswald might have been around his age when he died, but now, he could hear an irritating amount of youth in his laugh. This guy couldn't have made it to much more than twenty years old. You could catch a lot in a laugh: the view someone had of themselves was usually well-reflected in it, and the amount of reservations held. Oswald apparently had no reservations. His laugh echoed across the cemetery, tinny and free.

"Well, because it's fun, obviously," Oswald said. "I mean, I'm constantly collecting, so I'm not gonna fade. Why not have some fun on this plane while I can? Make the most of every life circumstance—or death circumstance!" He burst out laughing again, pretty pleased with himself.

"So you collect people's energy in order to use it to scare people?" Lydia murmured. She did not sound amused.

"Or, you know, get in fist fights with other tweens when they're being asshats." Oswald snickered. "Some of them really deserve it, too. Oh, come on!" he cried, sensing his audience had not warmed up to the idea. "Other people use it to reconnect with their loved ones. Why can't I use it to have a little fun?"

"Because there are plenty of people who are actually, um, trying to move on," Lydia whispered. Her voice kept getting quieter and quieter.

Oswald snickered. "Right, because being a tween isn't depressing enough already, we have to be chastised for making the most of our time here. It's not like I can give out the energy I collect. I gotta use it for something."

"But you're preventing others from collecting that energy."

"How do you know?" Oswald said, a challenge in his voice. "How do you know I'm not the only one who's there for these deaths, huh? Ever think that maybe I'm just really good at finding people who are about to bite the dust?"

Lydia didn't answer. Don could tell that she was done engaging. Never mind the *why*, he thought. Lydia and Oswald could argue over that all day if they really wanted to. But first, Don wanted to know more about the *how*. "Oswald," he said, trying to break the tension, "How... corporeal... have you gotten?"

"I've gotten pretty damn corporeal," Oswald said. "I'm honestly surprised that I haven't moved on, in some cases. I thought once you collected enough, you would just go."

"Have you seen someone move on?"

Oswald shrugged. "I don't really stick around to find out," he scoffed. "Most of these douchebags didn't pass on for a reason. They're fucking boring, most of the time. Why try to make friends with a boring-ass tween?"

"I don't think we didn't move on because we're boring," Don said uncertainly.

"No way to prove that's not true. And if it is... of *course* I haven't been around to see someone actually move on." Oswald laughed again. "We probably don't even move on," he said. "That's probably just a myth, to give us a sense of purpose. To make us forget that we're just gonna roam this godforsaken ghost realm forever."

"You're a 'tween' too," Don reminded him, still not exactly fond of the phrase. "You can't rag on other people being boring if you're here for possibly the same reasons."

"Yeah," said Oswald, "but I've learned from my mistake. Maybe I did die a boring-ass human being, because I was too scared to live life. I didn't take any risks; I didn't do anything worthwhile. Well... I did, but it got me here. So now I'm here. And if that isn't the most depressing fucking thing, then I don't know what is. But now, I'm taking risks. I'm doing something worth my time. Capisce?"

Don and Lydia were both silent.

Don thought back on his own life. As Lydia had said, no one was one hundred percent sure what had prevented them from moving on, but Oswald's argument was a compelling one: Don had not done much with his life. He hadn't taken any risks, either—there weren't even any risks he had *wanted* to take, because he hadn't had much desire past lounging around and playing video games.

The thought had crossed his mind early on that his laziness had gotten him stuck. The fact that there was nothing he had enjoyed more on a Saturday night than playing Xbox, eating leftover pizza, and drinking beer sounded an awful lot like "boring".

He wondered if Lydia had ever taken any risks in her lifetime. He wondered whether he would find her boring in real life. But no, being boring was so relative. That couldn't be how they had gotten stuck there.

"Anyway, if you want to feel something, now you know how," Oswald said, taking note of their silence. "Live a little now that you're dead, will ya? Jesus Christ, guys."

And with that, Oswald made his way through the cemetery and away from the two of them, whistling as he went. Don turned to Lydia. "Fun guy, huh?"

Lydia didn't respond. She was still glaring after Oswald.

"Hey, you want to go back to the jetty?" Don whispered, trying to break her from her reverie.

"Sure," she said, her eyes still glued on the hill Oswald had disappeared over. After a moment, she turned, and Don stepped into line with her on their way out of the cemetery in silence.

"So, being corporeal," Don tried.

Lydia took a moment to respond. "I mean, it makes sense," she said slowly. "I don't think I've ever felt corporeal, but I do think I feel more... I don't know. I feel more *here* now than I did before. And when, um, when I thought I might be feeling the wind... maybe that's because I was slightly more corporeal."

"I wonder how long it takes to become... I don't know, corporeal enough. How close we are. What if we just start bumping into things soon?"

"I don't think we would bump into something unless we actually exerted our energy."

"Maybe we should test it out. I mean, I don't want to waste the energy I've collected, but..."

"What does it matter? We want to move on, not screw around with the living."

Another bout of silence came over them as they walked. Don didn't dare interrupt it.

"Why?" Lydia asked suddenly. "Would you want to talk to your family?"

Don thought for a moment. "I think it would probably freak them out. I mean, my sister, definitely... she would have a panic attack right then and there. And my mom... I think she would just spend the next ten years obsessing over the fact that her son hadn't made it to Jannah."

"Okay, but would you *want* to?"

"I mean.... yeah, I think that might be nice. Talk to them one last time." He glanced over at her. "How about you?"

Lydia was silent for a moment. For too long of a moment, actually.

Don tried to read her eyes. "I've never really asked about who you left behind," he said gently.

Lydia glanced at him fleetingly, then back out at the water. "Probably my husband," she mumbled. "Colby."

Don blinked. "Your husband."

He must have sounded surprised, because she gave him a look. "I just, um, told you I grew up in a Christian family and died during childbirth, and you, um, you think it's such a crazy idea that I was married? Catch up."

"No, I guess it's..." Don swallowed his words, not really sure why he wanted to verbalize the fact that he hadn't realized she was married. "Wait, is he the one you were visiting last night? A Tale of Two Cities guy? You said you were visiting a friend—"

"Okay, well, I was visiting my husband."

"That's... that's fine. Hey, maybe that's why you're still here."

"What do you mean?"

"Well, you were in love, right? So if the unfinished business theory has any merit... maybe you haven't moved on because you miss him. Maybe you have to tell him you love him. Or maybe it's the opposite, maybe there was trouble in paradise, and things ended badly, and you never got the chance to break free."

Lydia swiveled her head to stare at him. "I did love Colby," she said with a kind of quiet indignation. "I *do* love him. I didn't stop loving him."

"Okay, cool. I didn't mean anything weird by that. I, uh. So, okay, you'd visit Colby."

"Yes. I'd visit Colby."

"Well... well, I guess you've already visited him? I mean, not corporally, but you said you...?"

"Mmmhmmm."

"And? I mean, how's he doing?"

"He's living life."

"Did he, uh... has he moved on?"

"I mean... it's hard to tell, um, when someone moves on. There's not a specific moment when you can look at a person and think, yes, he's moved on. It's not a switch." She hesitated. "He hasn't started dating again, if that's what you mean."

"Oh, I didn't... okay, that's a little what I meant."

"Honestly, I, um, I don't know if I want to know when he does start. It's out of my control, you know. So, do I even want to see him with someone?"

"So you just want to continue reading over his shoulder and avoid learning about where he is in life."

"I'm dead," Lydia reminded him. "How is my knowing going to change anything? It's just, um, it's just going to make me feel worse."

"Well, by all means, then. Lie to yourself."

"It's not just that," Lydia said defensively. "I would also worry that, um, showing myself to him would disrupt his… his 'moving on' process."

"So you don't want to visit him because you want to remain ignorant, but also because you want him to remain ignorant?"

"You're saying this like it's a bad thing."

"Well… truth is usually a better thing."

"Think about all the people in your life who have died and have not come back to visit, and um, not distracted you and updated you on their process of death."

"Okay?"

"Would it make it easier to move on after losing, say, your father or mother? If you saw them again after they died?"

"I would love to see my father again."

"But if you saw him again, would you try to keep talking to him? And obsess over the fact that he's still here, that you could still try to talk to him if only you tried harder? Or you'd feel that he was watching over you, and you would never again feel like you were alone, because hey, Dad might be there. There are so many little ways that seeing a ghost could traumatize a person, and derail their life as it is, even apart from the whole 'boo, I'm a ghost' charade."

"Hmm."

"So maybe it's a little selfish to think that visiting someone would actually do any good. Let them move on."

"Lydia…" Don laughed. "People have claimed to see ghosts before, and have led perfectly normal lives after that. If you want to see Colby again, I mean, actually see him and talk to him, why not save for that? Yeah, you'll be here a little longer… but you could hang out with me." Don laughed feebly. "And uh, you'd get one last chance to say goodbye."

"I don't want to end up an energy junkie like Oswald," Lydia muttered.

"See, now I think you're just coming up with excuses."

Lydia stared intently at Don. "I have interacted with Oswald before, Don."

"I knew it! I mean, I know you said you had met him, but… Every time I've talked about anything related to him, you've… I don't know, frozen up."

"Well, I don't like the guy. Can you blame me? It was right after I died and was just beginning to figure out collecting. He seemed like he knew what he was doing, so I followed him to a bar to watch him, see if I could glean any more information about how this all worked. I watched him nearly kill an old man with a prank. He, um, he scared this man so much that he nearly had a heart attack. Right there on the spot. Oswald is a junkie.

He doesn't care about how his actions might affect the people around him, he cares about getting that high, and having fun."

"Okay, okay." Don shrugged. "Oswald is a junkie."

Lydia eyed him. "He is."

"Still doesn't mean you shouldn't make your peace with Colby."

"I have made my peace with Colby."

The edge in her voice made Don realize he should let it go. They had reached Englewood Beach; the sun had already given its wondrous display, and the dark had swept in during their walk. The two of them wound their way around the shore in dark silence, holding their tongues and pretending everything was okay.

What a day, thought Don. Let there be none like it… please, for the love of all that is good and sound, let there be none like it.

CHAPTER NINE

Cherry was so tired. She got tired most days, but she was pretty sure she hadn't been sleeping properly in the past week or so, because she kept on waking up the same amount of tired that she had been upon going to sleep.

She sat at her desk at work, propped up on her elbows with her back hunched, as she stared at the spreadsheet on the screen in front of her. She'd already had two cups of coffee, but she kept losing focus, the numbers sliding over each other like transparency pages on a projector. Normally this was her favorite part of the job—she had a weird thing for spreadsheets—and the office had been fairly quiet all morning, which usually helped get her in the zone, gently pulling her toward productivity like a current. But today the waters were calm and still, growing more and more stagnant by the minute. It wasn't even eleven o' clock.

Her mind wandered to the plans she had made for that night. She and Dee were going to visit Thiago off Cape and go to a tavern called The Tipsy Toboggan. None of them had ever been, but the name was too good to pass up, and Dee had been adamant about it on that qualification alone. But, Cherry thought with an inward sigh, before she could make that foray with her friends, she had to get through the day.

Dolores, the older woman who worked at the next cubicle over, approached Cherry's desk, her smile thin and strained. It had been apparent ever since Cherry had started working at the company that Dolores could be just as anxious as she was sometimes, which made it doubly nerve-wracking when she came over to her cubicle. "Error code again," she sighed. "Do you know what H5-01 means?"

"I think that's a jam?" Cherry faltered. She honestly never had any problems with the copy machine, and didn't have an answer for people when they did. She may have had some supernatural, unspoken arrangement with the copy machine, or so everyone kept urging her to admit, but that didn't mean that she knew how to fix it. She pulled out her phone. "I think Dave had that error code last week, hold on." Always pass them over to Dave, she thought. Get someone else to deal with it so I can get back to staring blankly at my spreadsheet.

She opened her phone and scrolled through her text conversations to find Dave.

And discovered Don in the lineup. His name sitting there, squeezed between her old college roommate and a doctor's appointment auto-reminder, with the words, "You've got to be kidding me" underneath. Cherry couldn't remember the context of what Don had been referring to—probably some meme she had found that reminded her of him—but despite the completely arbitrary meaning of the words, his name made her brain stick.

She felt a wave, like a dam had broken inside of her and everything started rushing, coursing rampant through her body, frothing at the tips as it crashed into the walls of her skin and bones, shaking their stability, breaking past the barrier of her eyelids and leaking down her cheeks as she sat there at her desk, helpless to the turmoil within.

Dolores stood in front of her with wide eyes, watching Cherry's sobs slowly overtake her body, the discreet shudders descending into short, ugly gasps as Cherry tried desperately to breathe.

"Can I get you something?" Dolores' voice sounded in the distance, and Cherry turned away, wiping her face furiously with her sleeve.

"I just need a minute," she heard herself mumble, and when she stood to flee to the bathroom, Dolores was already back at her desk, head down and trying to pretend that she wasn't staring at her sidelong.

The inside of the bathroom was cold and white and a bit blurred as Cherry slumped against the wall, waiting for her panic to subside. Each time she thought she was fine, another wave came, like a gag reflex. Her body was one big spasming muscle of grief.

She looked down at her hands and found her phone still in their clutch. Fumbling to unlock the screen, she opened Don's conversation and scrolled up past the meme and into the weeks and months prior, all the little jokes the two of them had made, offhand comments about ordinary life events that now seemed like half-buried coins, slowly sinking into the sand and waiting to be rescued. She gathered them up in her mind and relished the words as she scrolled. Funny how they had lived within ten minutes of each other and the majority of their interactions had been random texts. Well... funny, or pathetic.

Finally, she dropped the phone into her lap, her breathing somewhat regulated and the bathroom coming back into focus. She stared at the wall in front of her, feeling like she had just thrown up her lunch.

Well, at least this moment had come. At least she wasn't a hollow bell anymore.

It will never be the same, she thought. No matter how many memories I have in this text thread, a bunch of words on a screen pales in comparison to the real thing. She let out a deep, stilted sigh. She would never get to hear him laughing and making snarky comments, or see him try to balance a water bottle on his head like he did as a kid. She would never get to fight over the last fry with him, or watch him pull the one Jenga block that led to destruction. Those memories had taken place so long ago, and yet they flooded into her mind, as fresh as if they were only a few hours old.

There was no more room for new memories. That opportunity was capped, and no amount of picking at the seal would allow for anything new to be added to the barrel.

But she would also never get angry at him again. That was a weird thought. Her brother was now in the untouchable zone, that place where the mourning lifted their loved ones up, rearranged them so that only their good parts were visible. Maybe she would get mad at his death, but he would never dig his way under her skin, never say the wrong thing to tip her over the edge ever again. Even as she sat there, trying to think of something she hated about her brother, she knew it would only surface as sadness rather than anger.

The door burst open, and Cherry scrambled to her feet. The incoming employee balked at the door, seeing her red, tear-streaked face, then hurried into a stall, and Cherry knew it was time to return to her desk. She still felt herself teetering on the edge, but she was on company time right now. She could hold it in until she got home. Right now, she needed to revert to the callous form she had taken for the past month.

She approached the mirror, fixed her hijab, cleaned off her glasses, and opened the door, stepping back into the office.

Every pair of eyes in the room was on her.

It was too overwhelming. The eyes on her, the reminder of why the eyes were on her, and it all burst forth again, tears running down her face, giving them more reason to stare at her. She didn't want this; she wanted to put a stopper in her eyes; the last thing she wanted was to call attention to the fact that she was absolutely ruined and empty and could never get back the thing she needed to fix that, and god dammit, Don, I really hate you for dying right now.

She was going to be like this for the rest of her life, broken and prone to bursting into tears at any given moment, and—

"Cheryl." She looked up and saw her boss standing amongst the other cubicle buddies, a soft look on her face. "Why don't you take the rest of the day off?"

* * *

Don was beginning to believe he would fade away before he ever got the chance to collect again.

It had been a few days since the experience at the cemetery. He had thought so many times since then about using his energy to say goodbye to his sister, or do *something*, just to see what would happen, but with only one full collection under his belt, Don didn't think that expending any energy was worth it. He wasn't even sure how much of the first collection was left. How long did it last? No one knew. It would've been nice to have met a tween scientist, someone who had been willing to do the tests and collect the data, but alas.

Don had spent the last couple of nights off on his own. He thought he might need the time to collect his own thoughts; but instead of making him feel refreshed, the break just made him sullen and lonely. He supposed that came with the territory of being dead, but it was still an unpleasant feeling. So today, he wandered back to Englewood Beach.

He saw the thin outline of Lydia's form standing on the small strip of beach next to the docks, almost shimmering in the sun as he approached.

"Wow, what are the odds?" he joked.

She swiveled to stare at him. He cleared his throat uncomfortably.

"Hi, Don," she said finally.

"Looks like you've been busy collecting."

"Not since the last time I saw you," she replied curiously.

"Oh," Don said, falling into step beside her. "You just look more... sparkly. Like a Twilight vampire."

Lydia groaned.

"Geez, quick to judge, aren't we? It's not like I actually read the books."

"I think you're just glad to see me," Lydia goaded. Don tried to determine whether she was joking or not, but couldn't tell. She wasn't wrong.

"This beach is so peaceful." Lydia closed her eyes for a moment, leaving her shimmer as the only remnant of her presence. "You ever hear the footsteps story?"

"Nope."

"It's a Christian story. Not from the Bible, but... I guess a folk tale. It goes something like, a man walked a beach, and looked back over his shoulder at his walk throughout his life, and saw two sets of footsteps—one was his, and one was God's. But sometimes there was only one set, during the parts of his life where he had found the most difficulty. He asked God, 'Where were you when I needed you the most?' and God replied, 'I was there with you. When you were in need, I carried you.' "

Don let out a little laugh. Lydia glanced at him, and he quickly cleared his throat to mask his original intent.

"What's so funny?"

Okay, so he had failed. "Well, nothing. Just, you know, the stories we still hold on to."

"I was going to say, that story feels especially important now," Lydia said sharply, "because I feel like there has just been one set of footprints everywhere I walk recently."

"You don't even make footprints," Don whispered. The humor fell flat. Lydia stared out at the water for a long moment.

Don studied her thoughtfully. "Lydia," he started, then frowned. "Uh... do you still consider yourself a Christian?"

"Of course," Lydia said, her voice ringed with confusion and apprehension.

"Even after... after all this?"

"After all this?" she repeated. "Don, the fact that I'm stuck here like this doesn't negate the gospel. If anything, it proves that our souls actually do exist, and go somewhere when we die."

Don considered this for a moment. "Okay. But... Then why aren't you in heaven?"

"I don't know, Don, I don't make the rules. But I'm not denying their existence."

"I just—"

"Maybe we weren't right about everything. Maybe we're in purgatory, like the Catholics believe. Maybe—maybe—I don't know, Don, maybe this *is* hell, and I don't get to go to heaven, *I don't know*. And it kills me that I lived for so long thinking I knew for sure, and now I'm here, and..."

Lydia choked on her words and let out a growl that slowly stretched into a low, guttural scream. Don blinked and stopped in his tracks, unsure of what to do. She breathed heavily for a moment before continuing, and when she did, it was like the following moment hadn't even occurred. It was like she'd taken a moment to turn off the pain. "Every day I'm terrified that I'm wrong. But, um, if I'm honest with myself, if it does turn out that I'm believing a lie, I don't care. I'm trying to go through my days with the condition that whatever I believe, it better not make me give up hope. Because if I don't have hope, then it doesn't matter if what I believe is true or not."

"But if what you believe is wrong, then you wouldn't go to heaven once you leave here."

"So I trust that I'm believing the right thing."

"And by your standards, then I'm going to hell when I leave here."

"Well, what do you believe?"

"Not what you believe." He sighed. "I... I don't know."

"Well, then reason it out."

"I don't know, I believe..." Man. Couldn't an atheist just be left alone to not have an opinion about the universe? But alas, he should have seen this conversation coming. "I believe *now* that obviously there might be some sort of an afterlife."

"You can't say 'obviously' and 'might' in the same sentence."

"Why not?"

"Because 'might' is not obvious. It is unsure."

"Okay, fine. I believe that there might be some sort of an afterlife. Do those semantics track for you? I didn't believe that before, but hey. Here we are. And I have no idea what that means, *afterlife*. It could just be this, here. Or maybe we move on to something else when we're finished here. I don't know. I believe…" He sighed. "I guess I was closer to being right when I was a kid than during the majority of my adult life. I used to believe in a heaven, and… I guess that changed over the years. And now, well, I still don't know if I believe in heaven, and maybe that's what scares me so much about this place. Maybe being an atheist is still the only thing I'll ever adhere to. Maybe this is just the universe's way of playing a cruel trick on me, making me wonder one last time if I'm wrong about death being the end. Maybe I still believe this is my last chance at life."

"So you believe you'll just disappear once you leave here?"

"It's a possibility."

"Then, um, why are you collecting?"

"I don't fucking know. Because I'm scared."

"I know. I'm scared, too."

"But you just said that you'd rather believe—"

"Well, yeah. I hope that I'm right. That doesn't mean I'm not scared. Look…" She hesitated. "If this really is the last chance you get, then okay. You can decide what you believe, you know. If you don't want to believe you're just going to fade away, then don't believe that."

"Isn't that what religion is all about?" he said. "Fear of just fading away when you die?" He laughed. "So, what, I should just fake it 'til I make it?"

"No. Believe something."

"I can't believe something that I don't believe, Lydia. You're asking me to create my own religion, and I don't want to. I can't. I don't have any faith. Not in this world, not in the next. I have more evidence than I've ever had before, and still, all I feel is fear." He sighed, staring out across the water for a moment. "I remember the moment I realized I didn't believe in Allah anymore. It was seventh grade, and I was sitting on the bleachers before school, waiting for the bell to ring for first period. It wasn't anything concrete that had changed my mind—I was just sitting there, listening to David Bowie on my portable CD player, and suddenly I thought, you know, I just don't see any logic in the whole deity thing. And, you know, I remember this feeling of surging panic about coming to that realization: if I didn't believe in Allah, then I was going to go to Jahannam." He laughed. "Which is ridiculous, because if I didn't believe in Allah, then I couldn't really believe in Jahannam, now, could I? How could I possibly be afraid for my eternal wellbeing when I no longer believed in an afterlife? That really messed with me. It was a hard feeling to shake—I had to train myself to not be worried after that moment. But that doesn't mean that I don't have fear, you know? It just means I don't fear going to hell. I still fear whatever else is in store for me. Maybe nothing. Nothingness.

"And it sounds," he said, knowing it was going to sound a little accusatory, "that you feel the same fear, even with your philosophy. You say that no matter what, you're going to keep believing what you believe. And yet you just stood there and screamed because you admit, you're terrified that you could be wrong."

"Well, I'm only human," Lydia said curtly. "Stop belittling what I'm trying to do if you can't come up with anything better."

"I didn't mean to turn this into an argument," Don said, his voice softening. "Look, I would love to have that kind of hope. It'd be nice to cling to some kind of purpose, you know? Instead of wandering around aimlessly. It doesn't feel right dying without some sort of reason for it all, you know? But I never did come up with that reason. And maybe now it would be pointless to try. I already missed that opportunity in life." He sighed. "My mom and my sister were always happy following Islam, and it's not as if they aren't intelligent people—you know a lot of atheists will say that religion is for those who are just not smart enough to understand—but I never believed that. I just... couldn't believe in *it*."

"It's a conscious choice."

"What?"

"Religion. Belief."

"Oh."

"Um. I mean. We don't just fall into it. I didn't, anyway. Sure, I grew up with it, but I still stuck around after I turned eighteen."

"Yeah, a lot of people do stick around when their heart's not really into it, though."

"But that wasn't me."

Don couldn't argue with that.

Lydia's shimmering form sank to the sandy floor. Don joined her. She reached out and touched Don's nothingness numbly. Her fingers felt cold on his chest; but they had more feeling than when he had reached out and touched his own arm down at the jetty. Don couldn't help but smile. She was so fucking close, and he knew it scared her. She was becoming corporeal, and she wasn't sure what to do with it. When the goal for so long was to move on, there would always be doubts when you became too used to the life you were living. Even if it wasn't really living.

"What did you look like?" Lydia asked softly.

"What?"

"What, um, what did you look like before you died?"

Don wasn't expecting that question. *A hot mess*, he wanted to say. "I, uh, I had dark hair, brown eyes... kind of an olive-ish skin color... half-Iranian genes. And glasses... and I was trying to grow a beard."

"Trying?"

Don detected a smirk.

"Yeah, trying."

"What kind of clothes did you wear?"

"I don't know, T-shirts and stuff. Why do you... what's making you ask this?"

"Because I realized that I want to know what you look like."

"What did *you* look like?"

There was a pause. "I had what most people would call blonde hair, but I called it mousy gray. It was not very attractive."

"I didn't ask you for your opinion of how you looked, I asked what you looked like."

Lydia let out that tinkling laugh. "I had brown eyes. And I was terribly skinny, um, basically deathly skinny. I always worried about my weight."

"You were anorexic."

"No."

"Lydia."

"That's body shaming, Don." She hesitated. "And I was short, too, so I was just... small."

"Well, I knew that much," Don said, smiling. "Your eyes never come up past my shoulders."

"That's not true!" Lydia said.

"How would you know?" Don asked. "You've never seen my shoulders."

Lydia's frame bent forward. Don wished that she would collect more energy so he could get a better look at her facial expression. He imagined she was smiling. "I wore a lot of sweaters. I was always cold."

"Right. Anorexic."

"Shut up. And I wore skirts."

"Right. Christian."

"You really know nothing about Christians, do you?"

"I really don't."

"Well, there. That's what I looked like."

"Maybe someday I'll be able to see."

"Um. Same for you."

"Well, hopefully by that time you'll be gone," Don said without thinking, and suddenly a weird feeling bloomed in his gut. Lydia also seemed at odds with the words he had spoken, and fidgeted quietly.

Don cleared his throat, wanting so badly to break the awkwardness that had just fallen over them. "Do you, uh, want to go to Giardino's?"

"Yes," Lydia said quickly, and they both stood.

As they wandered down the street, Don had the nasty thought that the weird feeling in his chest was going to be a problem later on.

* * *

The number of stray objects that had ended up on the floor of Cherry's apartment in the past few weeks was becoming unbearable.

There, her floor lamp had fallen over, and there, an empty pizza box lay, wafting what was left of its greasy smell into the air. There, a crumpled-up tissue, and there, a small pile of shredded paper that she only hazily recollected, though she couldn't remember why she had shredded it in the first place. Probably in a fit of half-awake distress. Her phone lay on the carpet, blinking from some unknown message, and too far away for Cherry to check. She already felt the guilt of having missed noon and afternoon prayers today, so she assumed the blinking was from those reminders. She shut her eyes, as if that would shut everything out.

She had been curled up on her couch for the last eight hours, a blanket thrown over her legs and a glass of water on the coffee table in front of her face to tempt her because her mother had always said, if you're going to cry, at least stay hydrated. The only time she had moved was to go to the bathroom, and even that had proven a difficult task.

She heard a knock at the door, and squeezed her eyes even further shut. But somehow, the accountability of human contact stirred her to move. With a grunt, she slowly swung her legs to the floor and puttered to the door, wrapping her hijab around her as she went. The open door revealed Dee, biting her lip.

"Oh!"

Cherry must have had a look of confusion on her face, or maybe it was her smudged eyeliner, because Dee laughed a bit, though somewhat darkly. "Thanks for not answering your phone," she muttered, pushing past Cherry and into the apartment.

"I'm sorry."

"Are you?" Dee sighed. "Are we going to Fall River or not? You said yesterday you were gonna pick me up so we could carpool, and then today you just stopped responding. I thought you had gotten in a c—" She looked sheepish. "I thought you were ignoring me."

"I'm sorry, I forgot."

"You wouldn't have forgotten if you'd looked at your phone." She bent over, picked the device up, and tossed it over, then straightened and examined Cherry shrewdly. "You've been crying."

Cherry nodded.

Dee's demeanor softened. "You okay?"

"I... I went home early from work today."

Dee was silent for a moment. "Because of Don?"

The tears started to leak out again, and Cherry sighed, blinking them back ineffectually. "I know that life continues, and I need to act accordingly, but I just couldn't do it today. And I really am sorry I forgot about our plans tonight. I should've been more mindful, and instead I just caused an inconvenience—"

"Okay, hold on," Dee scolded, sitting Cherry down on the couch. "Cherry, you haven't shown this much emotion since your brother died three weeks ago. It's not an inconvenience, it's good. It's part of the process."

"But it's cutting into my life—"

There was that dark laugh again. "Yeah, so is his death. You wanna call that an inconvenience, too?" She slumped onto the couch, sighing. "Here I am, that asshole who gets mad at her best friend for grieving."

Cherry sat uncomfortably beside her, fidgeting. "Well, it won't happen again, so you don't have to be mad about it again."

Dee gave her a shove. "God, Cherry, you get so insecure when you're upset. You're allowed to grieve, and you're allowed to do it in more than just one sitting. That whole 'three days of mourning' thing is not an order to get all of your sad out only in that time slot."

"I know."

"Do you, though? You've been walking around like a zombie for three weeks, and I don't know why you feel the need to hold back like that."

"I wasn't holding back." Cherry bit her lip. "I don't understand it, but I just... didn't have any sad."

"Oh." Dee stared at her, her eyes wide. "Well..."

Cherry could hear the gears turning in her friend's head, as if she was trying to come up with a way to justify Cherry's bizarre behavior. Whatever came out of her mouth next, that's what it would be: a justification. She appreciated that Dee was trying, but she wasn't sure she really wanted it.

"Sad doesn't just mean blubbering, Cherry. Sad can mean feeling lost, or feeling empty, or angry, or indifferent." She picked at a seam on the couch. "Everyone tries to define sad as one emotion, but it's a whole umbrella."

Cherry bit her lip. What a sensible statement, when all she wanted was to dissolve and vanish into thin air. She had wanted to be mad and disregard whatever Dee said in that moment, but she had to admit that even if justification was her endgame, the argument was pretty sound. She kind of hated that.

"Okay." Dee clapped her hands to her knees resolutely. "What do you want? Fall River is out, right? I can text Thiago. Do you want me to stay and hang out, or do you want you-time?"

Cherry groaned. "Me-time, I think. I don't know. Is that okay?"

Dee rolled her eyes and stood, heading for the door. "Stop acting like it's not okay to mourn, Cherry. Or I'll come back here and eat all your food."

"You would've done that either way!" Cherry called after Dee as the door slammed behind her. She sighed and fell back onto the couch, curling back up and staring out at the void of her apartment.

She tried to think about what she had felt initially when Don had died. Overwhelmed, she recalled. Angry. Like she was about to explode. She *had* felt those things, which only stood to reason that she wasn't a waste of space for not feeling them at the funeral. No one could tame the ebb and flow of the ocean's tide, and no one could tame the way that Cherry Rind-Davis mourned a loved one. Not even her. As much as she wanted to control how she mourned, and feel the correct emotions at the right time, she was not her mother, nor did she even think her mother was that perfect—maybe she needed to call her mother, and remind her of the same thing she needed to hear.

What was frustrating to Cherry was that she never seemed to react in the same way to any death she'd ever encountered. When her dad had died, she had been so young, the only thing she could feel was lost and confused. It had taken probably six months for her to fully grasp that he was gone—she kept on feeling like he was just in the other room. Her mind had played some backwards game of object permanence, slowing down her process of coming to terms with the fact that he was gone. And then the tears had come.

And with her uncle's death, the tears had happened right away, so bad that she had been unable to stop crying. She had been sixteen, and Uncle Bobby had been kind of an odd duck, but she loved him, and she remembered it took twenty-three days to make it a full day without crying. She had kept track, for some reason, in that weird way that teenagers pass the time by giving themselves bizarre and useless tasks.

Cherry tried to think of any other deaths that might have thrown her for a loop. There had been the deaths of her grandparents, but she had been so young, she barely remembered them. Especially on her mother's side, because they had been in Iran her whole life. But she remembered crying when her Mamani had died, mostly because her mother had broken down while telling her she had passed.

But none of that really correlated to this situation, did it? Cherry thought dully. Just because she reacted one way to one person's death didn't automatically mean that was her default reaction. It was a messy combination of who it was and who *she* was at that moment, and what the circumstances were. Dee was right. The body was going to do what it needed to do, and sometimes that meant complete and utter breakdown, and sometimes that meant avoiding emotion and being heartless for a few weeks before cracking and spilling out of the casing. Maybe it was a form of protection. Maybe it was... well. She didn't actually care. She just knew it was what had happened, and she had to be okay with that. Even if it made her feel awful.

What really mattered was that she loved her brother. Even just thinking that made the ocean in her bubble up again. She loved Don. She could be upset with the way that she had acted for the past three weeks, or she could whisper that truth to herself as she slowly fell asleep on the couch, the clutter around her fading into the edges of her mind. I loved my brother. I loved my brother. I loved…

CHAPTER TEN

The next death that Don collected was downtown, outside of a pizza place. It was a heart attack. The man was in his sixties; he had a neatly trimmed mustache, Nantucket Red shorts, and boat shoes. He was sitting with his son, enjoying a slice while talking stocks, when suddenly he grabbed his chest, let out a strained groan, and slumped forward in his seat, his face turning beat red and his breath coming in shallow bursts.

His son, in shocked panic, called his name several times and shook his shoulder, then took about fifteen seconds to find his cell phone in his bag and call an ambulance. Don knew that later the man would question the event in his mind, question whether his father would have lived if he had already had his phone out on the table instead of stowed away. He wanted to tell him, those fifteen seconds meant nothing. It was a full five minutes before an ambulance arrived, and the man was dead within two minutes.

Don drank in the energy quickly and quietly, paranoid that someone else would come along and steal it from him. He felt lucky to have happened to pass by at the right moment. The man in the red shorts had not been so lucky.

Don felt a little lightheaded after that collection, and he sat down at the table the two had been sitting at before an ambulance had come and carted away the dead body. The molecules in the air around Don buzzed and vibrated, and he wasn't sure if that was just some weird reaction to the collection, or if he would feel each death differently, like different flavors at an ice cream parlor.

I've grown some thick skin, he thought with disgust after those things passed through his mind. I'm adapting to my surroundings, and to the form of survival that is available to me, and it's turning me into a monster.

But that was what Lydia had begged him to do. Get used to it.

Don wondered what would have happened to the energy if he had not been there to collect it. Did it just dissipate into the air around the body, or did it wander around until it found a host? Or did it somehow find its original owner in the afterlife? Every time Don turned around, he had a new question, one which would probably never be answered.

He kind of wished that there *was* someone in charge. Someone had to have realized how everything really worked and formed a system for relaying that information. Although, he considered, without the ability to write things down and communicate long distance like people did when they were alive, it would take a very long time to figure out how to organize the afterlife. It was kind of like he was in the Wild West: if people did have a reason to connect with others and somehow write a manifesto, they didn't seem to want to push it into reality. Everyone just made up the rules as they went along, and that seemed fine for everyone else.

But Don still wished.

It would make everything much simpler, much safer-feeling. Don couldn't help but wonder for the hundredth time if this was some special hell fashioned for him: watching people die had to be the opposite of heaven. He thought back to what Lydia had said, about purgatory. Maybe the world had gotten it wrong. Maybe purgatory had nothing to do with atoning for sins or trying to make right what was wrong—maybe it was simply the accidental place that some people went. Maybe there was no moving on, "achieving" the next level or whatever.

Don heard a commotion to his right and stared at the bizarre scene unfolding before him: a large, shimmering mass catapulted through the air, bulging and fluctuating as it hit the ground and broke apart into two human shapes. Their shimmer reminded Don of saran wrap, the way the sun glinted off of them. The two figures found their bearings, then jumped back up and plowed into each other again, locking arms in a fumbling sort of way as their slightly corporeal forms kind of phased into each other before finally resisting. It was like watching a 3D Venn diagram trying to find its perfect fit.

One figure snickered as the other slammed a fist into the side of his face. Don shook his head. He recognized that snicker... Oswald had picked himself a fight.

After a few more moments of tussling, Oswald hooked his arm around the other fighter's neck and squeezed, his arm nearly phasing right through the poor figure's neck. That had to be uncomfortable, Don thought. "All right, all right!" the other fighter pleaded, his voice strained, "Let me go, man, I'm fading too fast!"

Don could see the truth in that. It wasn't just the other fighter—both figures had significantly diminished in visibility. If they didn't stop now, either one or both of them had the risk of disappearing altogether.

Oswald gave another snicker, then released his fighting partner roughly. "That's what you get for picking on someone bigger than you, fucker." He glanced over, saw Don's eyes floating over the tabletop, and froze. "Hey stooge," he called. "Who goes there?"

"It's Don," Don called.

Oswald's beady little eyes blinked a few times. "Oh, Don! Man, I almost didn't see you there."

It figured that while Don was excited to collect his second death, Oswald had clearly gotten a few more under his belt. And apparently was quick to waste it, as well.

The other fighter took a few jagged breaths and then slumped off down the street, and Oswald came over to Don's table. He giggled. "Fuck, man, that feeling never disappoints," he said, and Don realized that the fight had given Oswald a blatant high. His eyes were red, and he swayed a bit as he stood there.

"We keep running into each other," he said, plopping down in the other seat, where the man in the red shorts had been. "Guess we've got the same haunts."

"What just happened there?"

"What do you mean?"

"Fighting that guy. What happened?"

"Oh." Oswald leaned back, and his eyes closed for a moment, as if he was feeling the sun on his face. Don wondered briefly if that might not be too far from the truth. "What, you never get into a fight before? Release some tension? Guy was pissing me off, so I punched him in the face."

"But you lost a ton of energy."

"Ah, it's fine, I've got plenty left. So does he, he was just being a baby. So what are you doing here? You shootin' the shit?"

"I just collected," Don said proudly.

The shimmer shifted as he leaned forward. "No shit! How many is that, now?"

"Just my second. Well... second whole collection."

"Let me guess. You shared a collection with some other fuckers?"

"Not this time. But yeah, earlier."

"Well, great, man. You'll get more. Hey, it took me a long time to get a whole one. First time I collected, I was following a bunch of assholes as they played wolfpack, which, gotta say, don't ever do that if you want to actually get anywhere with your collecting. Everybody in this town dies alone. There are fucking rare occasions where you might get lucky, but most times you're duking it out to see who gets the fucking prize."

"You just said 'you might get lucky' in reference to more than one person dying at once."

"Ah, fuck, you know what I mean," Oswald groaned, rolling his eyes. "You can't fucking control accidents. Most of the time. You can't get all bent out of shape when they happen, 'cause you can't fucking control 'em. That's the only time more than one person dies. Well, I guess there could be a school shooting or something—"

"Jesus Christ."

Oswald snickered. "What? Is what I'm saying not true?"

"You just say it so fucking casually. You're pretty messed up, Oswald."

Oswald was quiet for a moment. The air around him seemed to bristle. "Yeah, you're probably right. I've spent too long in this fucking hellhole. So how'd they die?"

Don took a second to understand that Oswald meant his latest collection. "Oh. Heart attack."

"Shit, man." Oswald glanced around. There were a few people who had wandered into view, some from the pizza shop and some just walking down the street. "Were there lots of people here when it happened?"

"Just his son," Don said slowly. "There wasn't anyone else outside."

"His son? Like, a little kid, or adult?"

"Adult."

"Oh. Yo, you going to Giardino's tonight?"

"I thought you didn't do places like that on weekdays."

Oswald snickered. "Yeah, but I want to be social tonight. I mean, watching bitches at the club is great and all, don't get me wrong, but I thought maybe I could hang out with you tonight. Is that where you're going?"

"Uh…" Truthfully, he and Lydia had planned on going to Giardino's, but Don had a feeling Lydia was not interested in carousing with Oswald. He made a split-second decision. "I was actually gonna try out a new bar, if you're interested. There's a place downtown that just opened up, called Jackson's."

Oswald scoffed. "You want to go to a new bar? God, that's so fucking lame."

"Why's that lame?"

"Because new bars are always so weird. They're still trying to find their identity. They're like a crazy bitch who just broke up with her boyfriend and wants to find herself. Which, I mean, if I was still alive, I'd make ample opportunity to take advantage, but, one, I'm not, and two, we're talkin' about a fucking building, not a crazy bitch." Oswald snickered.

Don couldn't even begin to describe how exhausting this kid was. "It's fine. If you don't want to come, don't come."

"Nah, man, what's the place like?"

Don sighed. "Honestly, I've only seen it from the outside. But it's a sports bar."

"Fucking sports bars."

"Like I said—"

"This'll be fun. I need to change it up tonight. I'm in. I'm fucking stoked."

Don tried very hard not to roll his eyes. Sounded like Oswald was fucking lonely.

Well, that was that, then. He wasn't going to see Lydia tonight. The thought was a little bit of a bummer, but Don reminded himself that he was dead—he had all the time in the world to hang out with people. Also, he wasn't entirely sure how he felt about the fact that they were getting to know each other so well. Could he be interested in someone in the afterlife? It probably wasn't a great idea to get attached to someone who would probably move on before you. And even if you happened to move on at the same time, there was no guarantee what would happen on the other side.

"Hey, you think that when we move on, there'll be a place we go? You know, like heaven or hell, or do we just cease to exist, or…"

Oswald sighed. "I don't know, man. I couldn't even decide this shit when I was still alive."

Don laughed. "Fair. But now we have some more concrete information."

"Do we?" Oswald snickered. "We know that souls are a thing that exists. That's the information we've got now."

"And we know," Don prodded, "that some souls don't… trigger the afterlife, so to speak."

Oswald leaned back in his seat. "Hey, you ever hear about that experiment?"

"Gotta be more specific."

"The one where the scientist said that souls have weight. And he like, measured people before and after they died."

Don wracked his brain. "Uh. You mean the twenty-one grams experiment?"

"Yeah, sure."

"The experiment where the guy only had six test subjects, and only one subject reflected his hypothesis?"

"No—it was more serious than that. This was a real experiment."

"I think you take the word 'real' lightly."

"Whatever. And they tested dogs, too, saying that dogs don't have souls—"

"Yeah, like, fifteen dogs that the guy probably poisoned."

"Shut the fuck up, dude, I'm trying to make a point!"

Don shook his head. If this was what Oswald was basing his picture of the afterlife on, this was going to be a fun conversation. Not that he could really provide an alternative explanation. "Okay. Oswald. Do you understand how problematic that experiment was? How completely not based on fact it was?"

Oswald's beady little eyes simmered. "I don't care if it's fucked up or not. Can you let me finish my point?"

"Okay. I'm just saying that your point is gonna be garbled by all the ridiculous fallacies attached to that case."

"My fucking point, Einstein, is that our souls weren't heavy enough. If our souls have weight, then the heavier they are, the more noticeable the difference when we die, and heaven, like, activates. But we sat on the fucking scale of life as we died, and we did not reach our weight goal. You know?"

"What's your point?"

"My point is, do we really want to pass on if we know we didn't make it the first time?"

Don sat for a moment, struck by Oswald's words. "So you're saying—"

"I'm fucking saying that maybe this is hell. Maybe we missed our chance with heaven, and by collecting, we're literally just killing ourselves. We didn't pass the test the first time, what makes you think they're gonna let us waltz through the doors?"

"You got all that from that experiment?"

"I've been a tween for a long fucking time, dude. I've had time to get all that from that experiment."

Don took a deep breath, trying to ebb the tide of panic that was building inside of him. There was always the possibility that what they were doing was in vain—that was something that he had discussed with Lydia already. But there was no way of knowing for sure.

"So, we're doomed," he said. "We're doomed either way, because if we stop collecting, we'll fade away and die, but if we keep collecting, and heaven or whatever doesn't accept us…"

"I never said 'stop collecting'," Oswald muttered. "That would be fucking stupid."

"You're right. Ultimately, we're still taking a risk, but we're taking a risk with more chance of survival by collecting. At least we're walking toward the unknown, instead of… well, I guess we don't know for sure either way. Maybe we don't just fade away to nothing. Maybe we *fade* to the afterlife. But see, no, because we specifically didn't make it to the afterlife because of our... weight... so...."

Oswald stood. "Jesus, Don, you talk too much. Just keep doing what you've been doing, all right? Now let's go fucking check this new bar out, all right?"

Jackson's was quiet—never a good sign for opening week. The inside was furnished with industrial decor: bare light bulbs hanging from chains, metal wall panels distressed to look like they had been there for years. It was very industrial chic, and very in-fashion, and very sparsely populated.

"Look at that, bud, you picked a bar that closes at nine," Oswald drawled accusingly, and Don rolled his eyes. As if ninety percent of the bars on the Cape didn't follow the same routine.

A few people chatted at the bar; a few couples were dotted here and there in the restaurant portion. "Anybody look entertaining to you?" Don asked, slightly nervous to hear Oswald's response.

"How about that group, over there," Oswald said, "by the stage—they fucking have a stage here? What, they gonna have concerts?"

"You want to go people-watch *them*?" Don asked, surprised. It was a group of middle-aged business professionals, with sweater vests and collared blouses. Maybe a work outing, maybe straight off the golf course, who knew? That was not at all the crowd he expected Oswald to gravitate towards.

"I'm here to have fun," came Oswald's reply. He began walking towards the group, and Don felt another wave of concern regarding his decision to go out with Oswald.

They sat at the table beside them, listening in on their small talk. One of the men was bragging about a new yacht he had just purchased, and how he was looking forward to taking it out once the weather warmed up. Don glanced over at Oswald and watched him as best he could. Oswald, for once, had given the group of strangers his rapt attention, though he could hardly be accused of enjoying the conversation. He squirmed in his spot, his head hunched forward seriously, eyeing the bar folk with his beady little eyes. There had to be some reason he was drawn to this particular crowd, but hell if Don knew what it was. Maybe he had known people like this in life.

"Hey, how'd you die?" Don asked suddenly.

Oswald's attention broke from the group, and he turned to stare at Don. "What the fuck did you just ask me?"

"Uh. It wasn't meant to be an attack, I was just curious. 'Cause, you know, I had a pretty traumatic death, and I'm pretty sure Lydia did too. So, I don't know, I just wondered if that theory had any traction. That's a common thing you see in movies, anyway, ghosts being people who died due to some sort of trauma." Don hesitated as Oswald's hard gaze lingered on him for another second. "You know, it's fine if you don't want to tell me how you—"

Oswald shrugged and looked back at the drinkers sitting before them. "In a fight," he said simply.

Don never would have guessed "in a fight" in a million years, but the idea made a certain kind of sense, with Oswald's blatantly reckless nature. "Oh. So, I guess, probably traumatic. Like a fist fight, or a… a gun fight, or…? You weren't in a gang, were you?"

Oswald snickered. "I'll leave that to your imagination."

"Ohhhh, you were in a gang!"

Oswald glanced over restlessly, his squirming intensifying, but he didn't respond. Don thought that was odd. He figured Oswald would be the type of person who would brag about being in a gang, especially since he wouldn't be in any danger here if he admitted it. There were no cops to come after him, and way fewer people to judge him for his past. If anything, being in a gang was an interesting topic, one which would probably pass lots of time if you had a rapt listener hanging on your every word, which at this point Don was ready to be. But Oswald suddenly didn't seem to be in a talking mood.

"What, did you get offed?" Don ribbed.

Oswald let out a cackle. "If I was offed, I wouldn't have died in a fight, would I have?"

Don frowned. "Valid point." He gave Oswald one last suspicious glance before looking back at the group of drinkers. The two of them watched the group clink glasses, laughing and talking.

"They remind me of my dad," Oswald said quietly, his voice tinged with acid. "He was such a fucker. Straight laced in the daylight, fuckin' sponging it up in the night."

"The Vineyard is just lovely this time of year," said one woman, probably in her late forties, her hair pinned up neatly with a brooch.

The man next to her, his white hair trimmed into a sailor cut, gave a doe-eyed smile and nodded, and Don heard Oswald feign a vomiting sound. "It sure is," he replied. "It's my favorite time of year to go."

"Why don't you just go together?" Oswald muttered. "Take a ferry, fuck in the bathroom, and then act like you're on your honeymoon once you get there."

Don watched Oswald's eyes bob above his seat uneasily, the shimmer in constant motion. He had known Oswald could be restless, but he had never seen him like this. There was something wrong, and he couldn't place his finger on it, but Oswald was not acting like Oswald. Don grimaced. He wasn't even sure if he knew him well enough to know that for sure, but there was something very off about how he was acting.

The woman with the brooch batted her eyelashes at the man with the sailor cut.

Oswald's shimmering form twitched. He stood resolutely and made his way over to the budding couple.

Don heard him snicker, but it was difficult to tell exactly what Oswald was doing. He did, however, have the benefit of context, and, after a moment of Oswald's hovering, a strange look came across the face of the woman with the brooch. She shifted in her seat and tried to pull her collar away from her neck, as if she felt uncomfortable.

"Oswald, what are you doing?"

"Hold on."

Suddenly, the woman jolted a little in her seat, tipping her martini over and sending its contents everywhere. An olive rolled lazily across the table.

The woman swore and tried to clean it up with her bar napkin.

"Here, let me help," the man with the sailor cut said, jumping up and rushing to the bar to get more napkins, sopping up the liquid and wiping the table down as best he could. A moment later, and they had all returned to their seats, the woman having gotten another drink and looking pretty embarrassed.

Oswald was still hovering around her. "Oswald," Don said again, this time with a little more urgency in his voice.

"Chill the fuck out, man, I'm trying to accomplish something." There was a pause, and the woman shifted uncomfortably again.

"Seriously, Oswald, whatever you're doing, it's clearly not a good idea."

The woman began to cough loudly, almost as if she had gotten something stuck in her throat.

"Oh, shit!" Oswald cried. "I didn't realize she'd have this good a reaction."

"To *what*, Oswald?"

Oswald didn't have enough time to answer—the woman suddenly slammed her drink on the table, coughed some more, and pushed her seat back roughly, standing and tenderly touching her fingers to her throat. The chair clattered to its side behind her.

The rest of the group stared at her, confused; Don heard Oswald snickering in the background. His shimmering orb shifted focus.

"Are you okay?" the man with the sailor cut asked gingerly, standing; and as he stood, what anyone else would have seen in the room was that his belt loop got caught on the table, and the front of his pants ripped open. He gasped and stooped forward, trying to cover himself up, while several others at the table stood, unsure.

But Don could see what those living could not see. The man's belt loop had not been near enough to the table, nor was there anything jutting out from the table to catch on.

Oswald howled with laughter, his body now barely visible as he took pleasure in his practical joke. Don studied his form carefully—it was, in fact, almost impossible to see now, Oswald having wasted the energy on what he deemed to be more important. His eyes were now the only visual clues left of his existence.

Don's stomach felt cold. "What the fuck are you doing?" he asked sharply.

"I'm showing you a good time," Oswald said between elated gasps. "You wanna know what's better than fucking fading away? This."

"Oswald…"

Oswald sensed his tone. "Wow, Donny, you need to chill. It was a harmless prank."

"Doesn't look so harmless."

"Oh, fuck off, Don, that guy's probably paid six times the amount of what he should've paid for those fuckin' khakis, and he won't hesitate to do it again."

"And her?" Don watched the woman, tufts of hair now falling from the brooch's grasp. She still massaged her throat gingerly. "Oswald, did you—"

Oswald's laughter dropped off. His eyes swung over to meet Don's gaze. "Come on, Don. Let's get the fuck out of here. I knew this place was gonna be a piece of shit."

"You just tried to—"

"Yeah, and now I've done it, so let's get the fuck out of here."

Don reluctantly followed Oswald out of the bar and into the street.

Outside, Oswald wandered down the sidewalk, his path wavering back and forth. "Oswald," Don said. Oswald continued, giggling and running haphazardly out into the middle of the street. Don heard him let out a whoop. "Oswald," he said, louder and more stern.

The eyes flicked back towards Don, flashing. Oswald was silent for a moment, and finally came back towards Don.

"Don't kill my buzz, fucker," he muttered, and Don noticed the red around his eyes. Was Oswald high, or had he been crying? Was that even possible?

"Oswald, I can't even begin to describe how horrified I am about what just happened in there."

"Okay, *Dad*," Oswald said woozily, giggling. "Are you *disappointed* in me? Are you gonna give me a piece of your mind?" He stepped forward, and Don felt an icy cold push at his chest. "You wanna fuck me up, Donny Boy? We might want a little more energy to do that."

"Oswald, you just wasted your energy to choke a woman and rip a man's pants."

"Yeah?" Oswald's voice dripped with a challenge.

"I…" Don sighed. "I guess I can't even be surprised, because I can't say I know you very well. But—"

"But. But, but. You don't want to hang out with me now? You don't want to associate yourself with a little bastard like me? Come on, let's hear what you were going to say. Am I despicable to your eyes? What I did, does it make you want to puke? Come on, lay it on me." Oswald snickered. "I don't give a fucking shit what you have to say. I feel great."

"That's because you're high off the loss of energy, dumbass."

"Yeah. I'm high. I'm livin' large, baby," Oswald crooned.

"Yeah, well. Now you're back to square one. You know, Lydia was right about you."

"Fucking Lydia," Oswald spat. He laughed. His eyes widened. "Are you fucking Lydia? I bet with a little more energy you might be able to do something—"

"Shut the fuck up, Oswald. You… you fucking need help, is what you need."

"Okay. I'll go see a therapist tomorrow." Oswald giggled. "You know, it's been ten years since I've been here. You wanna know how I know? Because I've been keeping track. And guess what? Ten years later, I'm still in the same fucking spot. Doing the same shit. It's not as fun as it used to be, you know? But this…" He giggled. "This is fun."

"What were you planning on doing if that woman actually did get hurt? You know she was really choking, right? What if you had gone too far?"

Oswald's eyes rolled. "Nothing I haven't done before, baby."

"What? Jesus, Oswald. How many times have you done this?"

Oswald burst into laughter. "I've been here for ten years, dipshit," he said between breaths. "Tweens don't last that long on their own. I would've faded a long time ago. I have been collecting for ten fucking years."

It was slowly beginning to dawn on Don what exactly was happening here, how truly horrifying this all was. "Oswald, how many people have you killed?"

"Wouldn't you like to know?"

"Oswald, *how many people have you killed?*"

"I don't know, man."

"You're unbelievable. You're a fucking junkie. I don't even—"

"So save me, Donny. Swoop in and come to the rescue. That's what you want to do, huh? You're trying to win your brownie points, like it'll do anything. Moving on doesn't have anything to do with wrong and right, asshat. It's a simple matter of quantity, and nothing to do with morals. You can be a goodie two-shoes all you fucking want, it's not gonna get you to fucking heaven."

"Jesus, Oswald, *you are killing people.*"

"No, I'm just seeing all the death in the living. Fuck, man. You see a tree with a rotting trunk, don't you want to kick it?

See if it'll come toppling down? That's all I can ever think about when I see a train wreck like this." Oswald giggled.

Don was silent—Don had frozen. Something had just clicked in his brain. He thought back to the crash site, when he had died. Oswald had been there. And a fucking toppled tree. Was there a possibility—?

No, of course not. That was ridiculous. Oswald hadn't seemed high when he had introduced himself, had he? He would've been high, having used the energy to knock over the tree.

It had been a pretty rotten tree, though. Don had thought the fall had been caused by the wind.

No. No, no, no. Don was wrong about this. Don needed to get the hell away from Oswald and go calm down. He was starting to hyperventilate again, and he had nothing left to say.

Oswald must have felt the mood turn. "Fine. You know, I could've had my fun without you, Don. I thought maybe you might enjoy loosening up a bit. You and I both know we're in it for the long haul. But if you're not ready to understand what this is all about, then I can't help you there."

Don sighed, turned, and walked away. He heard Oswald mumbling and giggling behind him, high as a kite, and tried to block out the sounds.

Every time Don turned around, there was something new to be horrified about in this place.

CHAPTER ELEVEN

Don's next collection was the next morning, at the beach.

He had wandered down to the waterfront to collect his thoughts after the previous night's disaster. The realization that Oswald was his murderer sat cold in his stomach, weighing him down; he desperately needed a distraction. Instead, he got more horror.

It was a surprisingly warm day for the living. A child was playing in the shallow waves, sticking his pudgy hands into the cold water and grabbing at the sand beneath while his mother and her new boyfriend lounged on towels a few yards away, making the most of the sun. Mother and boyfriend quickly became entangled in each other, and the child became brave and walked deeper into the ocean.

Don had never wished harder that he was more corporeal.

It happened very quickly: the child toppled over, sucked in water, and was not able to pick his head back up. The water reflected the glow of his energy as it escaped from his body.

Don stared at the glimmering cloud of light and felt a pit in his stomach as he assessed the situation. It was done, and he couldn't do anything about it now, except maybe extract the sullied silver lining from the situation and collect. He waded through the water to reach the glow, and drank it in. It clung to his throat, making him choke, and Don thought, good. The death of a baby shouldn't be easy to ingest. It is because of these moments that I want to leave this world.

And then the mother noticed her child, face down in the water. And Don was so angry. He was angry at the boyfriend for distracting the mother; he was angry at the mother for only noticing immediately after life had left her child's body. He was mad at both of them for not putting some damn floaties on the child.

And then he let the buzz wash over his body as fervently as the waves before him, and thought, am I any better than Oswald in this scenario? Ten years ago, did Oswald feel the way I do now?

He didn't quite understand how Oswald had ended up so flippant and carefree. Don was already feeling dragged along the bottom of the shore, and he imagined that ten years from now, if he was still in this hellhole, such a state of existence would have sanded him down even further. Was Oswald a psychopath? Or was he a piece of sea glass that didn't remember what bottle it was from?

One thing was for sure: he wasn't going to lose that part of him, the innate need to care about the world around him. Yes, it hurt to care, but he couldn't let himself become… *that*.

What was he saying? He was even more sure of this: he wouldn't still be here in ten years. He needed to be gone much earlier than that. Oswald shouldn't even still be here, but Don didn't think he had much control over that.

Imagine if Oswald hadn't been there.

Don felt a pressure in the cage of his chest, a pressure that told him he needed to do something about Oswald. He just wasn't sure what.

He allowed his brain to shut off as he wandered, and eventually found himself walking the Rail Trail across town. He wasn't going to have a very high chance of collecting there, but he didn't care. The path cut off his need to make a decision—which way to turn, what direction to head in. Shaded by the lanky scrub pines, he made his way slowly towards Old Town House Park, barely seeing the scenery around him.

He left the Rail Trail and walked past the basketball court and into the heart of the park, passing only a few joggers and bikers.

Up ahead, a bunch of teenagers sat huddled around a picnic table. They were playing with tarot cards, and probably had no idea what to do with them, but they were sitting, admiring the pictures, and chatting loudly amongst themselves. One of them seemed to know more about the occult than the rest, and was trying to describe what the tarot cards were used for.

It took a full minute of watching the group for Don to realize that a tween was sitting with them. They sat on the picnic table, bent over the teen describing the major arcana, shimmering with quite a bit of energy. Probably the most he had ever seen.

The tween caught Don's eye. "They'll get there soon enough," they said smoothly, a slight, unplaceable accent to their voice. "Bri is good at explaining to them."

Don watched them for a moment, standing there dumbly. "I'm Don," he offered finally.

"I'm Jordan. It's a beautiful day."

Don glanced around, as if he hadn't noticed. "Yeah, I guess."

"Is it also a tough day?"

He laughed. "Is there really any other adjective available for us?"

Jordan didn't answer, or at least not directly. They swung their legs up into a cross-legged position on the picnic table—it was amazing how effortlessly corporeal they were—patting the space beside them. "Why don't you sit?"

Don shuffled over slowly, eyeing the crowded table full of teenagers, but acquiesced. "Do you ever wonder how we can walk through walls, but sitting is no issue?" he said. "You'd think we'd fall through the earth or something."

Jordan shrugged. "When we were alive, even when we were resting, we would expend energy. Just by taking up space."

"What? No."

"Mmmhmm. The average person burns 50 calories an hour while sleeping. You still need to feed a person in a coma, right?"

Don couldn't argue with that. He hadn't been expecting a straight answer for his rambling question, but there it had been.

Jordan laughed. "I've been on this plane for sixty years, and a lot of that time has been spent sitting in on seminars at 4Cs. I'm filled to the brim with a lot of seemingly useless facts."

"Sixty years? I... wow. I mean, that's cool that you're sitting in on classes. I guess you don't have to stop learning just because you're dead." Don laughed nervously.

"The mind is able to process so much more than you'd think when its usual activities are taken away. But I also like to give it the tools it needs to process efficiently."

"So you've just been consuming entire doctorate degrees in your time here?"

"That really only happens in my spare time now. I've picked myself up a day job of sorts; I'm focusing on helping people."

"Oh." Don felt a prick of guilt at that. He was barely able to cope with being dead... he hadn't even thought about helping people or going back to college. He had mostly thought about helping himself get out of there. He stared at the tarot deck that the teenaged girl before him shuffled through. "Living people? How?"

"Oh, not the living. Though perhaps in an indirect fashion. I help people like yourself connect with loved ones to move on."

Don looked up, surprised. "You mean, you know another way to move on?"

Jordan eyed him thoughtfully. "I assume, given how corporeal you are, that you've discovered a way of sorts yourself.

Not strong, but it looks like you've come into some energy of your own."

Don looked down at himself, caught off guard for a moment. He did have a bit of a shimmer. He guessed that two collections in a row stacked up pretty quickly. He sighed. "Yeah, and it involves death, and I'm really sick and tired of it."

Jordan's eyes sparkled. "Well," they said, "I may be able to introduce you to another way. Soon, if today goes well."

Don felt his breath catch in his throat. Maybe this was some strange way of the world paying amends for the nightmare he had just experienced. Sorry about your murder, pal, but here's your way out. A wave of relief swept over him, and then a wave of guilt, which he couldn't quite place. He was so tired, and this world wasn't getting any easier. "How?"

"It depends on whether or not Bri here has a conversation with her friends. I hope she'll rally them together for a séance, but it's not short work to plant that thought. I and another like yourself have been working towards that."

Don frowned. Another like yourself. That was the origin of the guilt—there he was, with the possibility of finding a better way to move on, and yet there were others he needed to consider: Lydia, for one. He couldn't just up and leave, not without at the very least passing along the information to her. He couldn't strand her there.

And then there was Oswald. He couldn't dare to move on yet, knowing what Oswald had done to him, and what he was capable of doing to others. No, he had a bone to pick before he left this earth for good.

"I… I would like to hear more."

Jordan tilted their head. "I sense a 'but'."

"But… I can't believe I'm saying this, but I'm not ready to leave this place just yet. I have some things I need to do first. Wow, that sounds so cliché."

Jordan shrugged. "I'm in no rush. My work takes me to different parts of the Cape, but I do like this park. You'll find me here quite often, even when I'm not with a client. And I will always be available to help whoever asks for it. Including you, if you so choose."

Don nodded. "Okay, well… I appreciate that, I guess. I hope to run into you again. I mean, I feel like there's gonna be a catch, but that's a problem for tomorrow, right?"

"I'm not in the business of catching," Jordan cooed. "But you'll see that if you choose to. And yes, I'll probably be here quite often until this passing is complete—Bri and her friends tend to frequent this spot, and I'm tagging along with her until my client is ready. So for a little while, anyway, you'll find me here. But if your journey takes you the long route, I have a feeling we'll find each other again when the time comes."

Don nodded and stood. He had a lot to tell Lydia.

* * *

Don waited patiently at the jetty, soaking his feet in the water. The water felt stronger against his skin now, more crisp and less tingly. He tried kicking a foot out, but he couldn't tell the difference between the waves from the bay and any result that might have come from him. But with his slight shimmer, he at least had to try.

He heard a cough behind him.

Lydia shimmered in the fading sunlight, and it was startling to Don that he could actually see her outline so clearly. "You… must have collected today," he said slowly.

"Two," she said. "Um. In the past two days. You too."

Don nodded. "Also two."

"Lucky couple of days for us, huh?"

Lydia began to pick her way down the side of the jetty towards him. "And an unlucky couple of days for the living."

"Yeah, I guess."

With Oswald's antics fresh on his mind, Don decided to ease the building sense of paranoia in his chest. "How'd you collect two deaths in the past two days?"

Her shimmering form sat next to him, submerging her feet into the water. "The first one was, um. Just lucky. Car accident over on Higgins Crowell. But the second, I had gone to visit my aunt in the nursing home."

Don eyed Lydia. "Was it—was it your aunt who died?"

"Mmm. She was old, and her health was failing her."

"Wait, nursing home. Were there other tweens there?"

"Yeah."

"Did you have to split the energy?"

She sighed. "No… it's… there's a crew of tweens who go to this particular nursing home, and they've seen me come and visit my aunt before. They let me have her."

The words felt flat and void, and Don knew Lydia was struggling with what had happened. "Well… I mean, that's nice that they didn't try to rush you and take… Yeah. I'm sorry about your aunt."

"It's okay. She moved on."

"Well, obviously."

"It's better that she moved on and didn't have to get stuck." There was a grumble in Lydia's voice.

It seemed that Lydia needed a distraction. Good, Don thought. I've got one. "So… I have something important I need to talk to you about. Actually, two things, but… one at a time."

Lydia turned towards Don, giving him her full attention. She seemed relieved by the change of subject. Don wasn't sure she would be relieved after he explained.

"So, Oswald and I…" Lydia rolled her eyes at his words. "We went out last night. I tried to relieve you of having to hang out with him, so I suggested a different bar."

"Don, are you apologizing for hanging out with someone else?" Lydia asked flatly.

"No—no, there's more to it than that. He, uh, he tried some stuff at the bar, and riled some patrons up."

Lydia frowned. Don couldn't help but smile at the faint outline of her lips, barely visible against the bright sky.

"What do you mean, he, um, 'riled some patrons up'?"

"He played poltergeist. He used his energy to make things happen. And things got… well, he could have really hurt people, and intentionally, let's put it that way."

Don squinted and studied the shimmering outline of Lydia's face, trying to ascertain her reaction. If a living person could have seen what Don could see, they would have called her an angel, glinting in the sunlight. It was hard to see features—it was more like he saw a muddled sketch made of shine. Her face was petite, and very angled, and though Don couldn't make out much detail beyond that, he saw beauty in her features.

She sighed. "I knew he was capable of this," she muttered. "Do you see why I try to avoid hanging out with him?"

"Okay. There's more." Lydia waited silently. Don cleared his throat. "I, uh, I think he might've killed me."

There was a pause. "I thought you died in a car crash?"

Oswald quickly explained about the tree. "I know, it sounds ridiculous, but I think he was the one who knocked it over and set my death in motion."

"Okay. Wow, that's… um. I'm so sorry, Don."

"So here's my thing…" Don felt so strange saying it, but he pushed forward. "I think we need to stop him."

Lydia stared at him for a moment, silent. He hated when she did that. She may have been more visible now than she had ever been before, but that didn't mean he could read her facial expressions.

"Okay. I've been thinking about this a lot, and it's—there's no police to catch him, Lydia. No one investigating to find him, at least not on our side. No one living is going to suspect a tween, and even if they do think it's paranormal activity, what are they gonna do? Have a séance?" Don thought briefly about his talk with Jordan, and wondered why they were trying to get a séance going. But that was a conversation for another time, when there wasn't a murderer on the loose. He blinked. "Regardless, Oswald is going to get off scot-free, in 95% of these scenarios. Just like he did for me."

"Don, I wasn't silent because I disagree with you," Lydia said slowly. "I, um. I just don't know how to go about stopping him."

"Me either. I've been thinking about this all day. It's not like there's a justice system in the tween state. There isn't any way to imprison him so he can't go out and cause damage—I mean, we can walk through walls, for god's sake, it's not gonna be easy to lock Oswald up somewhere and hope he stays put."

"Maybe..." Lydia hesitated. "Maybe we need to, um, get rid of him."

Don stared. "Well, that's dark."

"Well, what else do you have in mind?" Lydia retorted, though her voice sounded full of dread. "We don't want him using more energy to hurt people, right? So we could, um... we could follow him around and make sure he misses out on collections until he fades away."

"What, just steer him away from possible deaths? Prevent him from murdering new people so he can have their energy? Or keep showing up and splitting whatever energy he's trying to collect? I mean, he'd still be collecting at that point."

"Okay, so the first thing. We could steer him away from collecting, and keep him from killing anyone."

"And then we would also miss out on collecting. Which means we would eventually fade too."

"Well, we could tag team it," Lydia shrugged. "If we kept switching off, collecting and babysitting, then—"

"You know he'd figure it out. He'd know what we were trying to do and take advantage of it. No, if we do something, it has to be quick. He can't understand that we're keeping the energy from him."

"So we do the opposite. We try to make him move on."

Don laughed. "Oswald doesn't want to move on. There's no way we could prevent him from using the energy he's collected whenever he wanted. And besides, he's even speculated that he doesn't believe people actually move on. What if he's right? We could, in effect, help him build up enough energy to 'move on' and instead make him even more corporeal and able to hurt even more people."

"Well, if he's right about that, we're in trouble for other reasons," Lydia lamented. "Okay… We could try to collect more than Oswald, and have the upper hand. Keep him in line."

"And then, for the rest of eternity, be Oswald's keepers. We are now working backwards in our line of thought."

"Thanks, Don. I'm trying."

"I know. Sorry."

Suddenly Lydia froze. "Don," she said.

"What?"

"Repeat what you said about the séance."

"What? I, uh… I don't know. I was mostly joking…"

"No, Don, think about it. Maybe séances are real. Maybe people actually do commune with spirits. I mean, I never believed it when I was alive, but this makes perfect sense. Maybe they actually do communicate with, um… with us. With tweens. You know all those stories about people communicating with, I don't know, pirates of yore or whatever."

"Okay, I'm gonna point out real quick that there don't seem to be any pirates around," Don said flatly.

"But that's exactly what someone like Oswald would want to make a living person believe if they were listening in on a séance."

That proverbial lightbulb switched on very quickly. He hesitated. "…I did speak with someone today who seems to think that séances might actually do something. But… what does this have to do with getting rid of Oswald? What, do you want someone who's living to give him a stern talking-to? Make him stop hurting people?"

"Hold on, I'm so close," Lydia said, her eyes a bit wild, like she was trying to do math equations in her head. They sat in silence for a minute, then Lydia laughed. "Okay. Okay, I've got it."

"Well, please, explain."

Lydia adjusted her position, trying to get more comfortable. Don smiled quietly at the fact that Lydia was reaching the point where she had to get comfortable. "Okay, so, priests will sometimes perform exorcisms, right?"

"Whoa. Okay."

"Don, just listen."

"*Okay.*"

"So think about that in context with what we know. Performing an exorcism, say that, in fact, whatever 'evil spirit' they're dealing with is actually a tween, right? And what are they really trying to do, Don? They'd basically try to create a shortcut to help that person move on."

"I don't think their intent is—"

"No, but that could very well be what's happening. I don't know. We only know so much about how all this works. Maybe there's some other key that we haven't stumbled upon for moving on. Maybe the living have some other trick up their sleeve, something that they've tapped into through exorcisms."

"That's a lot of maybes, Lydia." Don sighed. "Look, we can't exactly call Oswald over, tell a living person to exorcise him, and *hope* that something will happen."

"Maybe we can test it out first."

"Wait, what? You want to do a *test exorcism?*"

"Well, what other ideas do you have, Don?"

"This is ridiculous. We're not even going to be able to convince a priest to do an exorcism once, let alone twice. We're not even going to be able to convince a priest that *we're* not demons. They'd probably try to exorcise *us*. How about that? We could be our own test subjects, and if it works, then oops, we still can't exorcise Oswald because sorry, *we've* been exorcised."

It was Lydia's turn to sigh. "Then we'll move on," she said flippantly. She sounded exhausted, and ready to give up. "We'll have tried. And then Oswald becomes someone else's problem."

"Okay, but *we don't know that we'll move on.* We literally just conjured the idea of exorcism into existence, for all we know. Or what if exorcism actually traps you in some sort of demon-spawn hell level we're not aware of? This is getting more and more impossible by the second. Like, absolute, complete reach. Even if we got Oswald to a location and kept him around long enough for a living person to come and perform an exorcism, whatever the hell that actually means, we still don't actually know if said exorcism will do a damn thing. The fact that there are so many 'actuallys' in that sentence is really worrying, Lydia. It might not *actually* do *anything*, and then we've got a royally pissed off Oswald, who will then try to go after us, and everyone we love. Think action film bad guy, but probably high."

Lydia rolled her eyes. They were stuck. Out of reasonable options.

Except for Jordan. "I don't think we're going to be able to resolve this without outside help," Don said slowly. "But I know someone who might have more information."

"Who?"

"Well, like I said, I was talking with someone today."

"A tween?"

"Yeah. And they said they have been spending their time here helping people move on through séances."

"How?"

"I don't know, the conversation didn't get that far."

Lydia sighed. "Well, that honestly sounds like a load of crock. You said so yourself, Don, we can't talk Oswald to death."

"Okay, maybe it's bullshit. But what if it's not? And chances are, if someone knows about séances, they will probably have at least more information about exorcisms than we do. Maybe they'll even know how to perform one. It can't hurt to ask."

Lydia mulled this piece of news over. "I guess it would at least be moving forward, instead of stewing in our lack of ideas."

"That's the spirit."

So they were still fumbling in the dark, but they at least had an objective, and a first step, regardless of the lack of known steps beyond that. There were a million paths that could lead to a dead end, but hey. They had the time. They had until Oswald got bored again and tried to kill someone else, anyway. And Don was pretty sure Lydia was on board.

"Okay," she said. "Let's do it."

* * *

It was clear that Lydia was skeptical.

"So you, um, you had experience communicating with the dead even when you were alive?" she asked, her eyes intent on Jordan's shimmering form. It was as if she was searching for a slip in a poker face.

"Yes," came Jordan's reply. The three of them sat at the picnic table at the park, the teenagers having moved on to some other activity. Jordan had reassured them that they were keeping tabs on the one teenager, so this chat was not an interruption. And helping was helping, they said. They were intrigued by a request for an exorcism. Who wouldn't be?

Now Don sat between the two shimmering masses called Lydia and Jordan, and felt an odd kind of intensity in the conversation that was taking place.

"From… from what, séances?"

"I have performed multiple séances, both from this side and from the side of the living, yes." Jordan glanced back and forth between Don and Lydia. "But if I recall correctly, you weren't asking about a séance. You were asking about an exorcism."

"Well… yes, actually." Don couldn't see any reason why they shouldn't be blunt about it.

"And those, um… those experiences from the side of the living… they match up with your experiences now?" Lydia continued to be skeptical.

"I understand the process more now than I did when I was alive, if that's what you're asking," Jordan replied calmly. "I've had sixty years here to fine-tune it."

Lydia didn't seem to have a response to that. Don gave a little chuckle. He didn't share Lydia's skepticism. In fact, he was just excited to meet someone who seemed to have a better handle on the way things worked around here. Lydia could be skeptical all she wanted—and that was probably a good thing, for someone to play the pessimist and keep things in check—but Don felt a sense of relief that he hadn't realized was missing since he'd died.

"I haven't been asked to do an exorcism in a long time." Jordan shimmered curiosity. "Are you sure you don't want to just help someone move on?"

"Well... yes? We definitely want him to move on. I don't think he wants to move on, though," Don offered awkwardly, glancing at Lydia.

"Ah. Then yes, you want an exorcism."

"So the difference is in the tween's desires?"

"Tween?"

"Never mind. What's the difference?"

Jordan gazed out at the bustling park, full of people relaxing: lying on the grass, reading books; walking silently, hand in hand; a boy chasing a dog down the path. The weather this week had really drawn a crowd. Jordan took a moment to speak. "An exorcism is draining the energy, causing the being to fade away. And helping someone to pass on is boosting the energy so that they—"

"So they can trigger the afterlife. Huh."

"Yes. It's quite different, both in approach and in outcome."

"Well, the outcome is kind of the same, isn't it?"

Jordan tilted their head at Don. "We will never know for sure. But I believe, no. I'm not sure if fading away gets us to the next plane."

Lydia shifted uncomfortably. "How do you know all this? Are these just theories?"

Jordan laughed. "Like I said, I've been here for sixty years," they crooned. "I've helped many people move on. It takes a lot of effort, and often a lot of pain, emotionally speaking, but there are many who do not want to use the techniques that the wanderers use."

Lydia and Don exchanged glances. "The wanderers?" Don asked. "Oh, you mean collecting?"

Jordan's eyes flashed. "Such an unpleasant life to lead. Like vultures, preying on others' departures to reach their own destination."

Don thought it was less preying than it was scavenging, but he couldn't disagree with Jordan on the unpleasant nature of such an act. "So… you've found a different way?"

"Very different. One can be gifted energy from the living to move on. One gift is not as powerful as a… collection, as you say. Nor does it last as long. But when many come together, the gift becomes stronger. More powerful. Still just as brief. But… life, collectively, holds more power than death."

"Enough power to help someone move on?"

"In most cases, yes. I've had a few cases in which it wasn't quite enough, and we had to try it again. The more people at the séance, the more certain the passing is."

Don didn't feel great about that answer. The goal was to get rid of Oswald, not make him more powerful.

Jordan heaved a sigh, lost in their own train of thought. "But it does not come with the snap of a finger. The power is in the hands of those performing the séance. Many times, they don't realize that the individual wants to move on. And they simply end up speaking to them and not offering their gifts."

Don frowned. "Okay, look… I bet a séance is really interesting, but our ultimate goal is an exorcism, so can we just… can we skip to that part?"

Jordan stared at him for a moment, clearly deep in thought. Maybe they were annoyed at his impatience; or maybe they were trying to decide if Don and Lydia deserved to know more about the process of an exorcism. Don hoped he and Lydia would pass their test. "Who do you wish to extinguish from this world?" they asked slowly.

Well, when you put it like that. "A murderer," Don said breathlessly.

Jordan turned to Don and studied him for a moment. "A murderer who doesn't want to move on," they murmured. "Yes, you will need an exorcism. But you will also need to be very cautious."

"Why?"

"Because for those who know the rules, it is very easy to do whatever they want with them."

Don frowned. "Okay, I don't know what that means. None of us really know the rules. We're all just making it up as we go."

Lydia now leaned forward, having discerned the meaning of the tween's words. "It means that he'll be able to counteract our moves if he figures out what we're trying to do," she explained.

"Which is why you must perform the exorcism, and not aid them in moving on," Jordan said. "Otherwise, you will be giving power to a very angry being that you wanted extinguished. And they will wreak havoc."

Lydia sighed. "This doesn't sound like a very foolproof plan."

"Did I ever promise you one?" Don asked quietly.

Lydia swiveled her gaze toward him and blinked. She turned back to Jordan. "Sorry. Still not clear what an exorcism actually is. Like, um, what we have to do."

"An exorcism requires provoking the intended."

Don mulled this over. "So, we'd be agitating him into using his energy? How the hell would you do that?"

"It requires a lot of finessing," Jordan said. "It is not easy. But it can be done. I will walk you through the process."

"Well, great," Don said.

"Um. Can we see one performed before we jump in headfirst?" Lydia, the pragmatic.

"No. I can't perform an exorcism just for show."

"That's what I said," Don whispered, and Lydia rolled her eyes.

Jordan slowly stood and lifted their arms above their head, reaching up and up, as if they were able to actually feel the soothing effect of a good stretch. Don felt a twinge of jealousy. "But I can show you a séance. The students are holding one tonight," they said matter-of-factly. "Bri is their leader. She has taught them about all manners of the occult over the past few weeks. She has been hoping to hold a séance for a while now. It is finally confirmed. They will meet tonight at seven."

Don and Lydia exchanged glances. "Well, it can't hurt," Don whispered. "Even if it's not exactly what we're trying to do, it would probably help to feel more comfortable and understand how all of this works a bit more."

"Are they trying to reach anyone in particular?"

Jordan nodded. "Bri's brother, a young man named Billy. He died several months ago."

Don glanced around. "Is… Billy going to be there?"

"Yes. I have sent him to collect any extra energy he may be able to gather before the séance. A small amount of energy is required to be able to communicate with the living."

Don nodded. "So a séance is just a shortcut for intermediates."

"Yes. Unfortunately, finding relief will always involve some hardship."

"That sounds only natural," Lydia murmured.

"I must warn you," Jordan began, then hesitated. They cleared their throat. "This… this is a very serious business. You will be witnessing a very intimate moment between Billy and his sister—"

"And those she has present," Lydia muttered.

"—And interrupting it in any way will—"

"We understand," Lydia assured them. "We aren't going to get in the way. We, um, we want to see the process, in full. It would be silly to interrupt."

"Good," Jordan said. They seemed ruffled by Lydia's insistence on cutting them off. Or maybe they were just ruffled by Lydia. Don glanced at her curiously—there was some sort of resistance that he hadn't seen before. "But for the record," Jordan continued, "I will protect Billy's passing in any way possible. If you try in any way to intercept the gifts he is given—"

"Oh, god, we're not going to *steal*—"

"I have seen things that would chill most souls," Jordan said, a hint of disgust in their voice. "And I have ways of making you pay, if such things occur."

Don and Lydia quickly promised not to incur Jordan's wrath, curious though they were about what exactly that entailed. After a bit more conversation, Jordan instructed Don and Lydia to meet at 1501 North Pond Street at 6:00 p.m.

"Nervous?" Lydia asked as they walked away.

"A little," Don admitted, glancing over his shoulder at the picnic table receding into the distance behind them.

"Me too."

And their shared unease somehow, in some nonsensical way, lifted Don's spirits.

CHAPTER TWELVE

The house at 1501 North Pond Street was small, with darkened shingles and red shutters. The sounds of children playing in the street drifted to Don and Lydia's ears.

They approached the door, then paused. Don turned to Lydia, suddenly embarrassed. "Is there any form of etiquette for entering a house when you're a tween?"

Lydia laughed. Don watched as she reached her shimmering hand forward, pushing through the door and inside. She held her hand there for a moment, then cleared her throat. "Okay to enter?" she called loudly.

"Come on in!" came the reply.

Lydia glanced at Don. He smirked. "You just made that up, didn't you?"

"Shut up and get inside," came Lydia's reply. She disappeared into the house, and Don shook his head, laughing, and followed.

Jordan and another shimmering form—that must be Billy, Don thought—waited inside, standing in the middle of an eclectic, ornately dressed living room. Chinese lanterns hung from the ceiling, illuminating framed movie posters on the walls, and an old couch harboring no less than five blankets leaned against the wall adjacent to a tiny box TV set, which sat on top of a stack of large, dusty dictionaries. Don had to laugh at the idea of hosting your media center on top of the entirety of the written word.

A thin trail of smoke wafted from the dining room, where one of the teenagers from the park sat at the table, reading and burning incense. That must be Bri. Her dark brown hair hung around her face as she read. Surrounding the girl were maybe twenty candles, and a pink Bic lighter.

"Welcome," Jordan said warmly. "Billy, these are the souls I spoke of, Don and Lydia."

The lightly shimmering form waved awkwardly. His puppy dog eyes bounced back and forth between the two of them, and as they waved back, Billy spoke. "Welcome to my home," he said. "Or... well, my family's home."

"It's your home, too," Jordan reminded him.

Perhaps Billy had been having a bit of an identity crisis since his death, Don thought.

"Wow, I haven't had any guests since dying," Billy said, possibly just chatting to bolster his courage. He didn't seem very used to talking to people. "I would normally offer you some soda or... or milk, or..."

Lydia laughed. "We understand," she said, stepping further into the house. "Is it just, um, you and Bri who live here?"

"Well, I don't... *live*... but, well, no. My father will occasionally live here. He is a truck driver, so he's here every few days, when his routes bring him home." Billy laughed. "Bri has kind of taken over since I died, as you can see with some of her decorations."

"Were the dictionaries her idea?" Don asked.

"What? No, it—well, the dictionaries have always been there. We just never got around to buying a TV stand."

"Oh." Don shrugged. "I like it."

Billy looked confused as to why he would like a stack of dictionaries, and Don decided to let the moment pass. He looked over at Bri. "So, is she reading up on séances, or...?"

"Yeah, no, she just likes to read," Billy said. "I don't know, maybe she should be brushing up. Are we sure she knows what she's doing?" His nerves were really strung up, Don thought. But he supposed he would be acting the same way if he was about to move on.

"She does," Jordan said soothingly. "I've been watching and guiding her research, and honestly, most of the measures she'll be taking tonight are completely unnecessary, but she does have the requirements ready."

"What are the requirements?" Lydia asked.

Billy took a deep breath. "She's got to have some sort of object that I can respond to her questions with."

Lydia waited, but Billy didn't elaborate any further. "That's... that's it?"

Jordan let out a soft laugh. "That, and a number of people. Though you sometimes don't even need extra people, if your goal is only to communicate. The candles, the incense, these are all things that the living are often told will help with the séance. They do not understand that it is simply an exchange of energy. They don't understand the work we put into it on our side. But, of course, there is no way to convey that those instruments are unnecessary, so the living continue to use them. And I suppose it makes it more fun," they added, their eyes twinkling.

The doorbell rang, and Bri jumped up from the table, crossing to the door and letting in two teenage girls, one a short blonde, the other Hispanic. Don recognized them from the park.

Jordan's countenance seemed to droop a bit. They caught Don staring, and explained, "It would have been better if there were a few more people in the circle. Billy, we'll have to be careful about how much energy you use."

"Why's that?" Lydia asked.

"Because if I use too much of it," Billy said in an overwhelmed tone, "their gifts may not be enough energy to send me on to the next plane."

"It's possible that we'll be fine," Jordan said, "But we'll need to ensure that your sister has a very emotional reaction. Higher stakes, but nothing unmanageable."

Don and Lydia exchanged glances.

"Oooh, look at all the candles!" the blonde girl cried, picking one up from the table and examining it.

The other girl elbowed Bri. "Are you ready to communicate with the dead?" she asked in an exaggerated tone, a little grin on her face.

"I'm pretty nervous, I gotta say," Bri said, grinning.

The blonde girl fished a bag of Bugles out of her purse and opened it loudly.

"Sarah, ugh, you can't eat Bugles while we do a séance," the other girl scoffed.

Sarah rolled her eyes. "I'm not gonna eat *while* we do the séance, god, Jessie," she said, plopping herself down in one of the chairs around the table. She glanced around, sticking another Bugle in her mouth as she took in the room. "Shouldn't we be, like, sitting on the floor or something?"

"I don't think it matters," Bri said calmly, putting her book to the side and grabbing the lighter from the table. One by one, she lit the candles, a determined look on her face.

"Oh, geez, I guess we're getting started now," Jessie said, sitting at the table as well. Don, Lydia, Billy, and Jordan slowly gravitated toward the remaining open spots at the table, hovering around the three seated girls. Billy positioned himself directly across from his sister, and watched her nervously.

Sarah leaned forward and smelled the incense in front of her. "So what if we actually get a spirit? Like, what if one actually responds?"

"What do you mean, what?"

"Like, do we have an agenda? Do we know what questions we're going to ask?"

"We can ask whatever we'd like."

"You don't just ask spirits whatever you'd like, idiot," Sarah cried, a grin on her face. "That's how you get like, possessed or whatever."

Bri stood, taking something from her pocket: it was a small spiral seashell, hanging like a pendant from a thin chain. "We're not gonna get possessed. I told you, if anything, it would probably be my brother that would respond."

"Yeah, but like, we already discussed this, Bri," Jessie said, stealing a Bugle from Sarah's bag, "if it's not your brother, you're not gonna get all upset just because that's who you were hoping for. Like, if we get a different ghost, you gotta be cool."

"I know," Bri said quietly.

Don glanced at Billy. He was staring at his sister, his eyes wide and full of understanding. He knew, and she knew, and everyone in the room except for Jessie and Sarah knew that this séance was about Billy and Bri connecting again. Bri may have casually suggested it as a possibility, but of course she was hoping for it.

Don held his breath as Bri settled in her seat. Sarah put the bag of Bugles to the side and wiped her hands on her jeans. Bri reached out, and both Jessie and Sarah took her hands, also taking each others'. The circle was formed.

They closed their eyes. "We are gathered here tonight in hopes that we will receive a sign of a spirit's presence," Bri said slowly, evenly, though Don still detected a measure of anxiety in her tone. "We welcome any spirits—any good spirits—to our circle. Please feel welcome and join us when you're ready."

There was a long pause in which Don idly wondered how much of the speech that Bri had just uttered was actually necessary. He looked around, almost expecting something to change: the room temperature, maybe, or a breeze to pick up. But that, he thought, frowning, was coming from his preconceptions of what a séance was—which were admittedly limited, and all from popular fiction. Now that he knew what the tween state really was, everything had a completely different logic to it.

Bri's eyes flicked open. She squeezed her two friends' hands, and they pressed their fingers into her wrists, keeping the circle whole as she reached forward, taking the seashell pendant and dangling it in the air. The three girls watched as the pendant spun from the impact, then slowly came to a stop, and hung, idle.

"Is there anyone in the room who would like to speak?" Bri asked, her voice wavering slightly.

There was a pause. Billy's eyes were now at their widest, and his shimmering form reached forward tentatively, then pulled back.

"Go on," Jordan said.

Bri continued. "If there is someone in the room who would like to speak, please make the pendant move."

Billy cleared his throat, then leaned further in, his fingers brushing up against the pendant. Though Billy was not fully corporeal, there did seem to be a slight movement that was caused by his push.

The girls saw it. Sarah let out a gasp. "Did you see that?"

"Oh my god," Jessie breathed.

Bri was silent, her face white, her fingers trembling slightly.

"Stop shaking, Bri," Sarah whispered. "Was that you?"

"Ask again," Jessie said.

"Um… if you could make the pendant move again, please." Bri bit her bottom lip.

Billy reached forward, and, with a little more concentration, pushed on the pendant again. This time, it began to rock.

Sarah squealed. "Shut up," Jessie said.

"Are—are you—okay." Bri cleared her throat, every part of her body shaking faintly. "If you would like to answer 'yes', please make the pendant swing. If you would like to answer 'no', please make the pendant um, move in a circle. Are you the spirit of someone who died recently?"

"Why don't you just ask—"

"Shut up, Sarah!"

Billy swung the pendant.

Bri, unable to control it, let a little smile out. She took a deep breath. "Are you Billy?"

He made the pendant swing.

Sarah and Jessie let out whispers of excitement. Bri narrowed her eyes, hesitating.

Jordan translated: "She doesn't quite believe it's you. Not yet."

Billy glanced at Jordan. "Well, how do I prove it?"

"Remember… we said, if the living do not provide a more intricate form of communication, then we must find another object in the room that speaks what we want to communicate."

Billy let out a shaky breath. He glanced around the room quickly. His eyes landed on a framed family photo on the wall. It was hung crooked, its right corner slightly lower than its left.

Billy strode through the table towards the photo frame. He scrounged up his strength and slowly shifted the frame to a straight position.

The frame made a slight scuffling sound as he repositioned it. Bri whipped her head to look around and stared at the frame in shock.

"What was that?" Jessie asked, spooked.

"It was the picture frame," Bri replied. She smiled. "It's my brother."

She stood, looking like she was going to move towards the frame, but Sarah tugged at her hand. "I don't know if letting go is a good idea," she said nervously.

Bri stared at the frame thoughtfully for a moment. "Billy couldn't stand that it hung crooked," she said softly.

Jordan reached out to Billy. "Billy... I'm afraid your energy is starting to fade. Perhaps—"

"Can I help?" Lydia piped up.

Don turned to stare at her. "How?"

Lydia moved towards Billy. "I could move the pendant for Billy if, um, if any other questions need to be answered. I'm corporeal enough that I could probably make it move. I mean, um, I've never tried, but... and that way, Billy can save his energy for, um, for passing."

Jordan glanced at Billy. "Billy?"

"Yeah. Yeah, that'd be fine. Thank you."

Billy approached the table again, and Lydia moved to stand beside him. They stared down at the pendant, still hanging from Bri's hands.

Bri let out a long, shaky breath. "Billy. Is there something preventing you from moving on?"

Billy glanced at Bri nervously. He looked to Jordan, then to Lydia. "Swing the pendant?" he asked.

Lydia swung the pendant.

"What do you need?" Bri asked. "What... I mean..."

"That's not a yes or no question," Sarah whispered.

Bri closed her eyes, her head falling forward towards her chest in helplessness. "I don't know what to ask," she whispered.

"She'll get there in a minute," Jordan assured them.

"Well, like, did your brother have any unfinished business?" asked Sarah.

"I don't know," Bri moaned. "Did you, Billy?"

"Swing the pendant," Jordan whispered. "We want her to start guessing. Guessing is good."

Don was not really sure how this was going to help in the long run, but Lydia was already reaching forward and nudging the pendant.

Bri saw the movement and gave a deep, searching sigh.

"Was it Dylan?" Jessie prodded. "He hated Dylan, didn't he?"

"I'm not dating Dylan, anymore, if that's helpful," Bri giggled. "If you were feeling like, big-brother protective of me."

"I did hate that guy," Billy muttered.

Lydia reached toward the pendant, but Jordan put up a hand. "No, it has to be something more," they said. "Let her keep guessing."

"You always were protective of me," Bri murmured. "Is it because Dad isn't around? Are you worried about me?"

Every tween saw it at the same time: Bri began to glow.

Don gasped. She wasn't—she wasn't dying, was she? But that's what death looked like, he thought, glancing at Lydia. Her eyes were wide, as though she were thinking the same thing: that's what someone looked like right before they died.

But the glow didn't separate from her body. It floated around her like an aura, wispy and serene.

"Here we go. Swing the pendant," Jordan breathed sharply. Lydia swung the pendant. "Now get out of the way, please." Lydia took a step back.

Bri stared at the bobbing pendant and bit her lip thoughtfully. Jessie and Sarah watched with wide eyes, hands squeezed tight around each other, doing their best to be silent.

"He's been home more." Bri's eyes brimmed with tears. "He's been really good about it. But it's been really difficult without you. I've wanted to talk to you for two years now, and I... I guess I could've done this sooner. But I was afraid. I've missed you so much."

"Can you please move the pendant?" Billy whispered faintly. Lydia glanced at Billy, then at Jordan, then reached out and pushed the pendant. Ever so slightly, it rocked.

Don felt extremely uncomfortable being there. Jordan hadn't been kidding—this was supposed to be Billy's private conversation with his sister, and he and Lydia were butting in. Granted, Jessie and Sarah were also there, and Jordan too, and if Lydia wasn't here, then Billy would be wasting his energy and not be able to move on, but still. It felt weird.

A tear trickled down Bri's cheek, and she squeezed her eyes shut, as if somehow the world around her was too much to take in. "I love you so much, big brother," she mumbled. "I wish I was able to help somehow, when you were in the hospital. I'm sorry. But I'm okay now. You don't have to stick around and watch over me. Everything's gonna be okay."

As she spoke, her glow grew, and a faint cloud of energy began to emanate from Sarah and Jessie as well. It stretched above their heads and mingled, twisting together and becoming one glow, and then it began to spread out, like a slow-motion atomic bomb, hovering around the room.

"Everyone but Billy, back up," Jordan's voice came, loud and stern. The tweens followed their directions, giving the table a wide berth.

Billy stepped forward, his shimmering form resting directly in the middle of the table, and became surrounded by the glow. It twisted, spiraling around him, and arched, seeping into him and filling him. Billy breathed it in, eyes closed, embracing it. His eyes flicked open, and he gazed upon his sister, eyes wide and full of emotion. "Love you, bonehead," he whispered.

Bri's eyes flew open, and Don saw her eyes lock onto her brother's shimmering form. She gasped as he faded once again, no longer visible to even the tweens.

Don was suddenly aware that he was holding his breath. He let it go.

A bit of glow remained above the table. Don caught movement beside him, and watched Jordan step forward, walking through the table and absorbing the rest of the glow. They stretched their shimmering arms out around them and let out a satisfied sigh.

The three girls were still silent, still wrapped up in the energy of the séance.

"I think he's gone," Bri whispered.

It took a full moment for anyone to move. The girls still clasped hands, in awe, Bri still staring at the place where she could have sworn she had seen her brother's face. Then Jessie let out a quiet laugh, and the three of them began chatting.

As the girls regrouped, Don glanced over at Lydia and saw her zeroed in on Jordan. If it was possible, her outline bristled angrily. "So you're a leech," she muttered.

"I beg your pardon?"

"You only do this to collect whatever energy is left over."

Jordan stared Lydia down. "Do leeches provide a service to others?" they asked. "I see you don't believe my motives. But as I've said, I've been here for sixty years. I offer the knowledge one needs to reach out and connect with loved ones, and when they receive their gifts, I take whatever is leftover as a compensation in order to remain and help the next soul."

"But you're stealing their energy," Lydia spat.

"I'm not stealing anyone's energy. Billy moved on. What, do you think I get some sort of personal gain by staying here in this liminal space? You think I'm doing this for myself?"

"I don't know why you do what you do, but I think—"

"I don't care about what you think," Jordan snapped, "or about whatever hatred you hold in your heart. But it's not wanted here. Now, if you could be so kind as to leave. We are no longer welcome in this household without the presence of Billy. And I suggest we walk separate ways," they said stiffly.

Don and Lydia did as Jordan suggested, leaving 1501 North Pond Street with a bit more urgency than when they arrived. Don secretly wished he could have stayed and talked with Jordan. He had so many questions. But Lydia was furious, and they had done what they had come to do. And now it was time to regroup.

CHAPTER THIRTEEN

It had started to rain, and Don was glad that at least rain couldn't bring them down now. The droplets of water breezed right through him, splashing on the jetty around him. He snuck a glance over at Lydia's shimmery form, considerably less shimmery now, and wondered if she felt it at all.

"I don't want Jordan helping with the exorcism," Lydia said after a moment of stillness.

"Okay, I have to ask… what's your beef with Jordan?"

"Nothing's my… beef. I just—"

"Clearly something's wrong. I have never seen you act so weird."

"You haven't known me that long, Don."

All right. Change of tactics. "I know. Which is why I'm not sure why you acted the way you did. I'm not trying to pester you. I just want to know what you're thinking."

"I, um, I just don't trust them."

Don squinted at Lydia. "Oh my god. Did you get a high from helping Billy tonight?"

"I did *not*—"

"You did! You got high! Ohh, Lydia, you are an anxious stoner. Look how paranoid you are!"

"I'm paranoid because I don't trust Jordan? Ever think that it's possible they're just not trustworthy?"

"Why, because they took a finder's fee from their client's excess energy? I mean, it wasn't harming Billy."

"Whatever. Let's just... can we do the exorcism without Jordan?"

"Lydia... We don't even know what an exorcism would entail."

"Yes, we do. They said that it's provoking the person to use their energy."

"Yeah, but how? Pick a fight with him?"

"Oswald isn't going to use his energy on us, don't be stupid."

"Okay. Then give me something we can work with. Or we get Jordan back on our good side, you can apologize for yelling at them—"

"I just don't think that inviting someone whose goal is to stick around as long as possible in the tween state to exorcise someone who has taken a similar path is a good thing," Lydia spat out.

"What?" Don mulled that over. "But Jordan isn't killing people to stick around, Lydia."

"I just..." Her eyes closed momentarily. "I don't know if I trust anyone who wants to remain in this place."

Don let that sink in. "It's not staying here that is the problem, Lydia. It's not a sin to be here."

"I never said anything about it being a sin."

"But that's kind of what you're getting at, isn't it?"

Lydia was silent.

"Look, sure, we're kind of on borrowed time. But that doesn't make us bad people for being here. I mean, Oswald, yes. He's an objectively bad guy. But not us. Just because we're here doesn't make us... I don't know, *wrong*."

Lydia blinked a few times. "We need to scare him." Ah, she was just going to ignore that statement and move on. "Think about it. I bet Oswald has watched films about exorcism, or at least heard crazy stories, right?

Don sighed, accepting Lydia's avoidance and making a mental note to circle back. "Okay."

"So, um, if we got someone from the living to perform an exorcism, even if nothing actually happens, we need Oswald to think something is happening."

"But *why*, Lydia—"

"*Because then he'll fight back.*"

There went the hamster wheel of Don's brain. "And he'll use up his energy trying to stop us. We wouldn't be making him more powerful. And it would be a lot faster than fading away." He swallowed. "Or, alternate outcome: Oswald kills an exorcist."

"Not with, um, careful planning."

Don stared at Lydia. "Okay. Well, I just don't want to see us getting hurt in the process." And by us, I mean you, he thought.

"Which would you prefer? The safety of the dead, or the safety of the living?"

She made a good point.

"Fine. So, we contact someone. Get them to perform an exorcism."

"Who can we contact? What about, um, your sister?"

"My sister?" Don frowned. "Why not your husband?" There was enough of a hesitation there that Don knew they had a problem. "Uh, we're gonna have to seriously consider involving a third party, here, because I'm not willing to put my sister in the line of fire. And I bet that's the same for you and Colby."

Lydia thought for a moment. "No, this will work. Because what would both your sister and my husband do if we tried to contact them from the dead?"

"Freak out."

"Colby grew up Pentecostal. He would think we were demons. And your sister?"

"She would probably think I was a Jinni."

"What's that?"

"It's, uh, it's another type of being in Muslim custom that lives on another plane. Any time people talk about spirits or ghosts, Muslims always point to the Jinn."

"Would you exorcise a Jinni?"

"I mean, yeah."

"But neither would try to cast out a demon or Jinni on their own, right? Unless your sister has some sort of formal training. I know Colby wouldn't. He would reach out to others at the church and get help."

"Well..." Don frowned thoughtfully. "Cherry might try? But I don't know, not right away. I don't know if she even knows how. I think at the very least, she would do some reading, research, maybe reach out to others and ask their advice first. She wouldn't just... jump in." He sighed. "Which is good. That would give us the time we'd need." Still felt dangerous, though. "So, we're on the same path, then. My sister may try to exorcise me, your husband may try to exorcise you. But not without help, or time. Cool. Let's hope they do decide to bring reinforcements, or we may be shit out of luck."

"So we go ourselves, try to contact them, somehow trick them into preparing an exorcism, and then get Oswald there. Do a switch."

"That sounds risky."

"It's simple... we make a show. Scare them enough to take action. I have a little more energy collected than you, but you are starting to get there... we should both have enough in us to spook them. And whoever's attention we succeed in getting first... once that happens, we find each other, and track Oswald down."

"I'll go to Cherry's apartment, see if I can catch her on a night she's staying in."

"And tonight is Tuesday, so that's prayer group. I'll head over to the church."

Don felt like he was in some sort of huddle in a high school gym class, where his fellow classmates were much better at devising a game plan than he ever was. He had the urge to grab Lydia's hand, throw it to the sky, and yell "Break!", but he resisted. "I'll see you soon," he managed, and the two parted ways. It was time for him to go have a chat with his sister.

* * *

Cherry dug around in her purse for her keys absentmindedly. She always put the keys back in her purse after entering the building, for some idiotic reason, and by the time she reached her apartment, had to go cave-diving to get the keys back from their deep frolic. She should have gotten wise to the tradition by now, but alas, she went through this every time.

Footsteps down the hall indicated the approach of a neighbor, and Cherry, muttering a small prayer, turned to see Josie. The angelic form of a woman smiled down at her from her tall frame.

"Hi, Cheryl!" she said smoothly, pulling out her own keys like she had somehow tamed the beasts to come at her beck and call.

Cherry winced. "Hi," she said openly, while inwardly cursing herself for still not being entirely sure what the woman's name was. "How are you?"

"Pretty good." She opened the door to her apartment and studied Cherry shrewdly for a moment. "Can't find your keys?"

And lo, there they were. Cherry pulled them up and jingled them. "Found 'em!" she said, her tone a little too high-pitched.

Julie smiled, and a strange look flickered over her face. Cherry would undoubtedly analyze that look for the next hour. "Well, have a good one," she said, and turned to go into her apartment. She stopped halfway through the door, her hand on the knob, lost in thought, then turned back to Cherry, biting her lip.

"Hey, we should actually go get that drink sometime," she said. "I'd love to get to know my neighbor."

Cherry stared at her, electrically aware of the fact that Johanna had said "love" in her sentence. Something in the back of her brain prodded her, making note of the fact that Justine was waiting for a response, and she forced her chin to move mechanically up and down. She swallowed. "That sounds great," she said faintly.

Jo raised an eyebrow, gave a thin-lipped smile, and put her apartment door between them. Cherry leaned her forehead on her own door, turned the key in the lock, and fell into her apartment.

Don was waiting patiently inside when she entered. He had heard the conversation between Cherry and her neighbor and rolled his eyes. Cherry never had been good at making conversation, especially with people that she wanted to make conversation with. He watched Cherry put down her purse, slip her shoes and hijab off, and wander into the kitchen. He heard the sound of running water. Cherry came back into the living room, placed the glass on the coffee table, and collapsed on the couch, immediately closing her eyes.

No, no, no, Don thought, you can't go to sleep yet. I have to haunt you first.

He concentrated, reaching out to touch the water glass. The idea of being able to tip a glass over was so ridiculous, and yet, simultaneously exciting—with only a few collections under his belt, he wanted to see how corporeal he had become.

Unfortunately, tipping the glass was a lot harder than he thought. His fingers kept gliding through its surface, ignoring physics. Don scrounged up all of his concentration and tried again. This time he managed a good nudge, and let out an excited whoop as the glass made a noise on the coffee table, the water sloshing around a bit.

It was enough to rouse Cherry's attention. Her eyes fluttered open, and she stared out at the glass curiously, as if maybe she had somehow knocked the glass in her prone state and made the water lap at the sides.

But after another moment, Cherry closed her eyes.

Damn it, thought Don, and he glanced around, trying to find a better source of movement. He only had so much energy. If he kept on making the glass move, and it wasn't enough to stop her from rolling over and falling asleep, then this whole night would be a waste. He needed something else, something that took the same amount of effort but would produce a bigger, louder result.

His gaze landed on the old, retro-style radio in the corner of the room. Cherry had received this radio for her seventeenth birthday, and for some godforsaken reason, had kept it all these years. Don approached the old beast of a machine, with its fabric-covered speaker and two clunky dials on either end of the contraption. Easy-to-move dials, he hoped.

With a little effort, Don worked at the left dial, his fingers slipping and sliding on it as if it were covered in butter. After a long, agonizing moment, he finally heard a click and felt resistance ebb as the dial turned. The sound of static filled the room.

Cherry's eyes flew open; she propped herself up on the couch and stared, a bewildered look on her face.

Don couldn't help but smile. Maybe he was just feeling the natural high from expending energy, but he was pretty pleased with himself. He imagined himself as one of those cartoon ghosts, floating in the air, his bottom half petering down to a wisp. Say hello to your Casper, he thought. Though he could literally feel the drain of energy in every action he made, it was still exciting, nonetheless, to see results.

Cherry slowly stood, her eyes trained on the radio. Bits of two separate stations played simultaneously, fighting for attention, with the prickly static sound of error keeping the beat in the background.

Cherry took a few steps towards the radio, then stopped. She looked stunned.

Then she ran to the door of her apartment, grabbing her hijab on the way, and left.

Don grimaced. Damn it.

Sticking his head through the door, he quietly thanked Cherry's stupid crush: Cherry had not, as Don had feared, fled from her home in the middle of the night. She had, in fact, knocked on her neighbor's door, and was now fidgeting impatiently.

The door opened. A tall blonde woman appeared, a guarded yet intrigued look on her face.

The two stared at each other for a moment.

"Um... I have a question," Cherry said, looking very dazed and completely not with it.

Don sighed. Come on, Cherry, what are you doing?

"Shoot," the neighbor replied, a smile pulling at her lips. She was watching Cherry with an amused, intent expression, and if Don hadn't been on a mission, he would have thought it was sweet.

"Okay. Okay, it's not really a question, more as it is a... a statement, I guess?"

"That was a question." The neighbor smiled. "Or it sounded like a question. Not that it *was* a question, but your inflection went up at the end, so..."

Cherry's brow furrowed. "My radio just turned on."

The neighbor shifted her weight, her amusement turning to puzzlement. "I'm afraid I'm not following."

"My..." Cherry bit her lip. "I didn't turn it on. But it turned on. By itself."

The neighbor's eyes went wide. "Do you have a ghost?"

"Do you believe in ghosts?"

"Um, I guess, yeah, do you?"

"No..." Cherry's voice had suddenly jumped an octave.

Her neighbor laughed. "Can I see?" she asked excitedly.

Don followed Cherry and her neighbor back into the apartment, full of excitement. He was not quite sure what his next move was—should he go find Lydia? Or should he wait until they started talking about exorcism?

He frowned. What if their first instinct wasn't exorcism? It seemed ridiculous that they would have assumed that, actually, now that he was watching the scenario unfold in front of him. It was highly unlikely that Cherry was going to scare the hell out of her neighbor by suggesting they perform an exorcism together. Cherry couldn't even make a phone call without writing a script for herself to follow. He was going to have to lead them to that conclusion, and give them more of a reason for an exorcism. He sighed. Did this mean he was going to have to break something? He really did not want to have to terrorize his sister to make this work.

The three of them entered the room, Cherry and her neighbor making a beeline for the radio.

"Maybe it was already on," her neighbor suggested, and Cherry shook her head.

"No, I haven't used the radio in a few weeks," she said.

The two of them stood silently for a moment, staring at the radio expectantly.

Don looked around the room in a panic. There had to be something else that would wow them. But something low-energy, because he really didn't want to fade away in the process.

There was a pinwheel hanging by the window that Cherry had fashioned into a curtain hook. That would do. He approached the pinwheel and tried blowing at it, but that didn't seem to do anything. He reached out and flicked at it, hard. The pinwheel slowly creaked its way into a spin. Don rolled his eyes. Well, it was something.

It was enough for Cherry's neighbor to notice. "Look!" she cried, and the two of them flocked to the pinwheel, eyes wide. No, Don thought, they look like they just stepped into Narnia. This is not the tone I'm trying to set.

He needed something scary.

He glanced around, and his eyes landed on the knife block on the counter. Ooh. That would do.

The knife block was a lot heavier than the pinwheel, or the glass. Luckily, its shape leaned forward, so he at least knew which way to push. It took a few tries, and probably longer than it needed to take because Don was starting to feel a little elated from the energy expenditure, but before they even lost interest in the pinwheel, he managed to tip the knife block just enough that momentum carried it the rest of the way forward. The block slammed into the counter, and a couple of knives slid out, clattering to the tile floor below.

That, thought Don, could not have been any more perfect.

The reaction was satisfactory. Cherry let out a little shriek, and the two of them peered from a distance at the knives. Don decided to add a little pizzazz to the show, kicking at one of the knives that lay on the floor, and the two women fell over each other on the way out of the apartment.

Don smiled. That ought to do it.

* * *

Cherry hurried with Jolene back into her apartment across the hall, slamming the door shut with relief. The two of them slouched over the kitchen counter for a moment, breathing heavily and exchanging wide-eyed glances. "Let's stay out of your place for now," Judy gasped, and they both let out a nervous laugh.

The thought occurred to Cherry that she had never been past the doorway of this apartment before. She glanced around, taking in the décor: a few dip-dyed plates hanging on the wall in the foyer, an overlarge, comfortable looking blue couch in the living room, the shaggy white rug partially covering the hardwood floor. A desk sat in the corner of the living room, with a fitness poster tacked above it. Goodness, this woman seemed to have her life much more together than Cherry ever would.

Janet motioned for Cherry to sit on the couch and disappeared into the kitchen, coming back out with hot mugs of tea. She shrugged. "I was boiling water when you knocked on my door," she said, sheepish at how quickly she had served her guest.

Cherry smiled and took the mug. She grimaced at her own vise-like grip, and took a deep breath. Her fingers were shaking, and she honestly was not sure if it was from the paranormal experience, or from being in her neighbor's apartment.

"Hey," Jessica said, "That was some wild shit, huh?" She cocked a half-smile, trying to foil Cherry's nerves.

"Oh, definitely," Cherry mumbled, sipping her tea. She groaned. "What if that happens every time I go home?"

"Probably not something you want, huh?" Jamie studied her for a moment, her eyes skimming over Cherry's hijab. "You're um…" She winced. "Muslim?"

Cherry raised an eyebrow at the wince. The poor girl was worried about being wrong. As if being wrongly called Muslim was an insult. "Yes."

"You guys don't believe in ghosts?"

"Once the soul has passed on, it doesn't come back. Demons and the Jinn, on the other hand…"

"Ah. What are Jinn?"

Cherry paused. "Like, beings from another plane, kind of," she said slowly. "We used to pass around horror stories about the Jinn when I was a kid."

"Okay, so kind of like ghosts, but evil."

Cherry squinted. "Not really. They are very much alive. And not all of them are evil. Though it is said that most of them are not friendly."

"Oh, good. Cool. I'm very excited about that piece of news. So what, do you think that's a Jinn in your apartment right now?"

"I don't know. Maybe it's a demon." Cherry shrugged. "I think I'd prefer it to be a Jinn. Though… I don't know. It's been a while since I've read up on the Jinn."

She smiled. "Guess you'll be reading up on it now, huh?"

Cherry laughed. "How about you?"

"Well I don't know anything about Jinn, but I do believe in ghosts. I've done a few séances in my day," she said excitedly. "They're always pretty spooky, but… enlightening." Her eyes held a mischief that told Cherry she was holding back the juicy details.

"You contacted spirits?" Cherry's eyes went wide. "That's like, a huge mistake if you believe in the Jinn. Appealing to the Jinn is impermissible."

"Well, that makes sense, if most of the Jinn are evil. Don't go poking evil spirits. But what if a Jinn is trying to contact you? What if it's a good Jinn?"

Cherry sighed. "It's very unlikely that a good Jinni would care to contact me."

"Hey, um. Shoot me down if this isn't my place, but... You just went through some sort of loss, didn't you?"

Cherry gave a slow nod. "My brother."

"Okay. Um..." She gave her a sympathetic, lingering, soft eyed stare. Cherry fidgeted uncomfortably. "Have you thought that maybe it's a weird coincidence that this happened so soon after his death?"

Cherry stared at Jill, at a loss for words. The two were silent for a moment.

Joanne leaned forward, her eyes suddenly glittering. "Okay, so humor me for a second. What would happen if you did contact them?"

Cherry studied her for a second. "You really want to try and contact them, don't you?"

She nodded. "I mean, like I said, I've done séances before. Docile stuff, for sure. But yeah. Didn't have any evil Jinn beating down my door, either." She smiled.

"What were some of your experiences?"

"Never really got too many details from the spirits. But I used a Ouija board once, and we got a name out of it."

"A name?"

"Yeah. Joshua. Pretty crazy. I figured, you know, if somebody was rigging the board, it would be something short, like Sam, or Joe. But no, this dude wanted us to know his name was Joshua."

"What else did he say?"

She bit her lip. "Not much. After he said his name, it kind of got quiet. Which was a bit disappointing, but… I don't know, I guess ghosts get tired, right? I bet it's exhausting, communicating from another realm." She saw the look on Cherry's face. "What? Okay, if it were a Jinn… Jinni? What was it doing… biding its time?"

"I don't know."

"Well, Jinn or spirit or whatever you want to call it, it's still in your apartment right now."

Cherry frowned. "You're right. And I'm worried that…" She stopped, then shook her head.

"What?"

Cherry sighed. "I'm worried that if I talk to it… it'll convince me that it *is* my brother."

Jackie's gaze softened again. "I'm sorry about your brother. Were you close?"

Cherry glanced up sharply. Part of her was ready to answer, yes. But determination had now set in—the other part of her screamed, *then prove it.* Don't play games with the Jinni, Cherry—but if you know your brother, you will know if it's

212

him. She wanted to play that game, terrifying though it sounded.

"You said you have a Ouija board?"

Janelle's eyes went wide. "You want to try to talk to the Jinn ghost?"

"Well, yeah. I thought that's what you were getting at."

She grinned. "I mean, I won't deny that would be a lot of fun," she said, pulling her legs into a crossed position on the couch, her back straightening and making her a few extra inches taller. Her body communicated her excitement. She thought for a moment. "But I don't have a Ouija board. The one I used way back when was a friend's. Shit, I wish I did have one. I mean, it's not necessary to have one, but it does allow for actual words to be spelled out. Communicating like a boss." She smiled.

Cherry's thoughts flickered to Don. The image of him jolted through her nervous system. "I think that would be best," she said quietly.

Jill examined her facial expression and nodded.

Cherry fidgeted uncomfortably. "I actually think my friend might have one," she said.

She stood, fishing her cell phone from her pocket. She was going to call Dee. Dee didn't believe in ghosts, or the Jinn—she believed in psychology. And that was, ironically, exactly why she had a Ouija board.

She pulled up Dee's number on her phone, then hesitated, sighing… she had to ask before things went any further.

"Hey—" she began, then fidgeted again. "I have a question."

"Shoot," came the smiling reply.

Cherry turned a deep shade of red. "What's your name?"

Something glinted in her eyes. She seemed more amused than upset at the question. "Gina," she replied.

"I'm so sorry. I'm the worst at names."

"It's absolutely no worry. I honestly don't know if I ever told you," Gina reassured her.

Cherry decided not to push the truth on her new friend—she had most definitely told her at one point, but... hey. New beginnings. "I'm Cheryl," she offered feebly.

Gina laughed, looked down. "I know."

"Well, that makes it feel even worse."

Gina's eyes flicked back up to lock with Cherry's. "No, hey. A name is a name is a name."

"I don't know what that means."

She grinned. "I don't either."

Cherry felt her face flush up and quickly turned to make her phone call.

CHAPTER FOURTEEN

Don could not have been more pleased about the fact that they would get to use a Ouija board. That would be so much easier than a seashell pendant. Noting how much time he might have before Cherry's friend would be able to find the board and bring it to the apartment, he quickly made a beeline for the Baptist church down the road.

The warm glow of the lobby welcomed him into the church, though no one was in sight. He glanced around at the room, noting the white walls adorned with wooden crosses and a corkboard heaped with bulletins and missionary photo cards.

A faint muttering reached his ears, and he guessed its direction, sticking his head through the door to the sanctuary. No one there.

He pulled himself back through the door and looked around. *"Lydia?"* he whispered, then laughed at himself, and called out with added volume. "Lydia?"

Don's eye caught movement from one of the doors, and he turned to see a shimmery hand—Lydia's, he presumed—sticking through the door, a finger raised as if to say, "One moment, please."

Don smirked and stepped through the door.

The instant he passed through, he knew something was up. A heavy cloud of energy hung in the air, swirling and shifting, its glow emanating from the group of people in a neat circle before him. They sat with heads bowed and eyes closed, one of them speaking quietly but firmly. The man was murmuring thanks to their god—the others hummed in agreement—and how holy he was—more hums—on and on about how wonderful their god was. The hums were like a quiet symphony.

Don peered through the haze and spotted Lydia sitting in the corner nearest to the door, spectating but still separate from the prayer circle.

He shook his head. He was having a hard time processing this new information. Lydia had made it sound like finding energy to collect was a struggle, and yet here she was, staring right at a jackpot. How had she not already moved on? And why hadn't she said anything about this?

He studied her for a moment. Her eyes were open, and he realized that probably meant she wasn't praying along with them. No, she had her eyes fixed on someone across the room. Don glanced over. That must be Colby. He was handsome enough, with thick, wavy blonde hair, kind of preppy looking, wearing a collared shirt. He had a bible on his lap. He reminded Don of 80% of the other Christian guys he knew.

Why was Lydia looking at him so sadly? It took Don a second to register the answer. Of the eight or nine people in the room, Colby was the only one who Don could see with perfect clarity amidst the clouds of energy; he was the only one from whom the energy wasn't seeping out of.

Lydia finally noticed that Don had entered the room. "Stop!" she hissed at him, jumping up. "Don't move any closer!" She joined Don at the door, giving the prayer circle a wide berth.

"What the fuck is this?" Don muttered, his eyes wide.

Lydia gave him a glare. "This is a place of worship," she chided.

"Lydia," Don breathed. "There is energy everywhere."

"Mmhmm. They're praying."

"This is what happens when people pray?"

"It, um. It makes so much more sense, now that we've seen what happened with Bri and Billy."

"...Lydia, how long have you known this is a thing? You have an endless supply of energy right—"

Lydia rolled her eyes. "Out," she said, "And don't you dare touch." She passed through the door, and Don sighed, following her out.

"You are not to touch that energy, Don, do you understand me?"

"Why?"

"Because it's not ours, that's why," she whispered, "It's God's."

Don laughed. "What?"

"Those people are praying to God. I won't pretend to fully understand it, but I just… um, it's not for us, okay?"

"Are you kidding me? How many people have we watched die, Lydia? And you've known about this the whole time? Just loads of extra energy, there for the taking, that could help us move on, I don't care if it's for God or not—"

"Well, then, that's the difference between you and me, Don," Lydia said, trying fruitlessly to keep her voice level. "These people come and pour their hearts out to God, they worship him, they pray to him, and you want to take that? Don't you think that's a little barbaric?"

"It's not like God is walking around, collecting the energy. And what is he gonna do with it?"

"We don't know where the energy goes, Don. We don't understand how any of this works."

"We certainly know enough to collect energy at other times. What's the big fucking difference?"

"Fine, Don!" Lydia's voice was very high-pitched now. "Fine, if that's what you want to do, then go ahead, take it all. Go on back in that room and collect the energy, go move on to wherever you think you're moving on to. It's not as if you believe there's a God who will judge you for your actions. But I can't, okay?"

Don stared at Lydia for a moment, at a loss for words. So, this was what it was like to have beliefs that counteracted your desires. When he had become an atheist, he had figured that religion was just this thing people used to fight the fear deep inside of them. You feared death, so you came up with a solution. But then… it ended up dictating more than the afterlife, didn't it? It gave you rules to live by, and rules to be constrained by, and when it hurt you more than helped you, what could you do? It was your religion.

Here Lydia was, worried about offending a god that, even after death, was still out of reach. What was to say that her god didn't want her to take that energy, so she could move on to heaven? He bit his tongue—he wasn't about to say that out loud. He didn't think that would go over well.

But, Don admitted, they did have a mission to complete. It wasn't as if he could just jump in there and move on. They had an Oswald to exorcise. And he especially wasn't going to move on if Lydia wasn't. Maybe when this was all said and done, he could come back there with Lydia, and somehow convince her that it was harmless to take the energy.

"Okay, this is…" He sighed. "This is a conversation for another time, and I will most certainly circle back, but right now, we need to rush to my sister's apartment."

"Why, what happened?"

"They want to do a séance."

"They? Wait—but I thought we were trying to get them to call an exorcist."

"Well, I tried my best, I threw knives at them. But I guess they want to try to talk it out first, and they want to do *that* tonight. It's Cherry and her neighbor, and they're waiting for Cherry's friend from college to show up with a Ouija board, so that's the kind of time we have."

"Okay, well, I guess you can play the bad guy in a séance and see if that does anything," Lydia said doubtfully. Don noted that she had said "you", and realized she wasn't quite ready to leave the prayer circle. He felt a little guilty. Of course, Lydia should be able to enjoy something that she enjoyed when she was alive. But she could enjoy it later.

"I think I'm going to need your help," Don pleaded. "I lost a lot of energy trying to communicate earlier—"

"Okay, yeah," Lydia said. She was just as shimmery as she had been since the last time he'd seen her, and he faltered for a second.

"Any luck with Colby?"

Lydia bowed her head and shook it. "No. I haven't been able to get him alone to try. I was going to follow him home after…"

Don had a sneaking suspicion she had had plenty of opportunities to try, but now was not the time to discuss it. "Okay, no worries, we've got a lead now," he said urgently, and within a few minutes, they were on their way back to the apartment building.

Cherry and Gina and another woman—Don vaguely recognized her, and figured she was Dee—were already setting the Ouija board up on Cherry's dining table when they arrived. Cherry lit a few candles and turned off the overhead light before sitting at the table with the other two women.

"Cutting it close, I guess," Lydia said, and they quickly situated themselves around the board, exchanging nervous glances.

"Wait, so you think a ghostie threw knives at you, and you want to call it forth?" Dee was saying, a look of disbelief on her face.

"We already removed all the knives and anything that might double as a weapon from the apartment, just in case," Gina assured her, smiling.

"Not to be the downer, here," Dee said, her voice tinged with doubt. "I don't know what you saw, but I'm gonna tell you right now, you may be disappointed with the results."

Cherry rolled her eyes. "Look, I get it, Dee, you don't believe—"

"I don't believe, I don't believe," Dee parroted, laughing. "It's not that. I mean, okay, it is that, but—"

"Wait, sorry, what don't you believe?" Gina asked.

"Dee studied psychology in college," Cherry explained.

"You make it sound like I'm the one with misinformation," Dee cried. "Okay, Gina? Gina. That's your name?"

"Yes," Gina said flatly. She didn't seem too thrilled at Dee's flippant, skeptical attitude.

"Okay," Dee began, fully relishing the fact that she got to explain, "so the Ouija board is a real thing. It gets results. But it doesn't get results from spirits, or demons or ghosts or whatever you want to call them. It's a great tool, it just connects you with your subconscious, not the 'Great Beyond'." She waved her fingers for effect.

Gina's eyes flicked back and forth between Dee and Cherry. "I'm still not following you."

Dee sighed. "Okay, so there've been experiments with Ouija boards before. It's the ideomotor effect. People think there's something else, or someone else, controlling the planchette, and technically, there is... it's our subconscious."

Dee grabbed hold of the planchette sitting on the table, and Cherry raised an eyebrow at Gina. "She's going to get really technical now," she joked.

Dee stuck her tongue out at Cherry.

"The ideomotor effect is when we move when we're not trying to move, right? So, we want to hear words from passed loved ones, and we subconsciously guide the planchette to give an answer." Dee slowly pushed the planchette forward. "Your body responds to your brain without you actually telling it to do so, and your muscles literally move the planchette to the answers that you want to receive."

"So what you're saying is, it's bogus?" Gina asked, eyes in slits.

Don and Lydia glanced at each other. "Um. I'm not sure if this conversation is helpful," Lydia muttered. "The last thing we need is for them to get into an argument and talk themselves out of doing the séance."

"It's not bogus. It's an answer. It's just not from the dead. We used the Ouija board in one of my psych classes, it was really informative."

Cherry put her head in her hands. "But we saw movement. My radio turned on, and then the knives just came flying out of the knife board—"

"So maybe it's our subconscious talking, like Dee says," Gina said, glancing at Cherry. She smiled. "Or maybe it's a Jinn, like you say, Cheryl. But maybe not. We'll test it out."

"What do you mean, test it out?"

Gina shrugged. "You have a suspicion it's your brother, right?"

Cherry blushed. "No, you have a suspicion it's my brother."

Gina grinned. "Fair. So then, when we start the séance, let's ask questions that only you would know the answer to—you and your brother, that is—and it'll just be me and Dee touching the planchette."

"But if it's a Jinni—"

"Do the Jinn have the ability to read your mind?"

"I... no. I don't think so."

Gina nodded. "Then we'll dig deep."

"That's if we even get a response," Dee protested.

Gina turned and gave her a level stare. "Well, we would definitely get a response, if it's the ideomotor effect. Right?"

Dee stared back. "Yeah, I guess."

"Right. So that's why only you and I will touch the planchette."

Cherry let out a deep breath.

"Okay," Dee said slowly, "But I'm saying this more for Cherry's sake... If we get a response, please, please, please don't put all your hope into it actually being your brother."

Cherry sighed. "Oh, I'm with you on that."

Dee smiled. "Also, you should buy a new knife block, because ghost or not, that is incredibly dangerous to have just tipping over like that."

Gina took a deep breath, and smiled at Dee. "Look, I understand your desire to be practical, but let's just see what happens, all right?"

Lydia turned to Don, her eyes reflecting amusement. "What did I miss?"

Don let out a little laugh. "I think we've got a case of 'protective friend vs. love interest'," he muttered. Lydia's eyes widened.

Gina and Dee placed their hands on the planchette. Cherry's mind raced. "Should I participate now?" she asked. The thought occurred to her that maybe once they started, some sort of bond would be made, and letting go of the planchette would break it. But she desperately wanted to be a part of the séance.

The women around her gave the expected reactions: Dee gave an impatient glance, and Gina kind of looked through her, sending shivers down her spine that had nothing to do with the séance. Okay, kiddo, Cherry thought, you're on your own in this decision. Be a big girl and keep your anxiety in check.

She leaned forward and placed her hands over theirs.

In the tween state, Don and Lydia nodded to each other, and pressed their hands over the knot of fingers guarding the planchette, their cold fingers brushing up against each other. Don felt the prickly feeling of Lydia interlaced with him. Below them, the warm hands of the living vibrated with the energy of life.

Gina took the initiative. "We invite any good spirits within this home to feel welcome and be present with us. We are in search of the one who made the pinwheel and the knives move and turned on the radio. We heard your call to communicate, and are ready to do so, in a nonviolent manner."

Silence. Don coughed. "Are we supposed to respond?"

Lydia hesitated. "Not yet."

The circle of women breathed in shallow breaths, eyes flitting from face to face as they built up their courage for the first question. Gina opened her mouth to speak.

"If you are here, and listening, can you tell us your name?"

The planchette began to move.

D.

O.

N.

Cherry let out a small whimper, and Dee closed her eyes, breathing a deep sigh. She looked uneasy.

Lydia glanced at Don, her eyes wild. "What are you doing?" she hissed. "I thought we were going to say Oswald's name."

"I can't lie to her," Don breathed. "She's my sister. I can't—"

Lydia groaned. "We need her to believe you're a Jinni, Don. That's the entire purpose of this plan. She won't call an exorcist if she thinks it's you."

"Okay, fine," he cried feebly. "But I... But I want to talk to her." It was strange, now that he was actually in the room with her, the opportunity before him, how real the urge was to just wave his arms and yell, "I'm here, I'm here!" This was family. He needed... he didn't know what he needed, honestly. He needed closure. Even if he hadn't realized that was what he needed before, he realized it now.

"We only have so much energy," Lydia muttered.

His mind scrambled to come up with a solution that would fix the situation. "Okay, I... I won't be stupid. But I want to try for honesty."

He could feel Lydia close off, trying to hold back her anger. Or was it fear? Hard to tell when you could only see a shimmering body.

"Trust me," he said simply, hoping Lydia would take him up on the offer. He couldn't even trust himself—he didn't have any idea how "honesty" was going to get them what they wanted, but... he hoped. Maybe that was what belief was: doing incredibly stupid things and banking on a hope. Well, he'd get an ear-load later if his hope turned around and bit him in the ass.

"Don," Cherry said unsteadily, "If this is you, I... I need proof. I'm going to remove my hands and ask a question. Please stay with us."

After a moment's hesitation, her fingers slipped from the pile.

"What was the game we used to play every time it rained as we grew up?"

In the tween state, Lydia's eyes flicked over to Don's. She was waiting for him. She no longer had control of this game; it was him calling the shots. Fuck.

Cherry stared anxiously at the board in front of her. Dee and Gina touched the motionless planchette, holding their breaths. There was a long, lingering silence in the room. Get a hold of yourself, Cherry thought. So what if it's a different answer? What does that prove—that you're crazy? That you imagined the radio turning on? That it's a Jinn, trying to trick you? What even for? This was stupid, anyway, she thought, just a way to get Gina to talk to her, she probably did imagine—

The planchette began to move.

It slid over the board. Letter by letter, it spelled:

R.

A.

C.

E.

Cherry felt her breath catch in her chest.

"You raced around the house?" Gina guessed.

Cherry shook her head. "We would watch the windows," she whispered. "We'd pick a raindrop and race each other to the bottom of the pane. Somehow, Donny always won."

Her heart slammed up against her rib cage. So it had gotten it right. Was it a guess? "Race" really did have multiple meanings, as Gina had just revealed. Maybe the Jinn had picked a generic word and hoped for the best.

"Ask another question," Gina prodded.

Cherry thought for a moment. She had to pick something harder, something less generic. "What did you give me for my nineteenth birthday?"

In the tween state, Don's heart plummeted into his stomach. Lydia glanced towards him. "Well?"

"I'm trying to figure out how to simplify," Don muttered. "I don't want to waste our energy."

After a moment, the planchette moved.

0.

Cherry stared at the board, lost in thought.

"Uhhh." Dee chuckled. "Ghost boy is broken. Replying with a number? I told you, this is bullshit."

Cherry had been hoping to trick the Jinni into answering incorrectly. After all, who asks a question about a birthday gift and expects the response to be "zero"? Maybe the question had been a bit callous, but it was clear that whoever was moving the planchette at least had a very detailed insight into her home life.

So maybe this *was* Don. Cherry's stomach grew cold. This was bad, right? This was very bad. It couldn't be Don, but all signs were pointing towards… A wave of nausea swept through her body, and she closed her eyes, trembling.

"Cherry?" Gina whispered. "Are you okay?"

"I don't think we should be doing this," Cherry whispered.

"Was the answer correct or not?" Dee asked. Gina shot her a look, and she rolled her eyes. "Hon, we can stop if you want to stop. This is just an exercise. If you feel uncomfortable, all we have to do is turn the lights back on."

Cherry reached forward and touched the planchette. "It was correct," she said. "Don got me nothing for my nineteenth birthday."

Dee raised an eyebrow. "Hello, dick brother," she whispered, chuckling.

"Don never got me presents for my birthday," Cherry whispered. "He always said that birthday gifts were just meant to pacify people, surround them with things that would not actually have any significance after a few months. He would rather whoop me at Scrabble on my birthday than give me something that would sit in my room, collecting dust."

Lydia nudged Don lightly. "That's really sweet."

Don didn't say anything, but realized the irony of his own past thoughts. He had been so full of shit. He remembered that speech well every time he gave it, but he wasn't sure if he had actually believed it until now. He was pretty sure the ideology had been spawned by an incredible laziness, and an equally incredible desire to cover that up. But now, he wished he had enjoyed the outcome of it all the more wholeheartedly. The things that being dead will do for you.

Cherry gripped the planchette under her friends' fingers. She would continue with this séance, Allah help her. She always had the option of backing out at any time, but the eerie accuracy that the answers had made her want to at least explore a little further. At this point, if it was still a Jinni pretending to be her brother, then they had done a really good job of guessing correctly. And in that case, maybe it was a good Jinni who had connections to her brother and was sending a message from beyond, somehow. Maybe they were just trying to help. Could that be a possibility? Either way, this was an opportunity that Cherry didn't feel like missing. Even if simply for closure purposes.

But what to ask? she thought. What do you ask your dead brother? Do you ask him what life after death is like? Is that too impersonal? Or is that too painful? After all, there was always the possibility that Don had not made it to Jannah. She believed he had been a good person, but maybe there were some dark things she didn't know about. What if he hadn't made it to Jannah, and was trying to reach out from Jahannam? She bit her lip at the thought. Stop it, Cherry, that is your anxiety talking. Do this for closure. Don't waste your time worrying about Don's potential shortcomings.

She had, after all, barely spoken to him in the last few years, didn't try at all to guide him or be an influence on him, and Jannah or Jahannam aside, that was a pretty awful thing for a sister to do. And now here she was, with the audacity to—

"Are you happy?" she asked gingerly, surprising herself with the interruption of her own thoughts.

The planchette moved, slowly making its way to the top of the board. "NO."

"Oh." Gina drew in a sharp breath. "Okay. Wasn't expecting—"

"Well, what *do* you expect from a ghost?" Dee asked, a brow arched. "He's dead. I wouldn't be happy." Gina gave her a deprecating glance.

Cherry sat, immobilized.

So maybe Don was communicating from Jahannam. If Don had gone to Jannah, he would be happy. But if Don was a ghost… what did that mean? Did that mean there was an afterlife, or not? What if Cherry had been wrong the whole time about—no, it's probably not Don, it's just a really good guesser—

"Why?" she asked.

The planchette was still.

230

The women looked tentatively up at Cherry.

"I—I think that's too broad of a question," Gina ventured.

"Hon, you don't have to keep asking questions," Dee said nervously.

"You can't just leave it at that," Gina whispered. " 'Are you happy?' 'No.' Okay, bye, then."

Cherry took a deep breath. It was true. She needed to continue, otherwise she would have that last answer hanging over her for the rest of her life. Don wasn't happy. Even if Don wasn't Don, she couldn't walk away without pressing further. Okay. "How can I help you be happy?" she asked.

"Jesus," Dee muttered, "What kind of question is that?"

But Don knew exactly what their message needed to be. He spoke it aloud to Lydia, and she stared at him, eyes alert and excited, and nodded.

They pushed, and the planchette began to shift, gliding slowly across the board. They paused over each letter slowly but firmly:

E.

X.

O.

R.

C.

I.

S.

E.

"Holy fuck," Gina said, eyes wide.

But they weren't done yet. "Pause," Don whispered. "New word." Then, they pushed, and the planchette began to slide across the board again:

O.

S.

W.

A.

L.

D.

A heavy silence fell over the group as they stared at the planchette, a chill sweeping over the room.

"Who the fuck is Oswald?" Dee blurted out.

CHAPTER FIFTEEN

Cherry sat on her bed, staring at the opposite wall. Her brain was churning over the details of last night, of communicating with her *freaking dead brother*. Should she tell Mom? No. Mom would flip.

The better question is, she told herself, do you believe it was actually him?

It could have been any number of things. Maybe Dee was right, and they had been caught up in the moment—a good guess from Dee and Gina, and then their hands had decided the narrative of the night for them. A psychological party trick guided by their own hopes.

But it seemed unrealistic that they could have had such good guesses. And also a bit crazy that the three of them would have made the jump from Cherry's dead brother to calling for an exorcism for some unknown person, whether it was a subconscious decision or not. If it had just been a psychology game, then the board would have read something simpler, like "chair" or "past", something that would have been loosely interpretable, and that would have allowed Cherry to grieve her brother—not a list of demands.

Or maybe it was, as she had originally been so adamant about, a Jinni. Trying to trick them into doing something crazy.

Cherry frowned. That possibility left two questions in her mind: one, if a Jinni knew the answers to all those questions, wouldn't that mean they would have had to follow her and her brother around their entire lives? It seemed a bit weird. And two, it had told them to get an exorcist. That didn't sound like something a Jinni would want.

It all came back to that crazy request.

It was *all* very crazy. Cherry had been raised with the belief of an afterlife, but not with any way to come back from that afterlife and communicate. But that didn't seem to reflect what had happened last night. And Don… as far as Cherry was aware, Don had given up on Islam years ago. He had never been into the occult, either, but now he was on the hunt for an exorcist.

But why? Why did he want an exorcist? Was it crazy to even consider finding one?

She knew she could perform ruqyah on herself if need be, but she wasn't even sure where to begin. She mulled through her mind's catalog of ruqyah information: that if you needed to perform it, it was simple, and you could do it yourself—and in fact, you were encouraged to perform it yourself, if you wanted a chance to be included in the 70,000. And yet… a small knot of panic grew in Cherry's chest at the mere thought of doing it herself. She was sure to screw it up.

But wasn't that the whole point of ruqyah—trusting in God? That said more about her uncertainty than she could ever muster to say herself. If she did screw it up, it would be less about the words that she said, and more about the condition of her heart, and Cherry wasn't feeling very confident in her faith at the moment. She could probably perform ruqyah all day, every day for the next year, and it wouldn't do squat.

And besides, she didn't even know if it was ruqyah that she needed, or if it was even her that needed it. She hadn't been feeling ailments of any sort, and she was pretty sure she wasn't possessed, but... how was she to know? She had been mourning her brother for weeks; had the grief from that experience somehow overshadowed the symptoms of possession? It just didn't line up—other than a little situational depression, she felt fine. No, she didn't think that she, herself, needed ruqyah. But as for the right move, she was at a loss. Her apartment needed it, maybe?

She should probably call someone. At the very least, to ask for counsel. She was in unfamiliar waters here, and well above her head. An imam would at least have a better idea of what to do, whether the answer was ruqyah or something else.

But what was she even thinking? She couldn't tell an imam that a Ouija board had asked her to exorcise someone. She would absolutely be viewed as the one to blame. Cherry frowned. Come on now, she thought, you can't be scared to get help just because it will make you look bad. Have a little more humility than that.

More likely, she would find herself admitted to some psych ward somewhere. What imam would hear a cockamamie story about someone's dead brother requesting an exorcism?

Maybe she should call Imam Aasim. He had been the imam at the Islamic Center before Cherry had even been born, and was like an uncle to her. Although she did worry that reaching out to him could trigger a call from her mother… Imam Aasim may have been her imam for her entire life, but he had been her mother's imam for even longer, so there could be some sort of conflict of interest there. Cherry really didn't want her mother asking why she had even tried to contact Don in the first place. That would be a mess.

Cherry rolled her eyes. Her pride kept butting in. But, she supposed, imams probably had a code of conduct that they had to abide by. Like HPAA, but for spiritual matters. Maybe he wouldn't be able to tell her mother what she had done.

"Exorcise Oswald," Cherry said slowly, letting the vowels slowly spill out of her mouth. But seriously, *who is Oswald?*

Cherry stood, crossing to the mirror, and stared at her reflection for a moment. Her glasses framed wide eyes in a state of growing terror. She took off the glasses and rubbed her eyes, shutting the image of herself out of her mind. Think, Cherry. "Exorcise Oswald," she whispered again.

If that was her brother's last request, then she didn't mind trying. And if it wasn't her brother, then whoever Oswald was, sorry, dude. This was gonna happen.

She grabbed her phone and flipped through the contacts numbly. Imam Aasim was tucked away quietly in her contacts, and she self-consciously hit "call". It took four rings before she got a voicemail. "Hi, this is Cheryl Rind-Davis, calling for Imam Aasim. I wanted to talk to you, if that's possible. I think it might be better for me if we could talk in person. Give me a call back. Thanks."

She sat back on her bed, biting her lip absentmindedly. Okay. It was set in motion, now. She couldn't chicken out.

* * *

Cherry fidgeted at a table, checking her watch periodically. She had come early—she always did—but she still feared that Imam Asim's absence was a sign he wasn't coming. She had chosen the Optimist Café as a gentle reminder to the both of them to be open to possibilities, but it seemed her own reminder wasn't working.

Imam Aasim entered, a backpack slung over one shoulder, and smiled as he caught sight of Cherry. "Cheryl! Assalamu alaikum."

"Wa alaikum assalam."

"It is so good to see you." He sat down at the table, dropping his backpack at his feet, and patted her hands gently, and Cherry was reminded of moments in her childhood when the Rind-Davis family would have potluck dinners. Several members of the community would come, including Imam Aasim, who would always bring candy for the kids. He was a quiet but jolly man, always with a beaming smile on his face, and today seemed no different. Cherry took a deep breath. She would see how long that smile stayed there.

"Thank you for meeting with me on such short notice," Cherry said, and Imam Aasim waved his hand.

"I always designate lunches for meetings with mosque members. And it has been a while since we've had a good talk, I am glad to catch up. Though it seems there's more than catching up on your mind?"

Cherry laughed at his abruptness. "Uh… yeah. I'd say."

"Is it about Donald?"

Cherry stared at him, caught off guard. How did he know? After a second, her logic jumped in: he was talking about the impact of his death—not what had happened the other night. Of course, he thought that she was struggling with his death. Which she was. But that… why was this situation so complicated? She wished she could just be done with the explanation already, and be discussing the solution.

"Um, kind of," she said meekly. "I… Okay, I'm just going to come out and say it. I may have actually talked to him. Or not him. I don't know. I talked to someone who claimed to be him."

He raised an eyebrow. "In a dream?" he asked.

"No. In waking."

Imam Asim leaned back in his chair, scratching his head. "How long have you been hearing your brother?"

Cherry frowned. "Not hearing."

"You haven't been hearing voices?"

"No."

"Well, that's good, at least. How has your mental health been? Any confusion, feelings of heaviness…"

"I mean, my brother just died, so—"

"Apologies. I know it is hard to separate general mental health from your current situation." Imam Aasim cleared his throat. "Tell me more. Let's go back to the beginning."

"Okay. So, the other day, weird things started happening in my apartment." Cherry wondered how much of this story she was going to have to divulge. "Things started moving of their own accord. A radio turned on suddenly."

"But no voices?"

"No, the radio was just playing static. And… well…" She hesitated. "Imam Aasim… it has been a long time since I've studied the Jinn. I wanted to ask you… do the Jinn know things that normal people wouldn't?"

He furrowed his brow. "Well, the Jinn live on a different plane," he replied. "There are probably countless things they know that we don't, depending on how that plane works."

"But I mean, would they know things about my life?"

"There is only so much we know about the Jinn," Imam Aasim replied. "Why do you ask?"

Cherry bit her lip. Might as well get it over with. "Well, there was definitely some sort of presence in my apartment, that much was clear. Even my neighbor saw things. So… we communicated with it. With a Ouija board. My friends and I."

Imam Aasim frowned. "Cheryl. That was not wise. It is very dangerous to be in touch with a Jinni—you don't know what its intentions are, for good or for evil."

"I know." She sighed.

"Why did you do it?"

"Well, my friend had the idea that it might be Don, like his ghost. And I know, it couldn't possibly be, but I just… wanted to make sure."

Imam Asim gave her a gentle glance. "You know that it is not possible that it is your brother, Cheryl. There are no such things as ghosts. Our souls move immediately on to the afterlife." He frowned. "It does sound to me like a Jinni, or some sort of spirit, contacted you, and I do not know why, but… it is very dangerous to continue this contact. The Quran speaks of the Jinn as beings separate from men—like I said before, they are on another plane. Physical beings, but invisible to us. There is no reason for them to communicate with us, unless it is for mischief. Do you understand?"

Cherry nodded. "I mean, I get it, I definitely shouldn't have been messing with a Ouija board. Not my brightest move. But it spoke—or, well, it answered questions through the board—in a way that really made it seem like my brother."

"It cannot be."

"But I wanted it to be," Cherry said bluntly.

Imam Aasim opened his mouth to speak, then closed it. He was mulling over his words. He leaned forward and placed his hand on the table in an apologetic way.

"Look," Cherry said, "I know that I'm supposed to believe that we go straight to Jannah or Jahannam, I get it. But what if we're wrong? What if souls don't go straight there? Or what if it's Barzakh, and he's just in transition? Or what if there's just a really strange situation, and God for some reason allowed a passed soul to speak to me? And I'm not questioning my faith, Imam Aasim, I'm not, but I just—" Cherry stopped abruptly, her chest suddenly hit with the imagined impact of a full-force train, and suddenly she was counting, taking deep breaths, tears leaking from her face, and all with her imam watching. How embarrassing.

"Cheryl. What you are experiencing is the grieving process. I would never tell you that you are questioning your faith, not at a time like this, when everything is confusing and shattered. Your world has abruptly changed. That is not a question of faith, but of emotion. When my father died, I went to a mountain top and screamed at God, I believed my father was ripped from me, and I screamed and cursed and cried." He cleared his throat. "I had not lost my faith. I had lost my father."

Cherry stared at him, her breathing slowing.

"And you," Imam Aasim said, smiling kindly, "are allowed to feel these things. It is best to feel them, not to bottle them up. We all walk through the mist at some point. Our vision gets clouded; but eventually the mist will clear, insha'Allah, and we will still be walking in the same direction. Do you understand?"

"Yes." An image of her brother flashed into her mind, one of him smiling. It was even an image of him when he was still in college—the last time she had really felt like they had hung out. That was the image she would maintain of him in her mind, not this strange, desperate vision of him as the walking dead, moving things in her apartment. Imam Aasim was right.

"When you spoke to this being," Imam Aasim said, frowning, "what happened?"

Cherry bit her lip. "Um… Well, it asked for an exorcism."

"I beg your pardon?"

Cherry explained how the Ouija board had spelled out its request.

Imam Aasim looked bewildered. "So a Jinni asked for ruqyah? For itself?" He shook his head. "Something is not right there."

"Well—" Cherry frowned. "Not exactly its own ruqyah. It was referring to itself as my brother. But it was very specific that we should exorcise Oswald."

"Who is Oswald?"

"Exactly." She laughed nervously. "Have you…?"

"I have performed ruqyah, yes. Cheryl, you can perform it for yourself."

Cherry squeezed her eyes shut for a moment, then sighed and glanced timidly at Imam Aasim. "I know. It is better to perform it for yourself, unless you're unable to. And I'm not asking you to perform it for me!" she said quickly. "I was, however, wondering if you could go over the Arabic with me."

Imam Asim's brow had creased very deeply as she spoke. Cherry wasn't quite sure that he had been listening, so deep in thought did he appear. No longer was the jolly man shining through. "Possibly we are dealing with two Jinn," he muttered under his breath. "Perhaps a good Jinni and a bad Jinni. Perhaps someone is abusing their boundaries between this plane and the next. Or, possibly we are not dealing with a Jinni at all, but something completely different. It does not make sense. Something is not right."

"You already mentioned that."

"There are things I am not clear on," Imam Aasim said. "My first assumption would be that only a bad Jinni would claim to be someone else, such as your brother. So then who is Oswald? And does that mean he is good or bad? It is much like a puzzle, this story of yours."

"I wish it was just a story."

Imam Aasim shook his head, still trying to sort things out. He studied her for a moment, then reached into his backpack and pulled out his Quran. "I will go over the ayaat with you, so you can recite it smoothly. And… may I ask to come to your apartment before you recite ruqyah? Maybe we will bless your apartment, too. I do not like how strong of a presence this being has had. No matter whether it is a Jinni or not, good or bad, I do not like this interaction. Let Allah protect you, my child. He will discern what to do."

"But what if it… I mean, what if my brother *was* somehow involved?"

"If, by some strange miracle, it is your brother," Imam Aasim said gravely, "then he is not where he should be." He cleared his throat. "The words of Allah will put everything to rest."

In the tween state, Don let his focus fade as the conversation switched to reading from the Quran. Now that he knew that Imam Aasim was involved, he could stop worrying about whether his and Lydia's plan had succeeded, and start thinking about the insanity of it all. It was a loaded thought. He had absolutely no idea how this was going to pan out, and the prospect of screwing it up at *all*, let alone at a moment when his sister would be in a room with a no-fucks-left-to-give killer tween, was daunting.

Maybe this was a mistake. Maybe Don was just feeding the fire by trying to put it out. Maybe Oswald would eventually take care of himself, burning until he dwindled down to smoke and embers.

Don closed his eyes, and pictured himself lying on the highway, torn in two. That was a fire that had gone unfought, and look how that had gone. Only *you* can prevent forest fires, Don thought, in a Smokey the Bear kind of inner voice. No. Oswald didn't get to ruin anyone else's life. Don would make sure that was the case. The plan would work; he and Lydia would succeed, because success was the only thing that would allow him to rest easy. And god damn it, Don wanted to rest.

CHAPTER SIXTEEN

Old Town House Park had decided that it was officially springtime, dotted with picnics and laughter and the occasional sprinting pup. The sun was shining, and everyone was beaming. Don glanced around, blinking his eyes at the brightness of it all. Felt only right that he would feel out of sorts.

He felt a breeze flow through him as he stood, each little blade of grass rustling around his feet, the trees on the perimeter swaying softly, and it surprised him. Oh my god, he thought, did I just feel the legendary not-breeze that Lydia had spoken of? He puzzled over this. He hadn't imagined that; he had definitely felt it. How far along was he? Had he really gotten to the point where he was so solid that the breeze tickled him, even if just a little?

Don wandered around the green, strolling through the small clusters of social life. He smirked at a little girl having a tantrum at her mother, then zeroed in on a shimmer a few dozen yards away. Jordan. Or he hoped, anyway. He wasn't sure why he had tracked them down, but there was something digging at the back of his mind, and he had a feeling Jordan could help with it. As he got closer, he confirmed that it was them, lying in the grass, propped up on their elbows. He didn't approach at first, unsure of what he would say when he did. They were looking off the other way, watching a couple of seagulls fighting over a discarded McDonalds bag.

"I know you're there," Jordan said after a moment.

"Sorry. Hi," he said sheepishly. He came to sit next to them in the grass. "What are you doing?"

"I'm resting," Jordan said.

"I would've thought you'd be off, looking for a new person to help. Didn't you say the energy derived from séances doesn't last as long?"

Jordan eyed him for a moment. "Your friend's skepticism is rubbing off on you. You're correct, the energy from a séance fades much faster than the energy collected from a death. But over the past sixty years, it has been people such as yourself who have found me, not the other way around. If the universe wants me to fade away, then I will fade away. But if it wants me to help one more person, I will." They looked back out over the park idly. "I get the impression that you haven't found me to ask for my services."

"I do want to ask you something though," Don said slowly, mulling the thought over in his mind. He was silent for a long moment, and Jordan didn't press him. He sighed, finally. "Sorry, I don't really know what I want to ask you."

"Were you an atheist when you were alive, Don?"

"Yeah. Yeah, how did you know?"

"How about now?"

Don hesitated. "I… I think so. I mean, just because we're still walking around like ghosts doesn't mean there's a god that caused it all."

"But you are questioning it," Jordan said smugly.

Don rolled his eyes. This was not the kind of conversation he had been hoping for.

Jordan recognized this. "Don't worry, I won't try to convert you," they said. "I don't even know what I would convert you to. My worldviews have also changed a bit since coming to this liminal state. But I suspect your confusion, or frustration, or whatever it is that made you pause, stems from that cognitive dissonance, yes?"

"What did you believe in before dying?"

"Reincarnation."

"I take it that doesn't line up with all this?"

"That depends on how you try to line it up. Same for any religion. If you try to go by the book, then no, it doesn't line up. But you could try. For reincarnation, there's a possibility that I'm simply stuck in my past life, unable for some reason to move on to the next."

"Six of one, half a dozen of the other," Don muttered.

"But going by the book only seems to make things messy here."

"How did you die?"

"Twelve years of cancer. Luckily, I went peacefully in the end."

Don frowned. Well, that completely disproved his idea of ghosts caused by sudden trauma.

"Why do *you* think we're stuck here? Because I've heard a range of answers."

Jordan chuckled. "I assume most of them depend on what we did wrong to get here, or revolve around the idea that we were wrong."

"I mean, we all kind of have to be wrong, right?"

"I don't believe that. You can beat yourself up for the rest of time over what the exact moment was that you condemned yourself to being stuck here, or what you could have done to avoid this. But do we blame people who get Parkinson's, or Alzheimer's? Do we get mad at entropy for existing? I don't believe we're here for any specific reason. It is not our fate that we are here. If we get Parkinson's, it's not our doing. It's not a god punishing us for being bad, or karmic debt. It's cells in our body mutating just for the hell of it. It's a malfunction. When we get stuck here, maybe it's the same."

"The glitch in the system. Like when something isn't working on your cell phone, but then you restart it and it's fine."

Jordan stared at him. "You are talking to the wrong person about that," they laughed. "We didn't have cell phones when I was alive."

"Ah. Okay, yeah. Cells in our body."

"The universe really is like a big living thing. And there are some things that happen that, when you put it under the microscope, we can't explain. Sometimes it's just because we don't have the right information. Or sometimes it's as you say, a glitch in the cell phone. It isn't supposed to happen. But it does." Jordan shook their head. "No, if you ask me, this liminal state of ours does not disprove any religion, nor does it prove any of them right. Just because something isn't explained in their books does not mean it is impossible. This is something different altogether. We are outliers. Or at least off the page. We are meant to be somewhere else."

"Then why do you stick around?"

"Because I was fortunate enough to understand a little more about the liminal world than most," Jordan said. "I studied energy when I was alive. Granted, not all of it was correct, or at least not on this plane, but I was able to understand it a lot better than your average—what did you call it?—tween. And so I offer up that knowledge for those unfortunate enough to get stuck here without a clue of what they're doing."

Don's thoughts suddenly gravitated to Giardino's—the small eyes barely peeking over the table, lost and confused and helpless.

"Jordan… have you ever dealt with the soul or spirit or whatever of someone who was miscarried?"

Jordan glanced at Don, surprised. "Have you?" Don didn't answer, and Jordan sighed. "What happened?"

"I just… I saw one. Sitting next to their mother. And I don't know if they fully understood what was happening. I… I didn't know how to help them."

Jordan was silent for a long moment. "When you watched Billy's departure, how do you think it worked?"

"What? Uh... I don't know, the girls gave him their energy somehow. And—"

"But how?"

"I don't know. They just did."

"They weren't aware they were helping him. Or, correction, they thought they were helping him, but in a very different way. They thought they were helping him to move on by bringing him to terms with his death and making him feel good about it. But it wasn't that, was it? You and I both know it was the energy exchange. So how did that energy exchange happen?"

Don thought for a moment. "It was like... it was like Bri was pouring her energy into her brother. By worrying about him, by connecting to him in that way."

"And the other girls?"

"...They felt for their friend. They weren't even giving him energy, they... poured their energy into her pouring her energy out."

Jordan nodded. "When we die, we leave behind any extra energy we might have, and that's what the wanderers collect. Like yourself and your friend. But left behind energy isn't very strong. The energy we have when we're alive, it is strong, and powerful, and influential. And we have the ability to give it freely, though we do it more rarely than you would think... for one thing, we don't know that we can, and once we learn that we can, we don't always know how to give it consciously. But when we need to, when our souls require it, we are able to give our energy. And when a gift is given freely, it is much stronger than when it's just leftover, is it not?"

"That makes sense."

"So what do you think happens when someone miscarries their child?"

Don put the pieces together. "They spend a lot of time thinking about their baby. And pouring their energy into mourning them."

"I would place money on the idea that the baby you saw has already moved on. It may just have taken a bit for the parents to know how to pour out their energy."

Don nodded. He didn't have anything to say.

Jordan turned to look Don in the eye. "You and your friend aren't going to let me help you with your exorcism, are you?"

Don laughed. "Lydia doesn't like you, for some reason. I'm sorry."

"It's no problem for me. But you should know what you're getting into. An exorcism is a big undertaking."

"Have any advice?"

Jordan was silent for a moment. "You need to consider an exorcism as a battle," they said slowly. "You will have to make the subject expel their own energy. But in order to do that, you will have to try a series of tactics. They may lash out in fear at first; this is good. Use their fear. But at some point, when what they are trying is not working, then they will change tactics. And that is when you will have to change tactics, as well."

"What do you mean?"

"In order to bend them to your will, you need to know what their will is. They will never stray from what their will is—most likely, that will be to survive—but you can use it against them. Once you can decipher their motive, and their tactic, you will have a better grasp of how to counter their moves."

"I still don't understand."

"Excuse me," a voice said behind them, "is one of you named Jordan?"

Jordan and Don turned to see a pair of eyes floating behind them.

"That's me." Jordan swiveled in their spot on the grass, patted the ground in front of them, and exchanged glances with Don.

Right, Don thought, that's my cue to leave. "I'd better get going," he mumbled. "Thank you, Jordan."

He began to walk away, looking over his shoulder at Jordan as they spoke with the new tween. Well, he had no idea what they meant about changing tactics, but he was still glad he had come. It was nice, after weeks of feeling like he was floating around in outer space, to chat with someone whose toes had found the ground.

He wandered out of the park and began walking down the road. The least he could do was head back to the jetty, see if Lydia was there, and try to make sense of what Jordan had said. Without mentioning he had gone and talked to Jordan, of course. He couldn't wrap his head around Lydia's reasons for not liking Jordan, and he guessed he probably never would. Maybe that was something he was just going to have to live with. Or whatever.

Up ahead, he saw a shimmering figure, and wondered if he had gotten lucky—maybe he wouldn't have to go all the way back to the jetty to meet Lydia.

He was incorrect. It was Oswald.

The fact that Oswald was still fairly corporeal filled Don with nausea. Perhaps it was just leftover from when he last saw him— Don could believe that Oswald had taken a break. Even if that wasn't the truth, there was nothing Don could do about it now.

"Hey, loser," Oswald said, snickering. His eyes looked smiling and inviting, but carried a tinge of tension, as if Oswald was on guard. Which made perfect sense, Don thought, since the last time he had seen him, Oswald had acted like—scratch that, he had *been* a fucking lunatic. "You still mad at me?"

Don's voice caught in his throat. He wasn't sure if he should lie or not. On the one hand, lying would mean not having to have that conversation; it would allow him to play along with Oswald's game until he could get away from him, keeping the plan for exorcism fully intact. But on the other hand, he wanted to yell at Oswald, explain to him what his moral dilemma was. Who knows, maybe Oswald would see the light, make amends. Even though Don thought that was highly unlikely.

"Well?" Oswald pressed. "What, you can't be mad about something I did for fun. We've all done shit like that."

"No, we haven't, Oswald," Don replied quietly.

"Okay. Well, maybe not you, or your goody two-shoes girlfriend, but lots of other tweens. Okay?"

Don couldn't help it. A mix of curiosity and rage pushed him to ask the question, even though he already knew the answer.

"Oswald… have you actually followed through? Have you killed people?"

Even with a question like that, Don could see the wheels turning behind Oswald's gaze. He took a while to answer. "I mean, yeah. Not like it was on purpose." Bullshit. "But—"

"But you still see if you can do it."

Oswald rolled his eyes. One shimmering hand reached up and scratched at his scalp self-consciously. "I know I can do it, asshole. But what the fuck else are we supposed to do with our time?"

Don sighed. "Plenty of things." That was a lie… he was quickly learning that there were a very limited amount of things to do. But he feared he had already thrown a log onto the fire.

Oswald scoffed. "Okay, what, I promise not to do any shit like that around you again, all right?"

"That doesn't make it better, Oswald. Killing, whether in private or public, is still killing."

"I didn't actually kill anybody that night," Oswald snapped. "It's not like you actually watched me kill somebody."

He really didn't get it, did he? "No, but that was your intent."

"So fucking what? We're all dead, Don. All of us. Even the living." Oswald hesitated, his eyes blinking in and out. "I learned that from my dad. He should've been the one fucking stuck here, you know? Instead, he got to live another eight years. And then he just… I mean, when he died, he just… died. How's that for fair? He got eight extra fucking years to live, and I could've done so much more with that, you know? None of us deserve the time we had, and none of them deserve the time they have left. But you know what else? Not a fucking one of us deserves what's beyond."

Don stared at him silently. He watched Oswald's figure bristle, alive with the height of whatever emotion was sweeping through him right now. He hoped it was guilt.

And then, Oswald faltered. "Okay, you're right, man," he whispered. "I'm sorry. It is pretty fucked up, huh? That in order to feel something now, I've got to stoop to that level?" He stared off into the distance cagily. "Sometimes I can't fucking wait to leave this place."

Don blinked. "Really?"

Oswald glanced over at Don. He snickered. "Nah, I like it here. I like being around, 'cause you know, we still don't know what's beyond this. I'll take fucking misery over the unknown any day."

Don studied Oswald for a moment. His eyes betrayed a truth about him that Don wasn't even sure Oswald knew, exactly. This damn kid was lonely. He was scared. And what's more, he was restless. "How long did you say you'd been a tween?" Don asked softly.

"Ten years last week. What's up! I've hit an anniversary. Guess I should've celebrated. Oh wait—" Oswald winked. "I did." He snickered.

"Messing with the living was your version of a celebration, I guess." Don shook his head.

Oswald was silent for a moment. He sighed. "Not much of a celebration, if I can be honest."

Afraid of death. That's what Oswald was. That was the problem with being in the tween state: it didn't disconnect you from all the fears you had when you were living. Your fear of death could still exist, because you had constant reminders of the potential to fade out of existence.

Don understood it. His fear of death when he was alive had been subtle, but present. He could remember his mother asking him what major he wanted to pick when he went off to college, and he'd had a flash of existential crisis—he was only in this world for so long, and he didn't know what he wanted to do with his time. And that was back when he thought he'd have at least longer than this. He had imagined he would at least make it to fifty. That fear was exhausting, terrifying. And he felt the same way now, not sure if he was doing the right thing or making the best use of his time... the tween state was just as exhausting.

Was that a good enough reason to exorcise someone? To blot them out? They all feared what might be behind the veil, even those who had every confidence. Oswald was just a scared kid clinging to his fear for survival. Don couldn't say much more about himself in that regard. It was clear that Oswald had had some sort of a troubled life. Maybe if he had been loved a little more, he wouldn't be like this. Don could say that about plenty of people he'd met over the years, who lived their lives with miserable, reckless abandon, because they didn't know how else to keep the fear at bay.

But then, Don supposed that not everyone expressed that fear by trying to kill people.

It was a matter of whether someone could be truly, irretrievably outside of the parameters of help. If Don found a way to help Oswald, then maybe they wouldn't have to exorcise him. Take him down.

But Oswald didn't have anything to lose. All he had left was self-interest. Don wasn't sure if someone could come out of that. The only thing that they, or anyone else on this plane, had to counteract the fear was to do exactly what Oswald was doing. You couldn't expect someone like him to sacrifice his own survival for the good of others. He had found his way to cheat death, and he was sticking to it.

The thought made Don want to leave. If he had to bring Oswald down, he didn't want to stick around and look him in the eye anymore. Focus instead, he thought, on doing what needs to be done. "Look, I've got to go."

"Go? Where do you have to go right now?"

"I've got some personal stuff to tend to." Don took a deep breath. "But hey, tomorrow night, you gonna be around?"

Oswald snickered. "Yeah, I'll be around. But I don't know if I want to go carousing with you again, bud. You weren't exactly a bucket of fun the last time."

"Well, uh… hey, I want to show you something tomorrow. You know that apartment complex in Hyannis, the one right by the Cape Mart?"

Oswald gave him a funny look. "You want me to meet you in Hyannis?"

"Yeah, I've been collecting over there. Better odds."

Oswald snorted. "All right. Yeah, I'll meet you there at sundown. We'll fuck some shit up." He winked at Don. "Without killing anyone."

Don's heart dropped into his stomach as Oswald walked away. If only he knew.

CHAPTER SEVENTEEN

Sitting on the jetty that night with Lydia was a muted experience. The water lapped at their shimmering feet as they sat in salty silence. The plan was set in motion, and now they just had to wait. Don figured they didn't have to leave for another few minutes to make it all the way to Hyannis. Imam Aasim was supposed to meet Cherry at her apartment at 6:00, and Oswald was supposed to arrive at around the same time, at sundown.

Don wondered what Lydia was thinking about. Maybe they were both thinking about the same thing. Maybe they were both thinking about what lay in store for them after all this—not only after the exorcism, but… beyond. He wished that for just one second, he didn't have to preoccupy himself with these thoughts. Thoughts of life. But he supposed that was a privilege reserved for the living.

"It's funny," he said aloud, maybe to Lydia, maybe just to himself. "It's funny how humans spend their entire lives telling stories about the afterlife, trying to discern where they're going to end up, or if there's anywhere to even end up, and we worry and worry about this but we'll never know for sure. And after we die… we're still not sure. Isn't death supposed to be a relief? Tearing away the uncertainty of life?"

Lydia glanced at him, then stared back out over the water. "Who was it, Franklin? He said nothing in this life is certain except death and taxes."

"Fuck. Are we gonna get taxed, do you think?"

"Imagine," Lydia said, laughing. But she quickly quieted, and the melancholy returned to her eyes.

"Lydia…" Don let the words sit in his mouth for a minute, scared to spit them out. "Did you actually talk to Colby?"

Lydia turned to stare at him. "I tried, yeah."

"But, uh… how did it go?"

"He wasn't responsive."

"What does that mean?"

Lydia eyed him for a moment. Her silence stretched out to what had to have been only a few seconds, but felt like eternity. "Why don't you just ask what you want to ask, Don?"

Ouch, the resolve of that challenge. "Look…" Don sighed. "If you want to ignore your unresolved issues with your husband, then fine, I don't care, Lydia. You don't *have* to talk to him, even though I think it would do you some good. But you were the one who *volunteered* to talk to him for this… this mission of ours. Okay? So I don't care how you do it, but it kind of sucks that you fell through on your word."

"I just told you, I tried."

"Like hell you tried, Lydia."

Lydia was silent for a moment. "Okay. Okay, you're right. I could have… um… tried harder." Don heard a sniffle. Oh, no, now he'd made her cry. "I, um… it's just… it's really hard to talk to him, because of, um, because I've just been…"

"I know it's hard to say goodbye to someone, Lydia. I'm sorry."

"No, it's…" She drew in a jagged breath. "I, um, it's because of you. I mean, meeting you. I mean, it's not your fault, it's, um… I just feel… guilty."

Don let those words sit for a long moment. He had no idea what to do with that. He felt that weird fluttering in his chest again.

"I—"

"We don't need to belabor this any more than we already have," Lydia said.

"But wait, I—"

"Don. Hi. We are two very dead people. And suffice it to say, we believe in two very different outcomes for all of this. So whatever happens, I don't think we're going to be spending an eternity together. So let me just, um, get these feelings out of my head, and then I, um, I can go talk to Colby. Yeah, I'll do that…"

"Shit, Lydia."

"Don't do that, okay? Don't, um, don't act like you haven't been thinking the same thing, okay? You do realize that once we do this exorcism, once we get rid of Oswald, then this little jaunt that we've been having, it's pointless. Pointless. Because

I'm nearly corporeal, Don, and you're getting to be, yourself, and then we're going to move on, and there's no point. There's just not. But I still…" She was silent for a moment. "I still feel guilty."

"I don't think this is going to make you feel any better, but I feel the same way."

"No. It doesn't."

"Look, I know it doesn't help with Colby. But… but in terms of the outcome… my mother and father came from different religious backgrounds. And… okay, he died pretty early on in my life, but they were happy. They fought and they had their moments, but they… loved each other. We could… we could make it work."

Lydia's eyes bored into him. "You're right," she said, her voice flat, "that doesn't help with Colby." She blinked. "And we can't make this work, Don. We would end up just like Oswald. Maybe he sticks around for different reasons, but… If we stay here to be together, then we are doing exactly what he's doing."

"Well, then we'll just spend the time we do have together. It'll be like life."

Lydia's eyes closed.

"Or," Don sighed, taking the hint, "we can continue to be friends and not make this any messier than we need to. You clearly still have feelings for Colby, and I wouldn't want to be the one who stood in the way of that."

"Stood in the way of what?"

"I don't want you to hurt, Lydia."

"You know what? I can't do this. I can't go talk to Colby. I don't have the ability, let alone the bandwidth, to reach out to him, get him to understand what's going on, tell him, ope, I've met a guy, and then say goodbye. I literally and metaphorically don't have the energy."

"Okay. Okay, you know what, forget about it. We'll just use the shot we already have. Cherry is on board, that's good. We should probably get going anyway." Don stood, and waited for Lydia to follow, but she continued to sit, her feet still hanging over the edge of the jetty. "We can worry about this afterwards, Lydia. Right now, we need to do what's right."

She nodded and slowly stood, and the two of them began their journey to Hyannis.

* * *

Cherry had stayed the night at Dee's apartment last night, upon instructions from Imam Aasim. He didn't like the idea of her being alone in the apartment with a being, whether Jinni or demon. Neither did Cherry, honestly.

But naturally, she didn't get much sleep at Dee's house. Dee was a talker, for sure, and the two of them had not had a sleepover since college. Dee had bemoaned early on that she was working the night of the big deed. Cherry had tried to explain the basics of ruqyah, and Dee kept muttering, "God, I'm gonna miss all the weird stuff," even though Cherry assured her that it wasn't that weird. And after that, Cherry keenly noted that Dee shifted the direction of the conversation, which Cherry guessed was her way of saying, hey, let's distract ourselves with less troubling matters. And so they talked about everything else.

The conversation ended up being excessively about Gina. And a little about existentialism, though Cherry had mainly steered the conversation towards that subject for Dee's own benefit. After all, it was her house. She should be allowed some comfort topics.

Eventually, they decided to put a movie on in the background while they tried to fall asleep. And so, at around two in the morning, as they lay sprawled on Dee's couch, watching The Man Who Fell To Earth, Cherry's mind began to wander. "Hey, Dee."

"Yep."

"What did you grow up believing about the dead?"

Dee hesitated. Cherry knew she hated talking about stuff like that. Dee came from a Brazilian Jewish family, and she and her mother had had some major drama around her dropping her beliefs to pick up the "cross of psychology"—Dee's words, not her mother's, though Cherry guessed that there had been a certain amount of betrayal felt by her mother. Dee tended to be pretty closed-mouthed about the whole thing. Cherry kicked herself for even bringing it up. But eventually, Dee responded. "There are a few different beliefs circulating in Jewish tradition about the dead. Some people believe that the Talmudic stories about the dead are more figurative than literal, like evil spirits were actually just mental illness, for example—"

"I didn't ask what all of Judaism believed, I asked what you believed."

Dee gave a quiet laugh, chewing her thoughts. "My mom is on the other side of the Jewish spectrum, in which those stories are very literal. She one hundred percent believes in angels and demons, and she absolutely believes that there are times when the dead appear in physical form. Not often, but in unique circumstances."

"Like what?"

Dee groaned. "Cherry, you're Muslim, you're not gonna start believing in ghosts just because I tell you Jewish custom."

Cherry felt something twist in her stomach. "I was just curious."

"I know."

Cherry fidgeted. "Maybe you're right. Maybe I do have a mental illness."

"What? When did I say that?"

"You said people who take Jewish stories more figuratively believe that evil spirits actually refer to mental illness. And I saw *something*—"

"Cherry, I don't think you have a mental illness just because you believe you saw something."

"But you don't believe I actually saw something."

Dee propped herself up on her elbows and stared at Cherry. "Hey. We have managed to be pretty great friends over the years while maintaining very different beliefs. Don't let this one situation destroy that." Cherry nodded, and she sighed. "I don't think you're crazy, okay? I mean, come on, you heard my explanation of the Ouija board. Everything has some logical explanation. And you are hardcore going through something, Cherry. I can't imagine what that does to your perceptual filter."

Cherry laughed. "Stop using your psychiatry-speak on me."

"Well, stop asking, then!" Dee grinned. "Seriously, I'm pretty sure you're mentally sound. But we're just going to have to acknowledge that we aren't going to agree past that point, at least not on this subject. I'm sorry if you wanted a better answer. Or a more appropriate friend whose couch you can crash on the night before your exorcism."

"Oh, shut up. You know this is exactly what I needed."

Dee bit her lip and gave Cherry side-eye. "You know, Jews are really big on asking questions. It's okay to doubt, to search for the answer." She shrugged. "That was the one thing I could relate to even after I stopped believing."

"What are you saying?"

"I don't know. That it's okay. To ask questions, I mean. Or have doubts."

"I'm nervous about tomorrow."

"Do you want me to take off from work?"

Cherry shook her head. "I'll have an imam there with me, I think it will be okay."

Dee settled back down in a slumbering pose, a smile on her face. "Well, then there you go. You said it yourself. It will work out. So stop being nervous. Do what you have to do. This is a big thing for you, you know. Everyone has their own idiosyncratic ways of moving on."

Dee passed out shortly after that, her arm wrapped around a bowl of popcorn, and so naturally, Cherry began to feel nervous. No, the more accurate description was that she felt slammed with dread. What if the ruqyah backfired somehow? Could ruqyah backfire? She knew that Allah would take care of them, and that nothing would happen that wasn't what He willed, but still, her mind quickly went to dark places without her permission. What if this being, whatever it was, retaliated? But no, she thought, then it was for Allah to deal with. She would trust. Ruqyah wouldn't work if she didn't trust.

She felt like she had already failed in that area. She had thought that it was her *brother*, and now she couldn't possibly see how she had been so stupid. Imam Aasim was right. No matter what was going on in this situation, it was best to invite it to leave, and let Allah protect them. How could she have possibly allowed herself to get into this kind of danger? Stupid, stupid.

And so sleep had not come until about three or four in the morning, when Cherry's brain had yammered on for so long that it finally ran out of steam.

And now here she was, having returned to her own home, terrified of what might happen, but apparently not enough to prevent her from falling asleep the instant she sank into the couch.

A knock sounded at the door, and Cherry rose, blurry-eyed. She opened the door and saw Gina standing there.

"Hi," Gina said, smiling. "I, uh… is that guy coming today?"

"Yeah, later tonight."

"Cool," Gina said. "Mind if I stick around for it?"

Cherry froze. She had not expected Gina to want to come for this. It would actually be really nice if she ended up being cool with a Muslim priest blessing her home, and even the idea of ruqyah, but chances were, it would end up being a perfect way to scare away an attractive woman, and the thought made her balk.

Not to mention, she didn't know the safety parameters when dealing with an unknown entity. She didn't want to put Gina in any danger. But a small ember in her heart had burst into flames when she had seen her at the door, and Cherry couldn't ignore that. "Uh, I mean, I guess. You don't have to—"

"Oh, I know," Gina laughed. "But I can't just sit on the other side of the hallway, wondering what in the world is going on. I might as well be here, you know, if you need any help. Am I allowed to be here?"

"I… I don't see why not." Cherry supposed that Imam Aasim would let them know if Gina needed to leave.

She let Gina into the apartment, feebly offering to make a cup of tea. Gina refused and sat on the couch. "What's the jar for?"

Cherry glanced over at the one-gallon jar sitting on the kitchen counter. "Oh, that's for… it will hold water for the ruqyah."

Gina's eyes betrayed that she didn't understand, but she didn't push. Cherry was glad of that; she didn't feel like getting into a long-winded, nervous explanation right before she had to actually perform.

"You nervous?"

"Am I human?" Cherry asked, laughing.

"As far as I know," Gina said, a smile tugging at her lips.

The little flame in her heart bloomed a bit at Gina's smile. But there wasn't any time to stoke that flame, because another knock sounded at the door.

This time, it was Imam Aasim. He smiled at Cherry and entered the apartment. He saw Gina standing in the corner, and a small frown flitted across his face, but he did not tell her to leave. Cherry breathed a sigh of relief.

Imam Aasim removed his jacket and glanced around the apartment. He got right to the point. "We first must remove all of your pictures from the room," he said, indicating the frames on the wall. "I would suggest you keep them down for a week or two." Cherry nodded and got to work taking the pictures down, Gina jumping in to help.

* * *

Just outside of the apartment, Don and Lydia sat, nervously listening to the living as they prepared inside. The night was slipping over them like a shade. The last night that Oswald would ever see, Don thought, and then desperately tried to think of something else. "Maybe you should wait inside," Don offered.

"Why?"

"Because I asked him to meet me here. If he shows up and you're here, too, he's going to get suspicious."

"Valid. I, um…" She was silent for a moment.

"What? Are you afraid that they're gonna exorcise you by accident or something?"

"No. I just… Um. Just be careful, that's all."

She didn't move to leave, and Don allowed the silence to swallow them for another moment. "Hey, no matter what the outcome of this… I just want you to know. We're doing the right thing."

"I know." Her voice wavered, and Don couldn't figure out why.

"What are you thinking?"

She laughed. "I just… I wish I had known you before we died. I wish our relationship didn't have to be based on all of this nonsense. We could've enjoyed getting to know each other without having to collect energy, and without trying to take down a rogue tween."

Don felt his heart twinge at that. "Well. I guess, no matter what, we would've had something to distract us. From getting to know each other, I mean."

"I don't understand."

Don sighed. "I don't think I would've been any better at getting to know you in life than in death. I'd love to say that I would, but… humans are useless at knowing what they should really be doing. I would've gotten caught up in something else, and completely taken you for granted."

"I don't feel like you've taken me for granted."

"I know, I just… I'm just glad you didn't meet me before all this. Maybe you would've liked to have known me back then, but I… I wasn't much to know. I'm glad you didn't see that side of me. I've gotten way cooler now that I'm dead."

Lydia let out a soft laugh. "You keep thinking that, Don." She got up and moved toward the door. "I'll see you soon."

And with that, she stepped through the door and into the apartment. Don stared out at the street, lost in thought. He hoped that things would go smoothly, just for once, and they could finish this business with Oswald so that he could, in fact, spend some quality time with Lydia. Before she went. Or before he went. Even though Lydia had explicitly stated that nothing would come of this, Don still felt like an old man who had just started dating, even though he knew he didn't have much time. Old men didn't think, better not to date, so why should he think that? He would make as much of the time they had left. Everything was temporary. And as much as that sucked, it was also okay. It was better than holding on like Oswald was doing.

Speaking of Oswald, where the hell was he?

* * *

Cherry closed her eyes and took a deep breath. She lifted her eyelids slightly, and Gina and Imam Aasim fluttered into shady view. They were staring at her. Great. She shut her eyes again and tried to forget that they were there. "Bismillah hir rahman nir raheem," she began, and her leg began to shake. It was a nervous reaction, and she instinctively put her hand down to steady it, as if grabbing her leg would suddenly release all of her nerves. It did not do any such thing.

Cherry sighed. The three of them sat cross-legged on the floor, the jar of water between them. She tried to focus on the task at hand… all she had to do was recite over the water, and then they would stop staring at her. "A'oothu billaahi minash Shaytaanir-rajeem. Alhamdu lillaahi Rabbil aalameen…" Breathe, Cherry, don't forget to breathe.

As she continued with the Surah Fatiha, her chest began to feel tight, and her skin felt hot. Well, that was just great. If she was going to have a panic attack, could it at least wait until after her guests were gone? Maybe she should have just recited ruqyah by herself. But no, then she would be more nervous, and the panic attack probably would have already happened.

She felt herself stumbling over her words, and blushed. Focus, Cherry.

Now onto the Surah Falaq. Now she was really in a whirlwind of a state, and she opened her eyes to read from the Arabic-to-English Quran in front of her. There. There wasn't anything that said she needed to recite from memory. Her arms were shaking, and she pinned them to her sides in an attempt to steady herself. This was getting ridiculous.

She made it all the way to the beginning of Surah Nas before the tears started, her lungs screwing up tight as she gasped for breath between sobs. "I'm sorry," she said, palms wiping at her eyes hopelessly, and gave a dark laugh. "This is normal, unfortunately."

Gina looked unsure of what to do. But Imam Aasim, in one swift, gentle movement, came over and kneeled in front of her, squeezing Cherry's shoulder quickly and then picking up where she left off.

As the lilt of his voice lifted the words of the Quran from the page, Cherry felt a calm sweep over her, followed by a strange twinge. What was that? Ah, that was anger that she couldn't finish the job herself. She tried to push that anger out and focus on the words that Imam Aasim was reciting.

* * *

Barely thirty seconds after Don heard the recitations start inside the apartment, Oswald appeared down the street. He glistened as he meandered towards the apartment complex. Once he was close enough to see the whites of his eyes, Don called out. Oswald's snicker bounced through the darkness.

"What are you doing, sitting in the dark?" Oswald said as he reached the steps.

"Better to see your glow, my dear," Don said, kicking himself as soon as the words were out of his mouth. Yes, Don, why don't you just up and tell him you're the big bad wolf?

Oswald's eyes glinted at him, full of confusion. "All right," he said, leaning against the side of the building. "What was it you wanted to show me?"

Don motioned for him to follow and led him through the front door, into the apartment complex, and down the hall. They breezed right through Cherry's door.

Imam Aasim had taken over the recitation, reading from the Quran over the large jug of water. Cherry and her friend sat side by side, both nervously fidgeting as they waited for Imam Aasim's work to take effect.

Oswald watched the scene with a quiet that, if Don was being honest, was a little scary. He had expected Oswald to laugh—or maybe he had expected the whole ordeal to fail miserably. He hadn't expected silence. And that was worse than what was to come.

CHAPTER EIGHTEEN

O swald eyed Don. He was still for a long time. Don was pretty sure he was cycling through all of the suspicious behavior of their last few interactions.

"Why did you ask me here?" Oswald asked quietly, the words of the Quran filling the room behind him. It was possible that this was the first time Don had ever heard him speak at a lower volume than the sass he normally spat out. "What the fuck is this?" His shimmering form moved forward, then pulled back, hesitating as he took in the scene.

Don planted himself firmly in the doorway.

"Nah, man, I'm out of here." Oswald made a move for the door, aiming to phase right through Don, but Don quickly braced himself to block him. He felt an icy cold push against him as Oswald tried but failed to plow through him.

"I see you've been collecting," Oswald said. There was no snicker in his voice this time. He stood, glaring at Don, a lean pillar of electric energy, radiant with anger. Don stood his ground.

Narrowing his eyes, Oswald shifted to the left and aimed for the wall. Don nearly missed him on his way out. He grabbed hold of Oswald's wrist, and when that slipped away, lunged and grabbed Oswald's ankle as he began passing through the wall. Oswald crashed to the floor, swearing, and Lydia rushed next to Don, joining him in the struggle. The two of them pulled Oswald back into the room feet first. Don couldn't decide if it felt more like Looney Toons, or a horror flick.

"What the fuck?" Oswald shouted angrily; then, he stopped struggling, and stood, glaring and kicking himself free of their hands. They quickly positioned themselves around him, eyeing him carefully.

Imam Aasim continued speaking his recitations. The words flowed out of him, and though Don's Arabic tutoring lessons had stopped at age twelve, he was still able to pick up words here and there.

Don glanced at Oswald, trying to gauge his reaction to the imam. He couldn't tell exactly what was going through his mind, but it was clear that Oswald was very tense.

"You guys are fucking nuts," Oswald hissed. He slowly approached Imam Aasim, like a trapped animal searching for another escape. "What's he saying?"

Don didn't reply. He glanced at Lydia, who shimmered nervously.

Oswald forced a laugh. "What, do you think I'm a demon or something?"

Don hesitated. "I think you act like one."

"You gonna exorcise me, Don?"

"You're out of control, Oswald."

Oswald's eyes snapped over to Don. "*I'm* out of control? I'm fucking out of control? But you're the one who sics a, what, an *exorcist*? On a *friend*. Fuck you, Don."

Don swallowed, keeping his eyes trained on Oswald. The thought dawned on him that ruqyah would only take so long, so they should probably get to the point.

"What's he fucking *doing*?" Oswald yelled. He made a lunge for Imam Aasim, and Don and Lydia rushed forward, grabbing onto his arms. Their reaction was a little too late, and Oswald's surprise momentum allowed him a swift kick at Imam Aasim's side.

The man coughed, doubling forward slightly, his eyes scanning the room in surprise. Maybe he hadn't believed Cherry, and thought the exorcism was for show. Don hoped he knew what he was doing, because they sure didn't.

Oswald struggled against Don and Lydia's grasp, swearing and swinging. The thought crossed Don's mind that if he didn't want to be called a demon, maybe he shouldn't act like one, but now was not the time for trite words. He felt Oswald's energy flickering as he strained against his captors, his limbs becoming slick, like they were oiled up, making them very difficult to hold on to. Not to mention that Don and Lydia were rapidly losing energy by holding him down.

With a sudden surge of strength, Oswald shoved Lydia off him. She staggered back, slamming into and through the wall, disappearing from sight. "Lydia!" Don cried, and he heard a faint call from the other side of the wall.

Another shove from Oswald, and Don was barely holding on. Without two people on him, Oswald was now free to assail Don with his free arm, sending blows down on his head, and Don felt pain for the first time since the car crash. He brandished one of his arms to protect himself and tried to gauge how much energy he had left, but it was hard to tell the difference in corporeality between his body and Oswald's. Shimmering energy swam in front of his eyes, little particles of being that didn't care to which soul they were connected. They bristled and buzzed, and Don knew he didn't have much time left.

The fact that his and Oswald's bodies were barely distinguishable worried Don. What if they had the same amount of energy left? Or even worse, what if Oswald had just slightly more energy than Don? It was so hard to tell in the jumble. But if Lydia didn't get back soon, he was pretty sure that Oswald was going to take Don with him.

Where the hell was she? Maybe she had gotten hurt when she fell through the wall. Don's head ached fully from Oswald's blows, but Lydia had been thrown against something physical while exerting her energy. An image of Lydia somehow splitting her head open on the wall crossed Don's mind. The thought of harm coming to her made Don sick, and for a moment, his grip loosened on Oswald's arm. Maybe it was an inadvertent thought to go check on Lydia. Maybe Don was just getting tired. But before he was able to recover, to remember that they had a mission, and the lives of Cherry and Imam Aasim and the other woman whose name Don now forgot and didn't quite care in that moment to remember were at stake—before he was able to tighten his grip, Oswald slipped out of his reach and barreled towards the imam, his shoulder slamming into his stomach.

The two of them toppled, Oswald forward and Imam Aasim backward, Oswald crouching over the man like a shimmering tiger, fangs bared. Don stumbled forward, trying to get a sense of what was happening. He saw one shimmery limb extended, pressing down on Imam Aasim's throat, and heard him choking, his words gurgling out in fear.

Beside the ghostly entanglement, Cherry and Gina fell onto their knees, staring in terror at Imam Aasim on the ground. "What do we do?" Gina asked dumbly, her hands twitching at her side as if ready to do something, but not quite sure what.

"Imam Aasim," Cherry whispered, her face filled with fright, "What's happening? How can we help?"

The panic in her voice brought Imam Aasim's gaze to her. With determination, he tried to continue speaking, but the words caught between his throat and the seemingly invisible force attacking him.

Don had his hands around Oswald's chest and neck. It was a pile of humans, dead and alive, and Don didn't know if his efforts were actually doing anything. He wasn't sure if trying to strangle a strangler would work, especially when the strangler wasn't alive to begin with. But he pulled, and as he felt his energy slipping away from him, his body becoming fainter, he felt another sensation: light and giddy, filling in the periphery of his conscience with an elated buzz. Damn it, Don thought, we're all going to be high as kites if we keep running around.

The high had already affected Oswald as well. He wasn't budging from his spot, clamped to the imam's throat, but his eyes were a bit wilder, a bit less focused. He let out a shriek of a laugh as he gripped tighter.

* * *

"Maybe we should call an ambulance," Gina said, jumping up and disappearing behind Cherry. Cherry felt tears running down her cheeks. She couldn't believe it; danger was upon them and she couldn't do anything but cry. Her breath still felt like it was caught in a cage, and her heart was rattling against her ribs, and with all her might, Cherry took a deep breath and started her counting exercises in her head. You're useless, she thought, this is what you need to focus on right now, is breathing exercises. Your friends need you, *do* something.

"Allah, protect us," she whispered, and took the Quran from Imam Asim, reading the words out loud, at first under her breath and then louder as her courage picked up momentum.

* * *

Don watched Oswald's wild gaze land on his sister, and a sudden surge of strength shot through him. "Oh, no you don't," he muttered as Oswald's one hand loosened its grip on the imam's neck and shot towards Cherry. Don let go of Oswald's chest and caught the kid's extending hand, using all his force to keep it from connecting with Cherry's neck. Between the high he felt, and the awkward angle his arms were contorted at, he knew this hold would not last for long.

"Don!" It was Lydia. She appeared through the wall, eyes wild. "Don, I'm sorry, I lost myself for a minute—"

"I don't care, just get over here," Don called with effort.

Oswald turned his bloodthirsty eyes on her and growled, fully letting go of Imam Aasim and standing, knocking Don backwards.

Imam Aasim let out a strained, pathetic noise, sucking air into his lungs as Don gathered himself, trying to lift himself off the ground. He felt wavery and unbalanced, the high having affected his coordination.

Oswald strode slowly towards Lydia. Cherry's recitations continued, and Don heard Imam Asim joining her, quietly but certainly in the background, but he didn't care about that now. He watched Oswald nervously, and Lydia as she stood her ground, staring Oswald down with a determination he had never seen before.

"Lydia," Oswald snarled, his eyes dancing, his body bristling. "Have you come to save your little exorcist friend? Couldn't hold on very long, could you?"

He glanced at Don, then back at Lydia. He snickered. "Well, well, well, neither of you are looking too good. I can barely see either of you." He turned his stare to Don. "And you," Oswald sang, "you little fucker, you need a lesson about biting the hand that feeds you. You do this to a friend?"

"I am not your friend."

"I can see that now. So what, this world wasn't big enough for you and me both? You two thought you would hire a fucking exorcist to take me out? You know he's not actually doing anything, right? He's just muttering a bunch of mumbo jumbo, it's not doing squat."

"Looks like it's done quite a bit, actually," Don said, gesturing to Oswald's diminishing glow. "You aren't looking too hot yourself."

Oswald glared at him. "He didn't do that. You did."

Don's heart sank. Up until this moment, their greatest weapon had been Oswald's fear. The worst thing that could happen, they'd surmised, was that Oswald would realize he had more control over the situation than he originally thought. Come on, Don thought, we need you to lash out. If Oswald didn't lash out, how could he lose all of his energy? Imam Aasim's words had worked on him for one reason and one reason only: the chant held power because of the fear, the uncertainty it struck in Oswald's heart. That power only remained if it made him fight back. And now, Oswald was catching on.

Change tactics, Don thought. Counter his moves. But how? Don had no idea what tactic to try next.

"No, you did it to yourself," Don shot back. "Because you're afraid that his words might actually do something, that maybe there's something you don't know. And you don't want to go, do you?"

"Shut up, asshole," Oswald muttered.

"No, I won't shut up," Don said. "What are you afraid of, Oswald? Everybody dies."

"Not this young," Oswald spat, and Don detected a hint of animalistic fear coming from his voice.

"You've had at least ten years to cheat your destiny, man. You've had the opportunity to live, to—"

"You know nothing about my opportunity. You think that playing practical jokes on the living is life? You think that somehow makes up for all the years I was jilted? Fuck you, Don. I've still got time left in me, and I will do with it what I fucking please. ' Oswald snickered. "You're such a fucking hypocrite, Don. You know the instant I'm gone, you're gonna feel such a sense of relief, 'cause the bad egg's gone, so you can continue doing what you were doing before. Except what the fuck have you been doing, Don? You're an atheist. Where are you gonna go when you finally cross over? Or are you gonna do what I did, and hold on for as long as possible? Kill Oswald and steal his plan."

Don felt his words like a sting. He was right. He had no idea what was in store for him. What if he did end up walking around for the next ten years like Oswald had done? He was no better than Oswald. He would've ended up just like him if he'd had the time.

Oswald snickered, his eyes wild. "Your plan was fucking stupid, anyway. That religious jackass wouldn't be enough to kill me!" he howled. "How many people have I killed, huh?" he asked. "How many people have I snuffed out? And I'm still around, pal. You think your fucking plan is so ingenious? You forgot… I'm a fuckin' resilient bitch. I have power you wouldn't even believe!"

Don almost laughed. The poor guy was so high, he sounded like a comic book villain. Always had to have the last word. But he was right. This plan had been lopsided right from the start. And suddenly, Don knew what he had to do.

"You're right," he said, holding out his hands. "This was a terrible idea. Lydia and I got really power hungry, and we just wanted to do you in. But I see now, that was really dumb of us."

Oswald hesitated, his eyes clouding with confusion.

"I'm sorry, man. And killing Imam Aasim isn't going to kill you, of course not. You're too powerful." Don laughed. "Or at least you were. I guess our little tumble took a bit out of you. Geez, Oswald, you *are* looking a little translucent right now. I'm sorry, man, that was a shitty thing to do. So shitty."

Oswald was tense again. He didn't know what to make of Don's sudden about-face.

"Don't even think of picking a fucking fight, Donny boy," Oswald growled. "You're just as wasted as me. You wouldn't stand a chance."

Don took a step forward. "Would you like to bet your life on that, Oswald?"

"Don?" Lydia murmured behind him.

Don knew his energy was even more spent than Oswald's. How much energy had Oswald actually collected? He still had a bold shimmer to him, whereas Don and Lydia were both barely visible. There was no way they would be able to overtake him.

"It seems like you're the lowest on energy that I've ever seen you," Don continued. "Sure would be nice to have a bit of an extra punch if someone was to, say, take a swing at you."

"You're not gonna try anything," Oswald spat. "You've got yourself a little girlfriend, you don't want to go disappearing on her, would you?"

"Who, Lydia?" Don laughed. "She's not my girlfriend. She just showed me how to collect. No, you're misunderstanding me… I'm not after you anymore. I don't want to fade away any more than you do, remember? There's nothing after this, man. I'm not taking that risk. You're right, I've done all I can do. But, I mean, there are a lot of crazy tweens out there. You know that, Oswald. You've gotten into fights with more than a few of them. Why don't you just get yourself some insurance energy?"

"What the fuck?"

"I mean, you were pretty close to doing in the religious freak here, weren't you? You could easily take him and be fine. Refill your tank, so to speak."

"Don, what are you doing?" Lydia hissed.

Don ignored her. He felt Oswald's beady little eyes on him for a long, hard minute. Finally, Oswald began to laugh. Not just a snicker, but a full-throated, hearty, relieved laugh. "I knew you would come around, Donny boy!" he shrieked. "Come on, I'll share this time. A little peace offering, if you will."

He turned towards Imam Aasim, and Lydia let out a yell, throwing herself at Oswald. With one swift shift of his body weight, Oswald tossed Lydia across the room, slamming her against the wall. She crumpled to the ground pitifully.

Oswald looked at Don, then turned back to the imam. He was still muttering Quranic verses, eyes closed, the two women huddled close to him. Cherry's chanting had faded to under her breath, and for this, Don silently thanked a nonexistent god.

Leisurely, Oswald approached Imam Aasim, and pushed him, watching the terrified man fall back onto the ground. Standing over him, he wrapped his hand around his throat and squeezed.

Cherry and her friend let out gasps of concern. Imam Aasim began grasping at the slippery energy around his throat, a gurgling sound escaping from his windpipe. Don glanced back at Lydia: the shimmering heap on the ground was barely moving, but her eyes threw daggers in his direction. He hoped she would figure out what he was doing soon. And he hoped she knew none of his cruel words were true.

Imam Aasim was growing faint, but so was Oswald's shimmer. Don hoped he hadn't pushed his luck. He had to find just the right moment—when Oswald had diminished himself just enough, but hadn't killed the imam yet.

Okay, that was probably enough. Don prayed that he had enough energy left in him to finish the job.

He jumped forward, grabbing Oswald roughly and yanking him off the imam, who collapsed very quickly to the floor.

Oswald's face revealed his lack of surprise in this turn of events. He let out a string of curses, turning his wrath on Don.

Don felt an icy grip around his throat now, and returned the favor, locking onto Oswald's jugular as best he could. Oswald's energy bristled beneath his fingers. He felt vibrant in that moment—whether it was the electricity coursing through his undead veins, or the excitement and terror of what was to come next, he couldn't be sure which, but Don had never felt more alive. That thought alone was disconcerting. As the two of them struggled with each other, he could feel his own energy slipping away from him, just as slippery as Oswald was becoming, and in that moment, Don knew that if he was going to finish the job, he was going to have to go, too. They were too close of a match for Don to come out ahead on this one, and he couldn't risk passing the baton onto Lydia… she looked so beaten up— barely visible at this point—no, this was up to him.

And you know what? He was okay with that.

Sure, he had no idea what was in store for him, but he hadn't known that in life either, so what was the difference?

He nearly laughed. The difference was, he had found his purpose. He had found an objective worth giving his life for. His entire life, none of his actions had ever chalked up to anything, but now—with the mysterious breath of death upon him, staring him in the eye with a ferocity and drive that should never have been associated with the dead—now, he knew that he had made a difference. He had expended his energy in a worthy way. He was going to stop Oswald from causing more pain, and if that meant the end of his existence, well… at least he would be remembered as the man who did it.

Maybe Cherry wouldn't know what he had done, and Imam Aasim wouldn't know, either—he also would have no idea that Don had offered him up on a silver platter, and Don was glad that at least that much was knowledge not imparted—but Lydia would know. She would know what Don had done for her, for everyone. And while it hurt him to think that this may be the end of their friendship, or the end of whatever it could have been, Don knew that it was the right decision.

Oswald let out a scream. His eyes blazed, his hatred burned bright, his grip never faltered, and in the same moment that Don felt the last of his energy spent, Oswald disappeared from sight, the end of his scream echoing off the walls.

* * *

The room was silent, but for the sound of heavy breathing, for just one long, confused, disheveled moment.

Lydia clambered to her feet, staring in shock at the empty space which had just moments ago held the person she most despised and the person she most held dear.

Imam Aasim, catching his breath, sat up and began chanting the words of the Quran again. He didn't know his work was done.

* * *

Cherry and Gina exchanged wide-eyed stares, quietly astonished at the series of events, as Imam Aasim kept chanting beside them.

Gina took a deep breath, closing her eyes, and Cherry realized she felt the same rush of relief. She didn't know why, but the air felt different around her. An energy shift. Maybe that Oswald fellow was gone, she thought.

Maybe they had done some good.

CHAPTER NINETEEN

Cherry opened her eyes, and bits and pieces of the night before flooded to the foreground of her mind: the strange energy she had felt in the apartment; Imam Aasim's gasping breath as he lay on the floor. She had never felt so scared in her entire life. When Imam Aasim had finally found his bearings and finished reciting the words from the Quran, he had collapsed heavily in a chair, closing his eyes for a moment, adding a personal prayer to the mix. Cherry didn't think it was part of the ruqyah… she thought he might have just been scared, and was praying for his own sake.

That was the point that an ambulance had arrived—Gina had, in fact, called. The paramedics fussed over Imam Aasim, who refused to be taken to the hospital, repeating over and over that he was fine, he promised. He finally convinced them to let him be, and the ambulance left.

After that, Imam Aasim gave Cherry a glass of the water from the jug and instructed her to drink it, and to keep drinking the water daily until it was gone. Then he packed up and left, leaving Cherry and Gina to fish out a bottle of wine from Gina's cupboard. Cherry couldn't remember the last time she had had any sort of alcoholic drink, and had serious misgivings about drinking alcohol right after the work they had just done, so she drank her ruqyah water instead, and Gina poured herself a glass of wine. The debriefing session was full of uncomfortable questions, plenty of laughter, and several instances of arms brushing against each other before both of them had fallen asleep on Cherry's bed.

Cherry glanced at Gina, still asleep beside her. She had used one arm as a pillow, and her other arm reached out towards Cherry, her fingers just grazing her stomach. Cherry shut her eyes and folded her hand into Gina's. The resulting rustle of movement told her that Gina was now awake, but her hand remained cupped in Cherry's. It was such a kiddish act, but the feel of their skin touching brought a smile to Cherry's lips. As hard as her brother's death had been, she felt that, in the end, he had given her one last gift: the gift of time well spent.

* * *

Tucked away in the house at 36 Berry Avenue, a man sat, curled up on the sofa in his living room, a blanket tossed over his knees, thumbing through a book.

It was A Tale Of Two Cities. He always read that book; he must have read it fifteen times. But it was a comfort read, one that reminded him of lazy Saturday mornings past, in the same trappings of comfort as he was now but with his late wife painted into the picture beside him, a warm mug of tea perched dangerously on the arm of the couch to his right, and Lydia's head pressing into his left shoulder, warm and comforting.

He didn't have Lydia anymore, but he could try to recreate the rest of the scene as best he could. The day was still and sleepy, and he imagined he would read one more chapter before calling it quits and going about the rest of his morning. But as he turned the page, he felt something shift around him, and felt a strange pressure on his left shoulder.

For a long moment, he sat, frozen, unable to make sense of the words on the page, his focus pulled. Finally, he cleared his throat, took a sip from his mug, and said aloud, "I miss you, too."

It took a few minutes of staring blankly out at the sun-streaked living room, silently chewing on the emotions that popped up, and when he finally looked back down at his book, he felt exhausted, as if he had spent all his energy on the toll. But he was able to continue reading.

And it was in those last minutes that Lydia finally found the energy to move on.

Finished reading Tween? Give it a review!

https://sammileighm.com/review-tween/

Stay up-to-date with what stories Sammi Leigh Melville is writing! Join the mailing list!

https://bit.ly/sammileighmnewsletter

PREVIEW:

THE FIELDS

SAMMI LEIGH MELVILLE

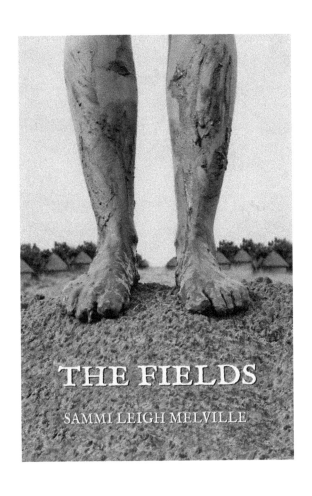

CHAPTER ONE – THE FALL

The day would officially begin with the unearthing of an elbow, an ear, a foot; a group of children would stumble across one of these prized possessions and begin to dig, peeling the mud away in hopes that the elbow would become an arm, the ear a head, the foot a leg. With increased effort, the body parts would lead to a body. This dazed being, usually a child, would be coaxed out of the mud by its proud saviors, who would giggle and whisper to each other in glee; the newcomer would then be escorted to the bathhouse by an adult.

It was always the little ones who were first to run onto the field, feet struggling against the mud's sucking pull, eyes searching for the rare individuals who already protruded from the ground. They loved the game of it, the fun of discovering new playmates in the mud. The adults had a different mindset as they methodically followed, one eye watching the children running out ahead of them and the other nervously scanning the sky for the winged specters. To them, digging the fields was an act of duty and necessity.

Just at the perimeter of the field, Marie Goodwin began her patrol. There was hardly ever anything that she needed to watch over—crime was low in a village where there wasn't much to steal, where everyone knew everyone and would not consider hurting anyone unless it was a foreigner—but watch she did, day in and day out, her baton safely tucked into the folds of her cotton blue dress just in case. It was her duty as Sheriff.

And there was the business of watching the specters. Their lithe, ghostly bodies gave the semblance of a small human but had the wings of a bat, diaphanous but strong and powerful, with raking talons, and razor-sharp teeth jutting from their snarls. Gliding lazily over the field of mud, they glowed an ethereal blue even in the daylight. The beasts thought they owned the place—and perhaps they did, in a way. Several circled overhead right now, flexing their talons, a constant reminder that an attack could occur at any given moment against these innocent humans residing in the village.

But they remained in the sky, which was just where Marie would rather. And so she returned her gaze to the field, that lot of mud in which the Southern Village's diggers so avidly worked, spanning nearly a quarter of a mile. They scooped handful after handful of the thick, clumpy, slippery mess and tossed it into piles behind them, watching the mud sink back into the hole they had just created—but a little progress was still made. The diggers averaged about five rescues a month, though they saw plenty more under the mud than that... the field, however sacred the villagers considered it, acted like a petulant child: it was jealous of its captives, and liked to give the diggers glimpses of them, revealing a foot or a shoulder but, as soon as more help came, sucking it back down into its depths, teasing the diggers in an ever-so-coy (but ever-so-irritating) way. And so the whole village would rejoice when they finally managed to unearth a newcomer from its grasp.

Marie swallowed the sigh that inevitably came to her lips during her daily patrol. Truth be told, she couldn't stand the sight of the field; it sometimes struck her that this community of beautiful people wasted their days living in servitude to the needs of the field. Day after day they returned, breaking their backs and risking their lives to pry others from its grasp... they didn't have to, but Marie saw the guilty conscience of the collective people, saw that they could not just sit back and let others lie unconscious underneath the mud, unable to open their eyes to the sunshine and stretch their legs on solid ground. No one with the same origins would wish that on anyone else... after all, what if the village had given up before they, themselves, were pulled from the mud? No, it was good that they fulfilled their duty; but still, Marie found herself secretly wishing the field wasn't there—that they could live in peace without knowledge of it. Or better yet, that it could be destroyed.

She gave a little shudder, amazed that the thought had even crossed her mind. Those thoughts were sacrilege. And besides, destruction was exactly what this village didn't need more of.

Marie caught a glimpse of Cecilia out on the field, gleefully helping the diggers, and a smile slowly edged its way back onto her face. Cecilia had been begging her to let her dig since she was four years old. "Mama, it's just mud! Mama, all the other kids got a chance. Mama, *I know how to dig*." Of course, initially Marie had refused—there would be too many whispers from the villagers about a flesh-born child running loose on the field. There was only so much Marie could do to shield her daughters from the spite of the villagers—defying the very act of creation that the field itself performed and being born of another womb was a direct violation of the village's stasis, and was why some villagers even referred to these children as bastards—but she could at least curb the spark of controversy by not sending them onto holy ground. Even the field seemed to agree; it was too dangerous for flesh-borns to try their hand at digging, especially with the specters watching so closely. While everyone felt the inherent risk of falling back under the mud, it was rare for a flesh-born child to make it past three years old without being knocked under, no matter what pains the parents took to prevent it.

Marie shuddered at the memory of the last flesh-born child to fall, two years ago: a specter had swooped down out of the sky and snatched little Sandy from the safety of his own front yard, flown to the center of the field, and simply dropped him. The field had devoured him within seconds, though the diggers spent hours trying to get him back. The villagers had eventually made their peace with the incident—after all, though the child had not come from the field, he was finally able to connect with the village's collective Womb on some level—but the thought of it still made Marie instinctively want to scoop Cecilia up in her arms and hold her tight.

But Cecilia was a tough child. The first time, only just a month ago, she had snuck onto the field against her mother's wishes. And of course Marie found out, scrounging up enough of her silent fury—not only at Cecilia for disobeying her, but also at Mukisa, Cecilia's older sister by twelve years, who was supposed to have been watching her. But by the time she had run out to Cecilia's spot on the field to give her a talking to, Cecilia had pulled up a little girl. You had to give it to her… she seemed to have a natural knack for digging, regardless of the heightened bounty that the specters sought for her kind. It brought a swell of pride to Marie's chest—*her daughter, a digger.*

A good number of villagers had to admit that, the stigma of illegitimate birth aside, the Goodwin family had a knack for everything they put their minds to. Mukisa was the finest hunter the village had seen for years; and Cecilia clearly would be a fine digger when Marie ascertained that she should dig full time. The jobs they had so deftly picked up certainly held the skeptics at bay; their greatest defense from their neighbors' spite was to earn their respect. Marie's position perhaps helped heighten that respect to some extent: she had hesitantly taken her position as sheriff when the previous sheriff, Lucas Clarke, had passed on; now here she was, twenty years later, and she could barely have a conversation about taking another vote for the position without people getting upset. Marie smiled at the thought of what one of the elders, Mama Nina, had said just a few days ago:

"Marie, you are a stronghold, born to mother whatever lost soul came across your path. You didn't have kids, so you figured you'd mother an entire village. And then Mukisa and Cecilia came along, and you just kept on doing a good job with the rest of us."

Out on the field, Cecilia hunched over a section of mud intently, her gaze fixed on something. With a muddied hand, she pushed the tight curls out of her face, uncompromising in her scrutiny of the ground before her. Marie shielded her eyes from the sun to get a better look as Cecilia's hand shot forward, reaching for something just under the surface of the mud; she looked up at the diggers around her, a smile spreading across her face. Shouting and motioning to those closest to her, she returned to her work with new vigor: she had excavated a hand.

The diggers around her smiled, nodding in approval at Cecilia, though they stuck to their own sections, hoping that they, too, could find a body part. Already Cecilia was showing up some of the most experienced diggers today... Marie could understand why they did not rush to her side to assist. Nobody wanted to be beaten by a seven-year-old, let alone a flesh-born seven-year-old. But Cecilia kept at it, and in a moment's time, Marie saw a head peeking out of the mud: a young boy's head, she could see. Now they would help her... getting the head to surface was half the battle, and the field would now be putting up a real fight.

But before Cecilia could even announce her victory, the head jerked back down into the mud. Cecilia stared in shock as the boy disappeared before her eyes, and plunged her hands into the mud around her, trying to find him.

Marie squinted, trying to make sense of the scene. Suddenly she saw a muddy hand shoot out of the space in front of Cecilia, and desperately grab hold of her arm—and then Cecilia lurched forward, screaming, yanked headfirst into the mud.

"Cecilia!" Marie bolted onto the field, making a beeline to the spot where her daughter had been. Other diggers who had seen the incident shouted and began reaching down, struggling to find her receding body in the mud. Marie shoved past them and reached her own arm down, into the slimy mess, into the heart of the field. Her fingers frantically clawed at the mud, grasping at nothing, over and over, and her heart began to climb into her throat.

After a while, Marie felt strong arms around her waist, pulling her away from the mud. It was possible that she kicked a man square in the jaw—she wasn't sure, but she didn't care—and the next thing she knew, she was on the edge of the field, seated on a tree stump and surrounded by people, a sea of comforting hands and a tangle of hushed words and everything was spinning and it was getting hot and the front of her dress was caked in mud and I'm sorry, Marie, but Cecilia is gone.

Mukisa peeked through the trees and smiled at the man before her, perched on a rock and minding his own business. Paul liked to have some time to himself, and she didn't usually like to disturb him… well, *sometimes* she liked to disturb him, but after her mother had lectured the two of them that their responsibilities should come before their personal lives, it was now more often than not that the disturbance was due to inevitability: she would be tracking a deer, or maybe a pheasant, and follow it right into his path, and suddenly she would see him there, off in his own little world. Not that he wasn't hunting—Mukisa knew that Paul was a great hunter—he just liked being alone sometimes.

Today must be one of those times. A particularly clever shaft of sunlight navigated past the shade of the oak trees and fell in Paul's general vicinity, allowing the man enough light with which to sharpen his spear. Mukisa frowned. She knew for a fact that Paul made it a habit of checking his weapons every night when they went back to the village, but perhaps he had been distracted last night. Very well. The entire village's next meal depended on what they and the rest of the hunters brought back, and she knew Paul wouldn't slack at his job.

He looked so content sitting there, scraping away at the slate with his whetstone, and Mukisa felt this same contentedness spread through her as she watched. He had told her once, she remembered, that sharpening his weapons was calming to him. She had laughed at him—Paul was not one to find pleasure in violence, and it was common knowledge that the only reason he had become a hunter was because it meant he could find some spare time to himself. He would even risk the dangers of the forest for it. So to her, it was funny that he found it a soothing practice.

She saw Paul suddenly freeze in his place on the rock, and grimaced; perhaps he had heard her breathing. Not that it mattered—Mukisa was one of the few people by whom Paul didn't mind being interrupted. But she liked seeing him so relaxed, and now that moment was gone.

She silently crept forward, an idea sprouting in her mind, and unsheathed the knife at her belt, reaching him before he even turned around and holding the weapon mere inches from his head. He turned, and nearly ran his nose straight into the tip of the knife. Mukisa let out a peal of laughter as he gasped and fell backwards off the rock, startled.

Paul jumped to his feet, fuming. Mukisa poised the knife in her hand nonchalantly, a mischievous grin splayed across her face. She shoved the knife back into its holster and gave Paul a coy look.

"Damn it, Mukisa, I told you to stop doing that!" Paul sputtered, picking up the spear that he had tossed inadvertently on the forest floor.

She smirked. "You're a hunter. You're supposed to hear me coming. Nice job dropping your weapon at the slightest surprise, by the way—"

"I didn't want to hurt you," Paul grumbled, sitting back down on the rock. But it was a good-natured grumble. Mukisa laughed and leaned in, trying to steal a kiss, and he pulled back, a scowl on his face. But the scowl didn't last long—that slow smile of his crept right onto his face like it always did.

She continued the game. "Fine, mope. *I'm* going hunting," she said, starting to move away. "Feel free to join me, whenever you've tended to your pride."

"Come here," he said, reaching to pull her in, but she laughed, pulling away.

"I'm sorry, *you* just killed the mood. So…"

She sauntered away, and heard him jump up, chasing after her. They ran through the forest, laughing, their feet expertly finding their way through the brush. "Slow down!" he called out, "I want to show you something!"

Mukisa ran for another second, then abruptly stopped and turned to Paul, still laughing. He nearly ran into her—he had been preoccupied with getting something out of his pocket.

Mukisa suddenly realized what he was holding and took a step back impulsively. It was a thin, threaded chain, with a bead in the center. It looked so meticulously made, the thin strips of leather woven together with such precision, the hole in the bead so painstakingly carved and threaded onto the chain.

Mukisa glanced up at Paul with wide eyes, her heart suddenly wreaking havoc in her chest. He seemed to be having his own little panic attack as well; his eyes nervously searched her face, begging for some sort of answer. She stared back down at the chain in shock, like it was a bomb, a fragile bomb, and she didn't know how to detonate it without blowing herself to bits.

"What… what is that?"

"I think you know what it is," he said breathlessly, and she knew it wasn't from the running.

Mukisa silently ordered her chest to maintain a steady rise and fall. He was right... she did know what it was. In fact, her mother used to have one of these. That didn't make it any less frightening that he was holding it out to her. Exhilarating, but frightening. "That's a wedding link, Paul."

"I know." His voice cracked, betraying him.

Her eyes flitted to his. "Paul, this isn't something to joke around with—"

"I'm not joking, Mukisa."

He looked so scared. Mukisa did a quick check, evaluating her reaction: perhaps her face was exhibiting the wrong emotions. She reached out and touched the bead gingerly. Not a bomb. Just a symbol of love and adoration. She smiled suddenly and lunged at Paul, hugging and kissing him as together they fell to the forest floor.

This was not at all what Mukisa had expected on such an average day, but she embraced the idea, taking in the warmth of his body as he returned her kiss, and the sound of his relieved laughter as she grabbed the link from his hands and fixed it around her head, the bead falling nicely onto her forehead.

That warmth stayed with her all throughout the day as they hunted; the spinning in her head didn't stop until they emerged from the woods with the other hunters, the carcasses of game slung over their shoulders, and hopped the fence surrounding the Southern Village. It stayed with her up until the moment that she realized that the village was unusually quiet, *unbearably* quiet; and the villagers greeting them when they arrived were not smiling, were only staring at her, saying, "I'm so sorry, child." The moment that she narrowed her eyes, saw her mother standing in the village green, and dropped her game before running to her.

The Fields is now available in paperback and e-book. To read more, go to https://sammileighm.com/the-fields/

ACKNOWLEDGEMENTS

Now that I have a second novel under my belt, I'd like to say that it gets easier. And in a sense, maybe it did... it took less time to write it, anyway. The Fields took a whopping ten years (and thank goodness I didn't try publishing it earlier than that... it would have been such a different book). Tween took about four. And the novella I've been working on has only taken about two years so far, so I think I'm getting better at the time thing, anyway! But there's still an arduous amount of work that gets put into each of these babies, and it's grueling, and it's gritty, and sometimes it causes tears. So no, it hasn't really gotten easier. But each time, I get a little bit better at reaching out and asking for help. And I am so, so grateful for those who have acted upon that request.

So who did I ask for help this time?

My first "thank you" has to go to my mother and my sister, who didn't know what they were getting into when they agreed to be beta readers and in fact ended up being alpha readers. Tween went through a lot of revisions, and I am unsure how many drafts I actually subjected them to.

Thank you to Mohammad Abu Shuleh from Dickinson College for sitting with me in a coffee shop and talking about

Islam so that I could write the story more realistically. And thank you to my sensitivity readers: Tay A. and Ilwad Zi, your suggestions were so helpful and so necessary; and to Abdullah Abu-Mahfouz, who talked story and accuracy with me, and reminded me that at the end of the day, I should tell the story instead of getting swamped in the details.

I want to thank my editor, Alex Woodroe, who, in several parts of the manuscript, watched me reject some of her edits and then come back complaining that she was right. My only hope, Alex, is that I never gave you too much of a headache. And thank you to my writing group, who was a hugely imperative sounding board when I needed it, and an all-around fantastic support group. I love you guys.

And finally, a very special thank you to Reade Scott Whinnem, who fostered my love for story in numerous ways in that little hole in the wall at the back of the library. I'm addicted to story because of you; I hope you're happy. I also hope you haven't changed your address, because otherwise some stranger will be receiving a free copy of Tween.

ABOUT THE AUTHOR

Sammi Leigh Melville lives in Harrisburg, PA with her cats, Loren, Charlie, and Billy. Aside from Tween, she is the author of the young adult fantasy book, The Fields, writes film reviews for The Burg, and has written and directed several short films through her production company, Screaming Pictures, in an attempt to work storytelling into every aspect of her life (except for the cats. Okay, maybe she tells stories to her cats).